Murder of the Cat's Meow

Center Point
Large Print

Also by Denise Swanson and available from
Center Point Large Print:

Scumble River Mysteries
  Murder of A Wedding Belle
  Murder of A Bookstore Babe
  Murder of A Creped Suzette

Devereaux Dime Store Mysteries
  Little Shop of Homicide

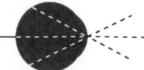

**This Large Print Book carries the
Seal of Approval of N.A.V.H.**

Murder of the Cat's Meow

A Scumble River Mystery

Denise Swanson

CENTER POINT LARGE PRINT
THORNDIKE, MAINE

This Center Point Large Print edition
is published in the year 2012 by arrangement with
NAL Signet, a member of Penguin Group (USA) Inc.

The text of this Large Print edition is unabridged.
In other aspects, this book may vary
from the original edition.
Printed in the United States of America
on permanent paper.
Set in 16-point Times New Roman type.

ISBN: 978-1-61173-580-2

Library of Congress Cataloging-in-Publication Data

Swanson, Denise.
Murder of the cat's meow : a Scumble River mystery / Denise
Swanson. — Center Point Large Print ed.
p. cm.
ISBN 978-1-61173-580-2 (lib. bdg. : alk. paper)
1. Denison, Skye (Fictitious character)—Fiction.
2. School psychologists—Fiction. 3. Women psychologists—Fiction.
4. Speed dating—Fiction. 5. Cat shows—Fiction.
6. Murder—Investigation—Fiction. 7. Large type books. I. Title.
PS3619.W36M897 2012
813'.6—dc23

2012033025

Author's Note

In July of 2000, when the first book in my Scumble River series, *Murder of a Small-Town Honey*, was published, it was written in "real time." It was the year 2000 in Skye's life as well as mine, but after several books in a series, time becomes a problem. It takes me from seven months to a year to write a book, and then it is usually another year from the time I turn that book in to my editor until the reader sees it on a bookstore shelf. This can make the timeline confusing. Different authors handle this matter in different ways. After a great deal of deliberation, I decided that Skye and her friends and family would age more slowly than those of us who don't live in Scumble River. So to catch everyone up, the following is when the books take place:

Murder of a Small-Town Honey—August 2000
Murder of a Sweet Old Lady—March 2001
Murder of a Sleeping Beauty—April 2002
Murder of a Snake in the Grass—August 2002
Murder of a Barbie and Ken—November 2002
Murder of a Pink Elephant—February 2003
Murder of a Smart Cookie—June 2003

And this is when the Scumble River short story and novella take place:

• • •

• • •

To my fellow cat lovers:
I promise you no kitties are harmed in this story.

CHAPTER 1

Raining Cats and Dogs

School psychologist Skye Denison stamped her bunny-slippered foot on the black-and-white-tiled floor of her newly remodeled kitchen and shouted, "If you keep doing that, I won't be able to convince Wally we should live here once we're married."

Silence greeted her threat. Not surprising, since she was the only person in the house. At least the only living person. Which was the problem.

Although Skye's fiancé, police chief Wally Boyd, claimed he didn't believe in ghosts, it was kind of hard to ignore the fact that nearly every time he and Skye started to get intimate, something in her house blew up, burst into flames, or broke into a thousand pieces.

Skye's gaze flitted from the granite counters to the stainless-steel fridge and came to rest on the cherrywood cupboards. She'd been renovating the house since she'd inherited it from Alma Griggs more than two and a half years ago. There was still a lot to do, and the process, so far, had been both frustrating and costly. But there was no way she was selling the place and moving into Wally's bungalow.

"Do you hear me, Mrs. Griggs?"

There was no response.

"Fine." Skye blew out an annoyed breath and grabbed the broom. As she swept up the shards of what *had* been her Grandma Leofanti's Jade-Ite cookie jar, she muttered under her breath, "You're leaving me no choice."

Skye had tolerated the situation for as long as she could. While she and Wally were engaged, it was all well and good for them to confine their lovemaking to nights spent at Wally's place. But once they were married, he needed to be able to move into her house without fear of some disaster forcing them out of bed just when things were getting interesting.

Like this morning, when Wally had stopped by to tell her that his annulment was in the final stages and Father Burns had assured him that it would be completed by the end of April. Skye had been on Wally's lap, celebrating the good news with a lingering kiss, when the cookie jar flew off the counter and smashed at their feet. It was a miracle neither of them had been injured by flying glass or Oreo shrapnel.

Wally had blamed Skye's cat for the incident, but she knew Bingo wasn't the culprit. The chubby feline had tried and failed on several occasions to leap onto the counter. It was too high, and he was too portly. Besides, there was no food sitting out, and without the enticement of something edible to motivate him, Bingo rarely moved farther than the next pool of sunlight.

Skye stepped out onto her back porch. "I'm giving you one more chance," she said, shivering in the cold March wind and rain, as she threw the sharp fragments of the dearly departed cookie jar into the trash can. "If so much as a door slams shut the next time Wally and I start to make love here, I'm getting rid of you." It was time to put an end to Mrs. Griggs's reign of terror—one way or another.

Marching back into the kitchen, Skye grabbed a thin blue folder from where she had hidden it at the bottom of her junk drawer, sat down at the table, and stared nervously at the file. Just as she inserted a finger beneath the tab, the telephone rang, and she jumped back. Could Mrs. Griggs be phoning to apologize?

Skye giggled at her own silliness. It was one thing to believe the spirit of the house's previous owner was present, but quite another to think the woman could call from the great beyond.

Halfway to her feet, Skye sank back in the chair. It was probably the same annoying tele-marketer that had been pestering her for the past week. A company claiming that it could lower her credit card rates had been calling her three or four times a day, and she'd finally resolved to let her answering machine act as a buffer.

Skye knew that at ten a.m. on a nonworkday morning her best friend, school librarian Trixie

Frayne, would still be fast asleep. Despite being married to a farmer, Trixie was not an early riser, so the call wouldn't be from her.

And it wouldn't be Wally, since he was on his way to Springfield to begin the last part of the Illinois police chief certification program. The first stage had required only documentation of his extensive law enforcement experience, including leadership abilities, education, and training. But for this final phase, he had to complete written tests that would take all afternoon and several hours the next day. He had told Skye that although the accreditation wasn't required, he felt it was important for him to have it in order to be a good role model for the officers under his command.

When the phone stopped ringing, then immediately started up again, Skye frowned. Maybe it wasn't the telemarketer. She doubted a computerized system would continue to redial again and again.

It couldn't be her brother, Vince. Saturday morning was the busiest time at his hair salon. The usual suspect would be her mother, but she and Skye's father had left last night for a weekend stay at Ho-Chunk Casino near the Wisconsin Dells.

Who did that leave? Skye's godfather, Charlie Patukas, would just hop in his Cadillac and drive over if he wanted to talk to her that urgently. Which meant . . .

Shoot! It had to be either Frannie or Justin, or

both. During their high school years, Frannie Ryan and Justin Boward had been coeditors of the school newspaper, which Skye and Trixie sponsored. Although they were no longer her students, Skye had remained close to them, and since they were attending Joliet Junior College and lived at home, they still frequently asked her for help.

Skye groaned in surrender, pushed the file aside, and rose from her chair. Figuring out how to get rid of Mrs. Griggs's ghost would have to wait a little longer. Peering at the phone where it hung on her kitchen wall, Skye focused on the caller ID—something she should have done several minutes ago.

The words BUNNY LANES appeared on the little screen. That was odd. Granted, Frannie worked there as a waitress in the grill, but the town bowling alley didn't open until the children's and teen leagues started at eleven.

Crap! Could her persistent caller be Bunny Reid—former Las Vegas dancer, current bowling alley manager, and mother of Skye's previous boyfriend? There was only one way to find out.

Snatching up the handset, Skye pushed the ON button and said, "Hello?"

"Ms. D, thank God you're home." Frannie's desperate voice was shrill in Skye's ear. "There's an emergency at the alley. Can you come right away?"

"Emergency? Are you okay? What happened?"

Skye gritted her teeth in aggravation when Frannie hung up without answering her questions.

No one responded to Skye's repeated attempts to call back, and after a couple of frustrating minutes, she gave up. As she slipped on tennis shoes and grabbed her jacket, purse, and keys from the coat stand, she told herself that at least she was dressed in nice jeans and a sweater, had French-braided her hair and put on a little makeup. Usually, in a crisis she was caught with a naked face, wearing a baggy sweatshirt, and with her chestnut curls in a bushy ponytail.

Happy that for once she looked presentable, Skye ran out of the house and jumped into her 1957 Bel Air convertible, a tank of a car that her father and godfather had rehabbed for her several years ago.

She stamped on the accelerator, and the Chevy flew down the blacktop, its windshield wipers at full speed to keep up with the pouring rain. Six minutes later, Skye squealed into the bowling alley's parking lot and skidded to a halt on the wet asphalt.

What in the world? Why was the lot filled with cars and trucks, and . . . Skye squinted through the deluge, trying to understand what she was seeing. Was that a row of RVs lined up like cows at the watering trough? Had Bunny opened a campsite? More to the point, did her son, Simon, know about it?

Three years ago, Bunny had reappeared in Simon's life after a twenty-year absence. And although he had already been the owner of Reid's Funeral Home and the coroner, he had bought the town bowling alley in order to provide his mother with the job and permanent address she needed to avoid going to jail for misusing prescription drugs. Simon had never admitted that he'd purchased the business solely to help Bunny, but Skye knew that had been his true motivation.

Although Simon and Skye were no longer a couple, she and Bunny were still friends. And Skye hated to see the flamboyant redhead damage the relationship she had finally forged with her son by getting involved in something he wouldn't approve of.

With that in mind, Skye flung herself out of the Bel Air, sprinted to the bowling alley's entrance, and shoved open the glass doors. As she stepped over the threshold, a wave of noise swept over her like a tsunami, nearly pushing her back out.

Skye paused in the entryway. Because of the way the place was designed, she couldn't see beyond the coatracks and the rows of cube-shaped lockers where the bowlers kept their equipment. Tilting her head, she tried to figure out what was going on.

The din she heard wasn't music; it was a cacophony of mostly indistinguishable voices, but every once in a while numbers were announced over a loudspeaker. What was happening in the rest of the alley? Could Bunny be holding an auction? But what could she be selling?

Deciding the best course of action would be to find Frannie, Skye took a left, heading toward the grill, which was the young woman's most likely location. Skye had planned to cut through the bar, but the door was locked. Peeking through the round, portholelike window, she saw that the bartender was absent and the room was empty of customers. The cocktail tables were lined up in rows, rather than placed in their usual scattered arrangement, and a digital countdown board had been set up on the stage next to a gigantic gong.

Skye gnawed on her lower lip. Was Bunny planning on some sort of game night?

Even though Skye wasn't very good at judging the direction that sounds were coming from, she thought the racket must be in the lounge area back by the alleys. While she was trying to decide whether to continue on to the grill or go toward the noise, she heard an angry male voice bellow Bunny's name. A few beats went by, and that same voice thundered an indistinguishable sentence. A nanosecond later, a woman screamed.

Okay. That definitely had not come from the alleys. Skye dashed down the narrow hallway into the grill, but it was empty. Where was the yelling coming from? Wait. The shouting had sounded echoey. The argument had to be taking place in the basement.

Several large rooms used for parties and banquets ran under the length of the bowling alley. Despite her bad memories of having been locked down there with Simon when their mothers had tried to reunite them, Skye raced through the open door and down the stairs.

At the bottom she stopped and stared. An extraordinarily large man wearing a gray suit jacket over a faded Metallica T-shirt and dark sweatpants with a white stripe down the leg was cuddling a fluffy white angora cat in one enormous arm while dangling a stunningly beautiful woman by her throat with the other hand.

It appeared that Skye had found Frannie's emergency.

CHAPTER 2

Quick As a Cat

Bunny was jumping around the man and woman like a rabbit trying to infiltrate a chicken-wire-enclosed garden. In between hops she screeched, "Elijah Jacobsen, you put Alexis down right this minute!"

The big guy ignored her, staring into his victim's sapphire blue eyes.

"She didn't mean it when she said Princess was seriously flawed," Bunny added, her red curls bouncing in time with her shouts. "Tell him you're sorry, Alexis."

Bunny's efforts to intervene went unheeded by the suspended woman, whose voice wheezed alarmingly as she unwisely said, "But I'm not sorry." Although Elijah tightened his hold, she gasped, "I meant every word."

The big man bellowed like an alpenhorn in a cough drop commercial and shook Alexis until her long, straight black hair swung from side to side, as if keeping time with some unheard melody.

Skye hesitated just long enough for Bunny to dart forward and grab an object that resembled a foot-long mini rake from a nearby table. As Bunny drew back like a little kid about to smash open a piñata, Skye saw that the weapon would hit Alexis, not Elijah. Intent on deflecting Bunny's attack, Skye flung herself forward.

Unfortunately, Skye's trajectory was as bad as Bunny's aim, and instead of knocking the redhead aside, Skye caught the brunt of Bunny's swing across the face. She sank to the floor, as flattened as a papier-mâché pony.

For a moment there was complete silence. The people bunched in the doorways and clustered in the basement hallway who had been excitedly commenting on the fight stood with their mouths open, seeming to wait for the next scene in a play.

Finally, Elijah dropped Alexis, shook his head, and, as if coming out of a deep sleep, blinked his pale gray eyes. He looked down at Skye and asked, "What happened to you?"

While Skye tried to figure out the answer—the blow seemed to have knocked the short-term memory out of her—the crowd started to chatter and Bunny wailed, "I'm so sorry. Are you all right? Skye, say you're all right. If you're not all right, Sonny Boy's going to kill me."

"Get a wet rag, some bandages, and a cold compress," Elijah ordered Bunny, pushing her out of his way.

The redhead leaped backward as if she were spring-loaded, then scurried off.

Elijah knelt by Skye's side and asked, "Do you need an ambulance?"

"No." Skye felt blood dripping from her cheek,

and the room was spinning. She was afraid she would vomit if she tried to say more.

"Let me get a good look." Elijah put a hand on her shoulder and pressed her back down when she tried to sit up. "Before my troubles, I used to be a doctor."

Skye fought to hold back tears of pain as he ran the fingers of one hand over her cheeks and nose. Was this the same guy who had nearly choked the brunette? He was still holding the cat, but otherwise seemed like an entirely different person—a calm and competent individual versus the raving maniac who had dangled Alexis like a ripe plum.

"I don't think anything is broken," Elijah reassured Skye. "Your nose seems intact and the scratches on your cheek are superficial."

A subdued Bunny returned with the first-aid items Elijah had asked for. Wordlessly, he took the wet cloth and gently wiped Skye's cheek. He murmured soothingly to her as he cleaned the blood from her face and applied several butterfly bandages to her wounds.

Bunny hovered near his shoulder, wringing her hands and begging him to say that Skye was okay.

At last Elijah handed Skye a cold compress and instructed: "Hold this across your nose and cheeks. It should lessen the bruising and swelling, but your pretty green eye is going to have quite a shiner."

Terrific! Skye's first thought was that she wouldn't be scheduling her engagement picture anytime soon. Her second was that she would have to avoid her mother until she healed. May Denison was not a huge fan of Bunny to begin with, and if she saw Skye's injuries, she'd probably skin the redhead alive and use her hide to wash windows.

"Ms. D, I'm so sorry." Frannie paced up and down in front of Skye's chair. "I should have met you at the door, but I had to pee so bad."

Frannie was tall and solidly built. Skye had spent several years trying to raise the young woman's self-esteem and help her to navigate high school, a world dominated by size 4 girls. Much of that work had been undone during Frannie's first semester at Loyola University. After a couple of months of feeling like an outcast and missing home, Frannie had returned to Scumble River. She was now completing her sophomore year at a local community college, and she'd applied to the University of Illinois journalism program.

"It's not your fault," Skye told Frannie for the third or fourth time. "No one forced me to get between Bunny and the object of her wrath. But why didn't you answer when I called you back?"

"I was helping to find Princess."

"Elijah's cat?"

"Yes," Frannie confirmed. "She escaped while Ms. Hightower had her out of her cage to judge her."

"And Ms. Hightower is?"

"The woman Mr. Jacobsen was trying to kill," Frannie clarified.

"The missing cat was the emergency, not the assault I walked in on?" Having seen Elijah Jacobsen manhandling Alexis, Skye understood how Frannie could have been panicked at his earlier agitation, but she wanted to make sure she understood the situation.

"Right." Frannie twisted a lock of glossy brown hair around her finger. When she went away to college, she had cut her nearly waist-long waves and flat-ironed the curl out of what was left. Now, almost two years later, she still didn't seem accustomed to the shorter length.

"Well," Skye said, "it looks as if everything is okay now, at least for the moment. Alexis refused to let us call the police and Elijah appears to have regained his composure."

Skye was sitting in Bunny's office. Through the open door, she had a clear view of the lounge and bowling alleys. Rows and rows of cages containing every kind of feline imaginable lined the lanes, and throngs of people wearing all styles of clothing from jeans to cocktail dresses milled around, many carrying cats in their arms.

"What is all this?" She gestured to the scene before her.

"A cat show," Frannie explained.

"And why is the bowling alley hosting a cat show?"

"It all started last September." Frannie's brown eyes sparkled. As a journalism student, she liked nothing more than to tell a good story. "Miss Bunny wanted to earn some extra money."

"For what?" Skye shuddered inwardly. An entrepreneurial Bunny was never a good thing. "Not more Botox treatments?" Bunny had gotten in trouble nine months ago when she'd accepted a kickback in her quest to pay for reclaiming her youthful appearance.

"That, too." Frannie finally stopped pacing. "Miss Bunny said that old age is like cheap underwear—it creeps up on you—so she makes sure she always wears Victoria's Secret V-strings." Frannie leaned against the edge of the desk facing Skye. "But mostly she wanted to take a singles cruise so she could hook a rich boyfriend."

"How did you get involved?" Skye refused to think about Bunny dressed in a string bikini on the high seas hunting millionaires.

"Well . . ." Frannie studied her white tennis shoes. "Miss Bunny, Justin, and I were all sitting around one night after the bowling alley closed and Miss Bunny was going on and on about how hard it was to meet men because she lived in a small town and was a little bit older and all."

"And?"

"I might have mentioned Internet dating." Frannie refused to meet Skye's gaze.

"Oh, my Lord," Skye moaned. Bunny loose in the virtual world was a recipe for catastrophe. "But how did you get from Bunny's lack of dates to this?" Skye pointed to the cages and people.

"Justin possibly brought up the idea that we could start an online matchmaking site of our own, and Miss Bunny could have her pick of the guys who signed up, *and* we could make money, too."

"Crap!" Skye still didn't see how an online dating service had morphed into a cat show, but she knew the answer wouldn't make her happy. "So Justin, as the resident computer genius, helped Bunny create a matchmaking service," Skye guessed.

"Right." Frannie grinned. "We decided it should specialize in people who lived in small Illinois towns and were over forty."

"Okay . . ." Skye frowned. Their idea actually sounded like a good one—sort of.

"Bunny decided to name the site CupidsCats Meow.com because *The Cat's Meow* was her most successful Las Vegas show." Frannie paused, as if Skye should be able to figure out the rest, but when she remained silent, the young woman continued. "Most of the people who signed up thought it was a service for single cat lovers looking to meet other single cat lovers. So we thought—what the heck."

"What the heck?" Skye cringed. That's why putting Bunny together with the young people was so dangerous; instead of careful consideration, all three of them leaped into the situation without considering the consequences. Not that Skye could criticize the trio, considering her own flying tackle half an hour ago.

"Uh-huh." Frannie nodded, beaming. "Why not have a combination cat show and speed-dating weekend right here in Scumble River? We had the bowling alley to hold the events—"

"And I researched cat shows," Justin Boward said, strolling into the office and taking over the story. "From what I read, cat shows can be held anywhere from high school gyms to five-star hotels."

At nineteen, Justin seemed to have had reached his full height of six-two. His weight was finally catching up with his height, though he would probably always have a slender build. He kept his nutmeg brown hair cut military short, but his new glasses no longer hid his long-lashed brown eyes. He hadn't been an attractive teenager, but he was turning into a nice-looking young man.

"And we could charge sixty bucks per cat for the show and seventy-five dollars for the speed dating," Frannie added. "We'd also make money from the cage rental, vendor table fee, and food and drinks."

"Does Simon know about this?" Skye was pretty darn sure he didn't.

"No." Frannie's expression was angelic. "Miss Bunny didn't want to bother him. He's spending the weekend with a friend in St. Louis."

The hairs on the back of Skye's neck stood at full attention. Was her reaction caused by the thought of what Simon would do to Bunny when he found out, or by the idea of a bunch of strangers invading Scumble River? From hard-learned experience, Skye knew for a fact that bringing in a crowd of out-of-towners nearly always resulted in murder.

CHAPTER 3

Who'll Bell the Cat?

Because the event had proven to need more manpower than they had expected, Bunny, Justin, and Frannie had begged Skye to stick around and help out. Although all the trio could offer was minimum wage and free meals in return, Skye had agreed to stay. She loved cats and didn't have any plans for the weekend. Besides, Trixie had given her a necklace engraved with the words LIFE BEGINS AT THE END OF YOUR COMFORT ZONE, and Skye was trying to take that advice to heart.

Her first assignment fell under Justin's purview. He was in charge of judging. On his computer, he kept track of all the scores and tabulated them for the final round. Skye's task was to find the contestants who didn't show up in the correct judging areas and to help catch any feline escape artists.

Justin had explained that because this was a small, unofficial show, all cats were being judged as pets. They would be evaluated on their beauty, character, demeanor, and grooming, rather than according to breed standards. There would be three rounds with three judges, so cats could collect up to four ribbons each—one for each round and one for the Best of the Best. And no one judge's opinion could influence that top prize.

Skye had asked if there was a danger of hard feelings developing among competitors that might hamper the contestants from making a love connection during the later speed-dating activity, but Bunny hadn't seemed worried.

As Skye approached the rows of cages lining the bowling lanes—which Frannie had informed her was known as the benching area—she hoped that Bunny had protected the wooden floors. She sighed in relief when she saw that plywood boards had been laid over the tarp-covered floors. At least Simon wouldn't have costly damages to add to his list of grievances against his mother's latest harebrained scheme.

Her mind at rest, Skye made her way down the aisles, admiring the imaginatively decorated pens and their cute kitty occupants. Stopping in front of a cage swathed in lilac satin, she peered through the bars. Inside, on a black velvet pedestal, lounged a pair of long, slender cats with short, sleek fur. As she studied the felines' trilateral heads and extra-large ears, their tails whipped back and forth and they narrowed their striking blue eyes.

A small sign edged in crystal beads read:

FAWNCATS
ORIENTAL SHORTHAIRS
FAWN IRVING
LAUREL, ILLINOIS

Entranced by the interesting-looking creatures, Skye jumped when a disembodied voice announced, "That's Fawncats Ice Pearl and Fawncats Ice Opal, but their call names are Miss Pearl and Miss Opal."

"They're amazing." For the second time that day Skye found herself talking to thin air. "I love their little pixyish faces."

"We call that wedge-shaped." A tall, thin woman in her late fifties emerged from behind the cage, catching the edge of the table with her hip and knocking over the oversize champagne glass full of tiny opalescent balls that had been perched on top of the crate. "Their heads should form perfect triangles," she explained while righting the glass and rounding up the escaped faux bubbles.

Her own face had high cheekbones and a pointy chin. Those features, along with her buzz-cut white-blond hair, made Skye wonder whether the woman had chosen the breed because of its resemblance to herself.

"Interesting," Skye murmured, then asked, "Are you Fawn Irving?"

"Yes."

"I'm Skye Denison. I'm here to escort you to the judging area for number seven."

"Great." Fawn opened the pen door and swooped up one of the cats. "I heard people were getting lost, and Miss Pearl here gets spooked easily."

Skye led the way to the basement door. Halfway down the steps, Fawn tripped and slammed into Skye. Luckily, for both women, Skye had a firm grip on the banister, and her substantially greater weight halted the lean breeder's momentum.

When they were all on solid ground, Skye escorted Fawn into one of the three rooms being used for judging. Skye stopped just inside the door, but Fawn placed Pearl in the only vacant cage of the nine set up along the rear wall.

A woman whom Skye immediately identified as Elijah Jacobsen's earlier victim, Alexis, stood with her back to the assembled cats, facing a long table. Attached to the front was a poster that read:

SCUMBLE RIVER CAT SHOW
JUDGE ALEXIS HIGHTOWER
RING #1 ROUND #1

Glancing over her shoulder, Alexis curled her lips and said, "I see the late Fawn Irving has decided to join us after all."

Two red circles formed on the gawky blonde's pale cheeks. "Sorry," she muttered. "I didn't hear my number being called."

Alexis raised a perfectly plucked sable eyebrow. "Perhaps if you had fewer holes in your head, your hearing would be better."

Fawn recoiled, her hands flying to the multiple pierced earrings she wore. "I, that's really . . ."

She stopped, swallowed, and straightened her spine. "Would it hurt you to be supportive once in a while?"

"I'd like to help you, Fawn," Alexis mocked, "because I know you need it, but I've mislaid my magic wand."

"Maybe one of your flying monkeys stole it." Fawn was breathing heavily and her fingernails dug into the tabletop, but she didn't back down.

Alexis gazed at a bruise on Fawn's forearm, then *tsk*ed. "Bump into something again—or did your husband come back?" Fawn gasped and Alexis smiled, shaking her head. "Your klutziness never ceases to amaze me."

"Why are you always so mean, Alexis?" The fragile woman finally lost the inner battle for strength that she'd been fighting, and whimpered, "What have I ever done to you?"

"Nothing. Nothing at all." Alexis bared her teeth in a self-satisfied smile. "How could you? You're such a colossal nobody, you and your second-rate cats aren't even a blip on my radar." With that, she plucked a cat from its cage and began the judging.

As Fawn slunk to a chair in the back without retaliating, Skye relaxed. She'd lingered, thinking that the gorgeous judge might provoke another physical altercation—this time by Fawn—but now that everything seemed calm, Skye left the room and returned upstairs.

As she continued to guide contestants to the correct areas, she thought about the most recent scene she'd witnessed in the basement. Why had Alexis insulted Fawn? There hadn't been any discernible reason for her verbal attack on the older woman. Was Alexis just plain mean? Didn't she care that her cruel words might make a bad impression that could damage her chances at the speeding-dating event? Maybe she thought the male participants would be blinded by her beauty and her bad behavior during the cat show wouldn't be an issue.

After Alexis's extreme nastiness, the rest of Skye's escort duties went smoothly. Princess had been the only feline fugitive. And although Skye saw Elijah several times that morning, he appeared calm and in control of himself, mostly texting or fiddling with his rosary beads.

During the past few months, Skye had been trying to mind her own business no matter what went on around her, but Alexis's treatment of Fawn continued to gnaw at her. So during the noon break, she looked for Bunny, determined to make her aware of the beautiful judge's bullying behavior.

When Skye couldn't find Bunny, she decided to ask Frannie if she knew where the elusive redhead had gone. Earlier, Frannie had explained that she was in charge of the food and nonalcoholic drink portion of the events, so Skye headed toward the grill.

The young entrepreneur was behind the counter selling cold sandwiches, chips, fruit, cookies, and sodas, and when Skye reached the front of the line, she asked, "Do you know where Bunny is? I haven't seen her in a while."

"She's in the bar working with the deejay for tonight." Frannie handed Skye a key, adding, "Here, you'll need this. The door's locked."

"Thanks." While Skye made her food selections, she noted that Frannie seemed to be in her element, managing the crowd with finesse and chatting easily with the customers as she took their money and made change. "Looks like you're doing a brisk business."

"Yep." Frannie leaned forward and whispered, "We deliberately only gave them forty-five minutes for lunch so they'd have to eat here if they didn't want to risk being late for the next round."

Skye started to speak, but held her tongue. Frannie was no longer her student, and as Skye slipped into the bar, then relocked the door behind her, she reassured herself that actions that seemed unscrupulous to her were just good business practices in the retail world.

Bunny was standing with a bearded guy wearing jeans, mirrored sunglasses, and a black T-shirt. Waving, Skye took a seat. As she removed her lunch from the brown bag Frannie had placed it in, she studied the man and woman in front of her as they moved around the stage talking and gesturing.

The DJ's appearance was unremarkable except for his dark brown hair, which was parted on the side and puffed out in the shape of a football helmet. Skye wondered how much hair spray he needed to hold his elaborate coiffure in place. She mentally scratched her head. Did he really think that was an attractive style?

Bunny held up a finger indicating that she'd be done in a minute, then turned back to the DJ. But that minute turned into fifteen, and Skye had finished eating her turkey wrap and chips by the time the redhead pulled out a chair and joined her.

"Phew." Bunny adjusted her black and purple spaghetti-strap top, pulling up the front while simultaneously tucking her boobs more firmly into the padded cups. "I hope he knows eighties music like he claims to, or tonight will be a catastrophe."

"Why are you worried?" Skye tore open her packet of cookies. "Isn't he a professional?"

"He's from Chicago." Bunny pronounced the name of the city with reverence. Small-town living would never have been the redhead's first choice if she hadn't run out of options. "Of course he's a pro, but the eighties was an extremely complex musical era."

"Sure it was." Skye crossed her fingers as she agreed. "But shouldn't you have soft music for speed dating? Something low and sexy to put the participants in the mood, and so they won't have to shout at each other to be heard?"

"Duh." Bunny snatched a ginger snap from Skye's pile. "DJ Wonka is for afterward. We're having a bowler disco party from ten till midnight. The servers are going to wear the cutest bowler hats."

"Where are you having the party?" Skye moved the remaining two cookies out of Bunny's reach. "The alleys are full of cages and feline paraphernalia."

"Round three ends at four, then the finalists are announced, and all cats and equipment must be removed by five." Bunny got up, went behind the bar, snagged a bottle of water from the cooler, and reseated herself. "Then the guys I hired to put down the tarps and plywood will remove them and the cages, and, voilà, we'll be ready for the bowler disco party."

"So you've got it under control." Skye was impressed with the redhead's planning. Preparedness was usually not her strong suit. "That sounds like fun." Then she frowned. "But how about tomorrow? Won't you have to put everything back for the final judging?"

"Nah." Bunny shook her head, making her magenta chandelier earrings swing. "There will only be nine cats in the Best of the Best round, and there's plenty of room for those cages in the lounge area where we now have the two vendors and the photographer."

"So this afternoon is rounds two and three, then dinner, and this evening is speed dating and the party?" Skye held up a finger for each activity.

"Right." Bunny's attention shifted to another topic and she tilted her head, examining Skye. "Elijah was wrong." She pursed her glossy mauve lips. "I don't think you're going to have a black eye after all, and I bet you could take off the bandages. You heal really fast."

"Thank goodness for small favors." Skye touched her cheek, wincing at how swollen it felt. "Hitting someone is never the solution to a problem. Even if they hit you first." She bit back a chuckle. She sounded like she was doing a social skills class at the elementary school, which was probably about the level Bunny would understand.

"And you, my darling, should never get between me and a man." The redhead giggled hysterically. "Especially one that I'm mad at."

"On that note, let's change the subject." Skye drained her can of Diet Coke and asked, "What's up with Alexis Hightower?"

"Well, she's working for free." Bunny attempted to flatten a crease in her black lace leggings and grimaced when she realized the wrinkle was in her thigh rather than in the fabric. "She waived her judging fee in return for food, drinks, and complimentary participation in the speed-dating portion of the weekend."

"Ever hear that you get what you pay for?" Skye crumpled a piece of wax paper. "You should have seen how nasty she was to that poor Fawn Irving."

"Hmm." Bunny frowned, then quickly used her pinky to smooth the line between her brows. "I know she really pressed Elijah's buttons, too, but she's always been okay with me. In fact, she gave me a lot of help organizing the cat show. We were on the phone every day for weeks. She told me all the stuff I needed to know about how to do things so the event would be fun even if it wasn't official."

Skye carefully considered her next words. "I don't want to jump to conclusions, but from what I've seen—her being verbally abusive to Elijah and Fawn, but nice to you—Alexis appears to bully people she considers less powerful than herself."

"That's something I won't tolerate." Bunny's brown eyes were suddenly serious. "Fawn's had a hard time lately. She told me she just got out of the hospital a week ago."

"I've just met Alexis today, and have only seen her in two situations, so it's hard to say if I just caught her at a bad time"—Skye bit her lip—"but it worries me that she appears to target the most vulnerable people."

CHAPTER 4

Cheshire Cat Smile

Skye delivered the last stray contestant to the judging room a few minutes after three thirty. Her assignment completed, she grabbed her purse from Bunny's office and headed toward the lounge to browse the vendor booths. She also wanted to check out the feline photographer, to see if she could arrange for him to do a portrait of Bingo the next day.

The first stand held cat toys, feline furniture, and kitty accessories of every conceivable—and a few inconceivable—kind. Who knew there were clothes for cats, let alone wigs? Didn't cats already have enough hair?

Skye closed her eyes, trying to envision Bingo in a tuxedo and a blond toupee, but the only image that came to mind was the bloody mess that her hand would become if she attempted to turn her cat into a dress-up doll.

Moving on, Skye studied a brightly colored package with the words KITTY-CASSO emblazoned on the top. She was struggling to imagine how the kit was used when she noticed a little old lady wearing a name tag that read, SANDY—EIGHTY YEARS OLD AND LOVING LIFE, approaching her.

The octogenarian smiled widely at Skye and asked, "Can I help you, dear?"

"Uh." Skye didn't want to insult the woman, so she said carefully, "Am I reading this right? This is a painting set for cats?"

"That's correct, dear." Sandy plucked the box from Skye's hand and said in a TV pitchman's singsong voice, "It's no mess and contains nontoxic paint. This wonderful product stimulates your pet's creativity, provides exercise, and is the hit of all my pet parties."

"Wow." A vision of the tiny woman in a finger-painting session with a group of cats wearing paper hats popped into Skye's head. "I'm not sure Bingo would enjoy it. He considers himself too macho to be an artist."

"How about our Jester Ribbon Wand?" Sandy held up a yellow and red striped baton with a blue and green donut on the end. Five objects hung from streamers attached to the ring. "This combines sound, scent, and movement to entice even the manliest cats."

"Well . . ." Skye looked around, hoping to see something that Bingo would deign to play with and her mother wouldn't mistake for a baby toy. All she needed was for May to think she was pregnant. Which reminded her, she needed to talk to Wally about children. Now that his annulment was nearly finalized, she had to find out his opinion of fatherhood.

Focusing back on the present, Skye pointed to a long stick with a feather attached to the end. But before she could ask Sandy about it, an identical little old lady joined them. This one's badge read, SONIA—I'M THE NICE TWIN. She was dressed in the same powder blue knit slacks and sweater set as her sister. Even the golden cathead pin above her right breast was an exact match.

Skye glanced down and noticed that although the women wore similar shoes—pale blue Mary Janes—Sandy's had a two-inch heel, and Sonia's were flat.

Sonia took Skye's elbow and said, "Forget these foolish bits and pieces. Your kitty will be happier if you give him a paper bag and a ball of yarn." She grinned. "You know the fifth cat law, don't you?"

Skye shook her head.

"A cat's attention level will rise and fall in reverse proportion to the amount of effort a human expends in trying to interest him."

Skye giggled. The older woman's assessment of Bingo's personality was dead-on.

Sonia guided Skye to a display of carpet-covered towers. "What you really need for your darling is a Kitty Kondo. I custom-build all of them myself, so you can mix and match the design and color scheme."

Sandy had followed them and was tugging on

Skye's hand. "Toys are better for your cat's health. I only stock the best brands."

"But you can make your own playthings." Sonia challenged her sister. "Whereas my creations are one of a kind, constructed especially for your best friend."

Skye was beginning to feel like the last can of Fancy Feast on the pet store shelf when Alexis strolled up, waved her hand at both sides of the booth's contents, and scoffed, "It's all crap for pathetic people who fail to realize that we own the animals, they don't own us. I've been breeding cats for years. All they need is a good diet, proper grooming, and a clean living area."

The twins gasped, then said in unison, "What about love?"

"That's so what old ladies would think." Alexis snorted.

The sisters glared at her as if she were something they'd scraped off the bottom of a litter box.

"I'm sure everyone here would agree that cats need affection," Skye said in support of the elderly women.

"Of course they would. Never underestimate the power of stupid people in large groups." Alexis snickered. "This crowd overindulges their pets."

"Caring deeply is not overindulging," Skye said, gazing steadily at Alexis.

"Their *animals* receive healthier food and more

attention than most *children* in this country." The nasty woman dared Skye to disagree.

"We all have a right to our beliefs." Skye kept her expression impassive, then said in an even tone, "But it really is rude to verbalize that opinion in a place where most people will be hurt by what you say."

"Only losers allow themselves to be hurt by others," Alexis retorted, then walked away, adding over her shoulder, "And clearly you're a loser."

Skye shrugged off Alexis's insults. In her years as a school psychologist, she'd grown a thick skin. However, she did feel bad for the twin vendors, who seemed crushed by the younger woman's boorishness. Figuring a sale would cheer them up, Skye ordered a cat tree that resembled a child's jungle gym. Beaming, Sonia assured her the tower would be ready in two days.

Then turning her attention to Sandy, Skye bought an object called Neko Flies. The woman assured her that the toy was designed to mimic the movements of the creatures cats loved to chase. Skye didn't mention that the only object Bingo was apt to pursue was a chicken nugget.

Having done her good deed for the day, and spent more money than she'd earned by working the cat show, Skye tucked the toy into her purse and moved on to the next booth, where she was instantly entranced by the jewelry. Unable to choose among all the wonderful pieces, she fingered necklaces made of tiger's eye, sleek silver pendants, and cute charm bracelets, debating the merits of each one.

Just as she slid a gold cat-shaped ring onto her finger, an elegant woman with a cascade of brown curls down her back stepped forward and said, "That's one of my best pieces, but it can't compete with your lovely engagement ring. Tiffany's, two carats, correct?"

"Right. Thank you." Skye inspected the olive-skinned beauty. "Do you make all the jewelry yourself?"

"Yes." She held out a slender hand. "I'm Lola Martinez, and you are?"

"Skye Denison."

"I liked how you handled Alexis." Lola's brown eyes were full of loathing. "She's always bitching about something, and if anyone says anything about it, she claims it's not complaining, it's motivational speaking."

"Really?" Skye wasn't surprised that Alexis considered her every word important and failed to understand that what she said affected others. The opinionated judge's total lack of empathy had been apparent in every encounter Skye had had with her.

"Alexis is such a witch." Lola's mouth tightened. "And no one ever stands up to her."

"I'm a school psychologist, so I'm used to handling mean girls."

"Then you should do just fine with Alexis. Her maturity level is about the same as a thirteen-year-old's, and that's probably being unfair to the teenager." Lola took a deep breath, shook her head, and changed the subject by holding up a pair of black-enameled cat-shaped earrings. "These would look good on you."

Skye agreed, but once she completed her purchase, Lola hesitated before giving her the gold-foil box. Skye held her palm out, waiting, and finally the jewelry maker handed her the package.

Skye turned to go, but Lola's voice stopped her. "Just FYI, keep your fiancé away from Alexis. Now that you've challenged her, she'll make it her purpose in life to steal him away from you."

"Thanks for the warning." Skye tucked the jewelry box into her purse. "I'll keep that in mind if they ever meet."

As she walked away, she dismissed Lola's concern. Wally would see through Alexis before the predatory woman could unsheathe her claws or fluff her fur. Besides, he'd never betray Skye. They'd gone through too much to be together for either of them to risk losing each other now. Not when they were so close to finally getting married.

While Skye made her way to the photographer's cubicle, she noted that most competitors had packed up and left. The participants who lived within a reasonable driving distance would go home, drop off their animals, clean up, and come back for dinner at six thirty.

The ones who lived farther away had brought their RVs or were staying at the Up A Lazy River Motor Court, the local motel owned by Skye's godfather, Charlie Patukas. He normally didn't allow pets, but Bunny had somehow charmed him into making an exception for this weekend.

Although a few people still lingered in the vendor area, the photographer was already putting away his equipment when Skye entered his space. He was a nice-looking man in his early forties, but he reminded Skye of the Munchkin cat she had seen earlier. Sitting or lying down, the breed appeared average, but once the animal stood up, its extremely short legs were evident.

"I see you're finished for the day," Skye said, gesturing to the gear that was already packed up in various containers. "But if you have a minute, could you answer a couple of questions for me?"

"Sure." He smiled pleasantly at her as she hovered at the entrance. "I'm Kyle O'Brien."

"Skye Denison." She shook his hand. "I'm working the event, not here as a contestant, but I'd love to have a picture taken of my cat. Would it be possible for me to bring him in before the show officially starts tomorrow?"

"Of course." Kyle slipped a camera into its case. "The Best of the Best judging is at ten. I could meet you at eight and do three or four setups."

"That would be great. I don't want anything overly elaborate. Just a nice photo for my wall." Skye hesitated, then said, "Bingo isn't a trained show cat, so he might be hard to manage."

"No problem." Kyle grinned. "They call me the cat whisperer."

"This is so bogus," Justin complained as he returned to the grill for another tray of plates. "Frannie was in charge of the food. My area was accounting and judging, and I didn't ask her to help me with any of that."

"The two servers Frannie hired never showed up," Skye explained. "So she drafted us."

But empathy had never been Justin's strong suit, and he muttered something about America having an all-volunteer army, then headed back to the bar to serve the remaining eight diners. One of whom was Bunny, who had elected to eat with her guests.

Justin's attitude made Skye sigh as she took a seat at the counter. Her feet were killing her. As soon as she finished eating and helped Frannie clean up, she was heading home. Her cell phone charge had run out without her noticing, and Wally was probably wondering where the heck she was.

Justin returned, still grumbling, and Frannie led him away for a little girlfriend-to-boyfriend chat. Skye watched the couple as she ate her dinner.

The spaghetti was surprisingly tasty and the salad had a nice light dressing, but she thought the garlic bread was probably a mistake—considering that the next event was speed dating.

After Skye finished eating and Frannie returned from her talk, the two women started to wash the dirty dishes that Justin had begun bringing into the kitchen from the bar.

As they worked Skye commented, "There seemed to be a lot of unique people at the cat show."

"I guess unique is one way of putting it." Frannie giggled. "I'd go with weird."

"Especially Elijah Jacobsen." Skye shook her head. "He seems to be the oddest of all."

"At least he has an excuse." Frannie's expression turned sober. "He was in a terrible auto accident twenty years ago and suffered a really bad head injury."

"How awful."

"It resulted in his fiancée's death and ended his career as a surgeon."

"That's awful." Skye's voice caught. "A traumatic brain injury can cause so much damage to cognitive functioning."

"Yeah. It really messed him up." Frannie handed Skye the last wet plate. "He said he has a lot of trouble with memory and concentration, and it's hard for him to make decisions."

"The poor man. It sounds as if he really has a lot

to deal with." Skye wiped the dish dry and slid it onto the towering stack on the shelf, then folded the towel and said, "That's it, and I'm heading home."

"Thanks, Ms. D." Frannie sounded tired and her shoulders slumped. "You sure you don't want to stick around for the bowler disco party?"

"I'm positive." Skye felt her head start to throb at the idea of the loud music and flashing lights. "The servers Bunny has lined up for that event are coming, right?" Both Justin and Frannie were too young to serve alcohol, and there was no way Skye was moonlighting as a cocktail waitress. She didn't have the figure or the tolerance for drunks that the job required.

"Yep." Frannie pushed a strand of hair off her cheek. "The weekend lounge workers are covering both the speed dating and the party."

"Are you staying?" Skye asked, wondering what Xavier thought about his daughter's business venture. He had been a single parent for a long time, and she guessed that he would have a hard time accepting the young woman's growing independence.

"Nah." Frannie shook her head. "I hate disco and Justin's off pouting somewhere." She frowned. "It wouldn't be any fun without him."

"Why's he in such a bad mood tonight?" Skye asked, giving in to her curiosity—her noninterference policy was driving her crazy. "He seemed just fine this afternoon."

"Ms. Hightower yelled at him," Frannie explained. "She wanted to see the scores so far, but the judges aren't allowed to know how the cats did in the other rounds." Frannie pursed her lips, indicating her disapproval of Alexis's attempt to break the rules. "When Justin said no, she tried to flirt with him, and when that didn't work, she called him incompetent."

"Ouch!" Skye winced. Justin prided himself on his intelligence and his computer ability. Alexis's words would have really wounded his ego.

"Yep. Major ouch."

"Hey." The discussion about Alexis reminded Skye of a question she'd been meaning to ask all day. "What kind of qualifications does someone need to be a cat show judge? Is there a class you have to take?"

"We looked it up online and found out that to become a legitimate judge a person needs to have been a successful breeder whose cats have won ribbons at several shows," Frannie explained.

"Is that all?"

"No." Frannie scrunched her face in deep thought. "If I remember right, they also have to be on committees, work as entry clerks, and serve as show managers. Then they have to be trainees, pass tests, and apprentice with certified teachers."

"That sounds like a lot of effort." Skye bit her lip. "Since Alexis doesn't seem as enamored of cats as everyone else here, I wonder why she went to so much trouble."

"Maybe it's the only place she can be the boss. I remember her saying she supports herself working temp jobs."

"Ah, that might explain it."

"Yeah. She said her last one was as some city official's assistant, and he was a real control freak. He had a special phone she wasn't allowed to touch, but he didn't tell her that it was off limits until she'd already answered it. He expected her to read his mind about her duties and was always yelling at her."

"Sounds like one of my bosses."

Frannie giggled, then dried her hands and walked toward the bar door. "You want to take a peek at the speed daters?"

"Just for a minute." Skye had only a vague idea of how the event worked.

When she joined Frannie in peering through the frosted-glass window, the young woman said, "See the men at all the little round tables?"

"Yes." Skye noted that there were twenty guys ranging in age from forty to seventy seated facing the stage. One of them was Elijah, who had added a black velvet fedora to his outfit. Beneath its brim, gray-blond dreadlocks poked out in all directions.

Kyle O'Brien sat one table over from the ex-doctor. The photographer was dressed in nicely pressed khakis and a designer kelly green polo shirt. Since he was long-waisted, his unusually short stature wasn't noticeable when he was seated.

"See the women standing by the other door?" Frannie pointed to the left.

"Uh-huh." Skye recognized Fawn, Alexis, and Lola among the group.

"At eight o'clock, the women will join the guys." Frannie indicated the huge timer on the stage. "After ten minutes the deejay sounds the gong and the women get up and move to the next table."

"Geesh!" Skye was astounded. "Ten minutes to decide if you like someone?"

"Yes." Frannie nodded. "At the end of the event, each person ranks the men or women they've met from one to fifteen, with one being the guy or gal they would most like to have a real date with."

"Putting couples together using that method sounds complicated."

"Justin designed some computer program to match up the couples," Frannie explained. "Which reminds me, he better remember he has to be in the bar at nine thirty to run the thing."

"Do the matchees attend the bowler disco party together?"

"Yep." Frannie nodded. "The only other people allowed in are the vendors and the judges." Frannie winked. "Miss Bunny even hired a bouncer for the front door to keep out the local riffraff and any gate-crashers. She wanted the party to be exclusive."

Skye rolled her eyes. Simon would have a fit when he found out his mother was excluding the regulars. Scumble Riverites didn't forget slights like that, and there would be hell to pay for Bunny's snubbing them.

CHAPTER 5

Curiosity Killed the Cat

Although Skye was tired, she found herself lingering until the conclusion of the speed-dating event. She was curious to see who would end up with whom. Frannie had to stick around as well. Justin was her ride home, and the computer wizard couldn't work his magic and come up with the final couples until the very end.

Everyone watched intently as Justin keyed the numbers from the rating sheets into his laptop. Bunny stood by his side keeping up a constant patter to entertain the audience while he worked. She had changed from her fairly modest daytime attire into a short black dress with a bodice made of buckles, straps, and grommets that looked a little like a sexy version of a straitjacket, minus the overlong restraining sleeves.

A few minutes later, the small printer attached to the computer spit out a single sheet of paper. Justin looked up from the monitor and announced in a dramatic voice, "The results are in."

Bunny snatched the page from the tray, squinted, then hissed at Justin, "I told you to make the font bigger."

"For crying out loud, it's Arial sixteen," Justin

protested. "If you can't see that, you need to go to the eye doctor."

Bunny's scarlet fingernails pressed into Justin's shoulder, but she addressed the spectators. "Everyone ready to find out their dream dates?"

Skye surveyed the crowd as they roared their consent to Bunny's question. Most of their faces, including Kyle's and Fawn's, held a mixture of anticipation, trepidation, and hopefulness, but a few of the participants' expressions were harder to gauge. Both Alexis and Lola were impassive, and Elijah stared at his cell phone with his brows drawn together and his eyes unfocused.

Bunny strutted over to the stage like the dancer she had once been, then ran up the three steps. Considering that the fifty-seven-year-old was wearing thigh-high black boots with four-inch spike heels, her swift ascent was nothing short of astounding. As were the red ribbons crisscrossing up the boots' calves that fluttered saucily in the breeze.

DJ Wonka banged the gong, and once Bunny was sure she had everyone's attention, she pulled a pair of rhinestone-encrusted glasses from her cleavage and started calling out names. As she slowly read from her list, pausing dramatically after each pair, there were screeches of excitement, groans of disappointment, and meaningful glances between the men and women.

Of the participants Skye could identify, Kyle

was partnered with a cute little blonde, Lola got a dashing man who needed only a sword and eye patch to be a dead ringer for Hollywood's version of a pirate, and Fawn and Elijah were put together—which actually made sense in a weird sort of way. The most astonishing combination was Alexis and a short, mousy guy wearing a cheap navy suit, thick glasses, and a really bad hairpiece. How had that happened?

Skye was surprised that Bunny hadn't participated in the activity, since the whole shebang had started as a way for her to find a date. But as Skye turned to leave, she noticed the redhead slide into a chair next to a vaguely familiar, handsome man in his sixties. He kissed her cheek and tipped his head to whisper in her ear. Bunny giggled; then they both stood and slipped quietly out of the bar.

Evidently the wily redhead had saved the best guy for herself. It reminded Skye of her mother's practice of setting aside the piece of chocolate she wanted before offering the box to everyone else. But at least Bunny hadn't poked holes in the other men to see what they were made of before making her selection, which is what May did with the candy.

There was a message from Wally on Skye's answering machine when she got home. Although it was close to ten thirty, she immediately called him back, and it was clear from his voice that he had been asleep.

"I'm so sorry I woke you up," Skye said. "We can talk in the morning."

"No, I just went to bed a few minutes ago." Wally cleared his throat. "I'm fine. Where have you been and why didn't you answer your cell?"

"I forgot to charge the battery," Skye explained, then went on to describe her day, ending with, "See, I can be spontaneous."

"I never said you couldn't." Wally's smooth baritone held a hint of amusement, but sobered when he asked, "How badly did Bunny injure you?"

"I have three scratches on my cheek"—Skye fingered the bandages as she spoke—"but at least I didn't get the shiner Elijah predicted."

"Elijah being the big guy who started out as a raving lunatic and then claimed to be a physician?" Wally's tone was incredulous.

"Yeah."

"I think you should go to a real doctor." Wally's voice was implacable.

"Why? I'm fine. Unless . . ."—Skye teased him, drawing out the word—"you're afraid you might be marrying a scarred woman?"

"You know it's not your outer beauty I care about." Wally's voice was sincere. "I just want to make sure your cuts don't get infected."

"That's sweet of you." Skye understood Wally's

concern, but he needed to understand that she had been taking care of herself for a long time without his help. "I'm perfectly okay. The scrapes are already healing."

"I still think you should check with a doctor who graduated from a medical school located somewhere other than in his imagination," Wally persisted. "This guy sounds messed up to me."

"His name is Elijah, and he cleaned the scratches and told me to apply Neosporin twice a day for the next seventy-two hours," Skye assured Wally. "He said as long as I'd had a recent tetanus shot, I'm good, but if the edges of the wound turn red, I need to have it looked at."

"Someone should report him for practicing medicine without a license," Wally muttered. "Maybe I'll look into that when I get back."

Shoot! Skye sat straight up in bed and looked at the clock on the nightstand. It was quarter to seven. She had forgotten today was Sunday. How was she going to get Bingo's picture taken, work the cat show, and still attend church?

Closing her eyes, she tried to remember the new worship schedule. Out of the blue, Father Burns had altered it a couple of months ago, and she was still getting used to the change. Services were now at six, nine, and twelve. The first one was nearly over, and there was no way she could make the second, but noon was a possibility.

The cat show officially ended at two p.m., after the final round of judging and the awards brunch, so she would have to leave at quarter to twelve, then come back and help with the meal and the cleanup. Bunny wouldn't be happy, and Skye hated to break her promise to work the entire event, but she wasn't missing Mass.

Speaking of missing, where was Bingo? He wasn't in his usual spot—perched on the pillow next to her head. She scanned the room, a little worried that he had read her mind and was hiding because he didn't want to be photographed. But a few seconds later she spotted him sitting in the doorway looking down the hall, his tail flicking impatiently back and forth. Undoubtedly, since it was past his breakfast time, he was waiting for her to get her butt up and feed him.

She swung her legs to the floor and stood. "We're in a hurry this morning." Stepping around him on her way to the shower, she added, "You'll have to wait for your food until I'm dressed."

After putting on black jeans, a gray sweater set, and black loafers—a compromise between appropriate work and church attire—Skye ran down the stairs with Bingo following so closely he nearly tripped her in his eagerness to get to the kitchen and his food bowl.

Skye popped open a can of Fancy Feast and scooped a third of it into his dish. While Bingo ate, Skye had a quick cup of tea and an English muffin hot from the toaster. She usually tried to eat a healthier breakfast, but she was in a hurry. At least that was her excuse as she smeared the muffin with butter and marmalade.

As Bingo occupied himself in his litter box, she darted into the sunroom, snatched his Pet Taxi, and hid it behind the table. As soon as the cat strolled back into the kitchen to see if perhaps more gushie food had appeared in his bowl while he was gone, Skye scooped him up and stuffed him into the canvas carrier.

He meowed sharply, then huddled on the bottom, chirping furiously.

Skye talked softly to him as she carried him to the car. "I'm sorry, Bingo." She settled him on the passenger seat. "I know you hate to leave the house and I promise you're not going to the vet." Sliding in behind the wheel, she cajoled, "I want a professional photo of you to show everyone what a pretty boy you are."

He hissed and turned so that his rear end was facing her. She patted him through the stiff fabric, then headed into town. Bingo was still muttering when they arrived at the bowling alley, and Skye wondered if this was a wasted trip. Could Kyle get the cat's cooperation long enough to take a decent photograph?

When Skye approached the entrance, she noticed that the interior was dark. Looking at her watch, she saw that it was a couple of minutes to eight. "Crap!" she said to the cat's hindquarters. "I forgot that the show's hours are nine to two today."

Bingo was silent.

"When I made the appointment for your picture, it didn't even cross my mind that the building might not be open at eight." Skye tipped her head. "Do you think Kyle forgot about that, too?"

Bingo's tail twitched.

"I can't see past the entryway, so maybe the lights are on in the other parts of the bowling alley." Skye continued to address the cat's rear end. "Kyle's probably in his booth waiting for us."

Bingo licked a paw.

"I hate being late for an appointment." Frustrated, she slapped the door, and to her surprise, it swung open. "See, Bingo." She pumped her fist in the air. "I told you Kyle didn't forget about us."

Skye edged carefully past the benches and lockers. Although the lights were on in the vendor area, no one was around. She poked her head into the photography cubicle, but it, too, was empty.

Bingo was getting heavy. Skye didn't want to leave him alone, so she cradled his crate in her arms and asked, "What should we do, boy?"

He had finally turned around and was staring at her with luminous green eyes.

"If Kyle was here, his equipment would be set up, or at least his cases would be in his space. And where's Bunny? If the alley's open, she should be here." Skye cocked her head, listening. "Maybe she ran upstairs to her apartment for something."

Bingo yawned.

"We'll wait ten minutes for Kyle." Skye looked around the vendor space for a seat. "If he doesn't show up by then, I'll take you home."

Just as Skye located a folding chair, Bingo let out a howl and a horrible odor filled the air. She looked down and saw something brown oozing from the mesh at the back of the cat carrier. Bingo had expressed his opinion about the whole situation.

"Bad kitty!" Skye scolded. "Bad, bad kitty." Holding the crate as far from her as possible, she tried to figure out what to do.

Before Skye could formulate a plan, Bunny materialized in front of her, squealing and holding her nose. "What is that god-awful stench?" The redhead's clingy black tank top boasted a rhinestone black widow spider with a faux ruby hourglass shape on its back.

"Bingo had an accident." Skye felt her face flame at her pet's faux pas.

"So I see." Bunny stepped daintily over a slime trail of poo.

"Uh!" Skye tried not to inhale. "Is there somewhere I can clean him up?"

"There's a sink and a pile of rags in the basement utility closet."

"Great." Skye tried to take a step.

"Wait." Bunny grabbed Skye's arm. "I'll get something you can use to stop the seepage."

"Thanks."

Bunny tottered away, her black patent leather ankle boots tapping merrily as she dashed into the bar. A second later she returned with a stack of paper napkins and thrust them at Skye.

Using the wad as a kind of diaper for the carrier, Skye made her way to the basement door, descended the stairs, then stopped and looked around. Okay, where was the utility closet? Two rooms to her right and a large one to her left were bisected by a narrow hallway. The closet had to be at the back.

Skye walked down the short, faintly lit passage. Squinting, she was relieved when she spotted a door at the end marked PRIVATE. Thankful that the brown waterfall had ceased to trickle from the rear of the Pet Taxi, she balanced the carrier in one arm and turned the knob.

The basement's lack of windows made it seem like midnight even on the sunniest days, and Skye had been glad that the area around the stairs was lit by low-wattage fixtures that always remained on. But it had grown dimmer and dimmer as she made her way down the corridor, and in the closet there was no illumination.

She felt along the walls on either side of the doorway for the light switch, but couldn't find any. *Hmm.* It had to be here somewhere. Maybe there was a string hanging from a bulb in the center of the room.

She shuffled toward where she thought the cord might be and waved her hand around the space in front of her. Finally, her fingers closed around a chain. She gave it a hard tug and the closet lit up.

As she turned, her foot nudged something soft. She looked down and jumped backward. Alexis Hightower was lying spread-eagled on the tile floor. A thin braided wire was wound tightly around her neck. The metal cord was connected to a glittery wand, which stuck up next to her ear like a video game joystick. A toy mouse attached to the wire was stuffed into her mouth.

CHAPTER 6

When a Black Cat
Crosses Your Path

Skye swallowed the scream that was threatening to burst from her throat. There was no doubt that Alexis was dead. The only question in Skye's mind was whether the murderer was still in the building.

After making sure that the hall was empty, she took a firm grip on Bingo's carrier and sprinted for the stairs. Once she reached the main floor, she rounded up Bunny and enlightened her about the situation as she propelled the three of them into the redhead's office and locked the door.

As Skye grabbed the phone and dialed 911, she sent up a silent prayer of gratitude that it was Sunday. At least she wouldn't have to deal with her mother, who was a police dispatcher. Thank goodness May worked the Monday-through-Friday second shift.

When Skye finished explaining the murder to the weekend dispatcher, she, along with Bunny and a vocally unhappy Bingo, sat in the office and watched the second hand on the wall clock inch around its oversize round face. The women didn't speak, and neither could translate the black cat's yowls. Although "Get me the hell out of this stinky carrier" would have been Skye's first guess.

Finally, Bunny jumped up, yanked open a file cabinet drawer and took out a bottle of José Cuervo and a shot glass. She unscrewed the cap, poured, and pounded down the tequila. She repeated the process, then offered the glass to Skye. "For most things," she said, "there's MasterCard, but for a situation like this, there's nothing like booze."

Although tempted, Skye refused the shooter, and another very long five minutes ticked by before they heard sirens, running feet, and authoritative voices shouting "Clear" over and over again.

Skye knew that they should remain in their present location until an officer informed them it was safe to come out. Bunny, on the other hand, wanted to see what was happening, and Skye was still clutching the redhead's arm, trying to stop her from leaving, when there was a knock on the door.

"The area has been cleared." Skye recognized the voice as belonging to Sergeant Roy Quirk, Wally's second in command. "There's no one here."

In order to release the lock, Skye had to let go of Bunny. She hid a grin when the redhead threw herself into the sergeant's arms as soon as he stepped into the room. Quirk was in his mid-thirties, young enough to be Bunny's son, but he was male, which qualified him for the redhead's full flirtation routine.

Quirk's face turned brick red as he peeled Bunny off his chest. He sat her down and asked, "Everyone okay in here?"

"No." Bunny popped out of her chair and pointed to Bingo. "The stink is closing up my sinuses. Can Skye wash him up in one of the bathrooms?"

"Nothing in the alley can be touched until after the techs from Laurel process the scene." There was an unbending resolve in Quirk's voice.

"But that's a good forty-five miles from here. It'll take them forever," Bunny complained.

"Yep." Quirk folded his arms across his muscular chest. With his beefy build and shaved head, all he needed was a bunch of gold chains, a Mohawk, and a really good tan to be a stunt double for Mr. T. "If forever is an hour."

"Sorry." Skye apologized for Bingo's dishabille. "Can I take him home? I could be back in fifteen or twenty minutes at the most."

"Well . . ." Quirk's tone was suddenly uncertain. "I really do need to get your information right away."

"Sure. I understand." Skye felt sorry for the sergeant. Not only was she his boss's fiancée, she was also the police department's psychological consultant. For an ex-military man like Quirk, it was disturbing when he couldn't figure out who outranked whom.

"Well, *I* don't understand." Bunny wrinkled her nose and fanned her hand in front of her face. "I'll never get the smell of cat poop out of these clothes if you don't let me out of here right this minute."

"Sit down, ma'am." Quirk ignored the older woman's grumbles. "There would have been a much worse odor if Skye hadn't found the victim."

It took a second before Bunny's expression darkened in comprehension. Swallowing back whatever protest she had been about to utter, she paled and sank into the chair behind the desk. For once, she didn't have a smart-alecky retort or an innuendo-laden comment.

With Bunny subdued, Quirk perched on the desktop and indicated that Skye should take the visitor's seat. He flipped open his notebook, clicked his pen, and asked, "Ready?"

"Yes."

Skye started to describe her actions, but when she got to the part about entering the bowling alley, Quirk interrupted to ask Bunny, "What time did you open the front entrance this morning?"

"I didn't. I only finished dressing a few minutes before I ran into Skye." She batted her false lashes at the sergeant. "I never leave my apartment without my war paint and full battle dress."

"So you forgot to lock the door last night?" Quirk's face was disapproving. "You know that's a very dangerous thing to overlook. Scumble

River may be a small town, but as Ms. Denison can attest, having found more than her share of murder victims, it's certainly not crime free."

"State the obvious much?" Bunny arched a brow. "And I didn't forget." She fluffed her curls. "The bowler disco party ended at midnight and the cleaning crew worked until two. Once they were finished, I paid them, escorted them out, and locked up behind them."

Quirk turned to Skye. "But the door was open when you got here?"

"Yes."

"And the photographer—" Quirk consulted his notes. "Kyle O'Brien wasn't here."

"Correct."

Quirk wrote something down, then asked Bunny, "Who has keys to the bowling alley?"

"Sonny Boy."

"And that is?"

"Her son, Simon Reid, the owner," Skye translated, then added, "I believe he's spending the weekend in Saint Louis. Right, Bunny?"

"Yep." The redhead nodded. "He's not due back until late this afternoon."

"I know." Quirk's mouth tightened. "Since Reid's the coroner, I had to call the medical examiner to come, and he was none too happy to have his Sunday disturbed."

Because there were so few murders in Stanley County—usually only two or three a year—the

ME was a part-timer. Since there was no rush for accident victims' autopsies, he wasn't used to having his weekend interrupted.

"Oh." Bunny grimaced. "Right. I forgot about Sonny Boy being the coroner."

"Anyone else have a key?" Quirk asked. "The bartender, one of the waitresses, the cleaning crew, maybe a gentleman friend or two?"

"Nope." Bunny patted her considerable cleavage. "And I keep mine right here."

"So only two keys and unless Reid lost his—"

"Sonny Boy never ever loses anything," Bunny declared.

"Then we'll assume both keys are accounted for." Quirk pursed his lips in thought. "Do you need one to unlock the door from the inside?"

"No. The dead bolt has a thumb turn." Bunny's heavily made-up eyes widened in alarm. "Are you saying the murderer was here after everyone was gone last night? When I was alone?"

"Maybe." Quirk shrugged. "Depends on what the ME determines as the time of death."

"But," Skye said, "isn't it more likely that someone killed Alexis during the party and left with the other guests?" She frowned. "Otherwise the murderer would have had to persuade her to hide from Bunny at closing. And why would she agree to do that?"

"Motivation is your area of expertise. I prefer to deal with the facts," Quirk said, stone-faced.

"Are we done?" Bunny whined, her brush with cold, harsh reality forgotten.

"No, we are not." Quirk turned his attention to the redhead. "Enlighten me as to what this cat show, speed-dating thing is all about."

Bunny's explanation was surprisingly concise and businesslike, and when she finished, Quirk had only a couple of follow-up questions. Then he got to his feet, walked to the door, and said to Skye, "Why don't you go get cleaned up and drop off the cat?"

"Okay."

"There's no rush, but when you get back, work with Mrs. Reid and the two kids helping her run this shindig to come up with a list of the people from yesterday's event who might have persuaded the vic to stay behind, and/or who may have had a reason to want her dead." Quirk paused, then said to Bunny, "And I need the names, addresses, and phone numbers of all the attendees."

Quirk didn't have to tell Skye twice that she could leave. She practically ran out of Bunny's office, hopped in her car, and sped home. Once in the house, her first order of business was to give the ticked-off feline a bath. When he was clean—and angrier than before—she bribed him with cat treats to forgive her for all the indignities he'd been put though that morning.

While Bingo was calming down, Skye threw the

ruined Pet Taxi into the outside trash can, then put her clothes directly into the washing machine. By the time the laundry was ready to go in the dryer, she was showered and redressed, Bingo was asleep, and she had half an hour to make noon Mass.

Skye lingered a few minutes after the service, but there was no buzz about the murder. Because gossip had interfered with several investigations in the past, Wally had issued a directive to use cell phones rather than the police radio to notify the officers when a serious crime was suspected.

Happy that his orders had apparently been followed even though he wasn't in town, Skye left church and drove to the bowling alley. When she arrived at a little after one, the county techs had been and gone.

Anthony, a part-time officer who worked the shifts no one else wanted, stood outside the glass doors. He tipped his hat and moved the yellow crime scene tape so Skye could enter.

"Anyone else still here?" she asked.

"Just me and Zelda." Anthony jerked his thumb toward the interior.

Zelda Martinez was both the youngest and the most recent hire on the Scumble River police force, and thus she was usually assigned all the boring duties. She was also the only female.

"Anything new on the case?" Skye asked Anthony before stepping over the threshold.

"Nah." He straightened his police hat. "We took names, addresses, and phone numbers as the folks arrived, then told them they couldn't come inside."

"Any problem with that?" Skye wondered how the contestants had taken the abrupt end of their weekend. "Did any of them get mad?"

"A couple started to demand their money back, but Miss Bunny held a speeded-up version of the final round in the parking lot. Good thing it warmed up some today and stopped raining." Anthony grinned. "There sure were some odd-looking cats. One didn't have any fur at all."

"What did Bunny do about the awards ceremony?" Skye asked, sure the clever redhead had come up with something. "It was supposed to have been a brunch."

"Miss Bunny called some guys and they brought tables and set them up in her garage. Sarge let her take out the food that had been stored in the grill, and she and Frannie cooked it in her apartment kitchen. The servers brought the meal down Bunny's outside staircase to the garage."

Skye wondered how they had navigated the rickety wooden steps.

As she walked inside, she said over her shoulder, "I'm glad it all worked out."

She found Bunny, Frannie, and Justin seated in the lounge. Justin was entering data into his laptop and Frannie was counting money. Bunny had her feet up, a cold compress over her eyes, and she clutched a half-empty martini glass to her chest.

After turning down Bunny's offer of a drink, Skye sat and pulled a yellow legal pad and pen from her tote bag. "You all ready to discuss who Alexis might have stayed behind with and/or who wanted her dead?"

"I don't think anyone could have talked Alexis into having a tryst in the basement," Bunny said, smirking. "She would have insisted on the Drake in Chicago, or at least the Hilton in Oak Brook. The only time she was hot for a man's company was when he owned it."

Frannie snickered, nodding her agreement.

"Definitely." Justin sneered. "That's why she liked the guy she got in speed dating. She ranked all the men by income, and he owns most of the businesses in Brooklyn."

"What's his name?" Skye asked, unable to recall meeting him during the show. "Maybe he persuaded Alexis it would be worth her while to take a walk on the wild side with him in the basement."

"Ivan Quigley," Bunny answered. "But he stormed out of here before the party really got started."

"Did Alexis go with him?" Skye asked. Maybe the beautiful judge had been killed elsewhere and then planted in the basement.

"Nope." Bunny drained her martini glass. "And

Alexis was ticked off because her date deserted her. She started hitting on other men."

"Anyone hit back?" Skye knew an angry woman was often an easy target.

"Uh-uh." Bunny shook her head. "Everyone was already paired up."

"Were the women whose dates she was flirting with upset?" Skye asked.

"Not exactly angry, since the guys didn't respond, just . . ." Bunny thought for a minute. "Just mildly annoyed."

"Is that how you felt?"

"I wasn't with anyone, so her behavior didn't bother me one way or the other."

"You weren't?" Skye tilted her head. "How about the man you left the bar with after the speed-dating event?"

"He wasn't my date." Bunny stared at Skye without blinking. "Just some guy asking me to show him where the bathrooms were at."

"But . . ." Skye trailed off. She didn't believe the older woman's explanation, but she'd wait until she and Bunny were alone to finesse the truth out of her.

The four of them talked a little more about whom Alexis had upset during the cat show, and as Skye wrote down the last name, she said to Bunny, "By the way, I've been meaning to ask you—don't you usually have bowling leagues here on both Saturday and Sunday?"

"Uh-huh."

"Did you cancel them?"

"Yeah."

"Weren't the bowlers annoyed?"

"A few were." Bunny shrugged. "It wasn't a big deal. I told them we'd make it up at the end of the season."

"Won't Simon be mad when he hears?"

"Yes." A male voice behind her made Skye whip her head around. "He will, and he is."

"Sonny Boy!" Bunny let out a shriek. "Uh, I wasn't expecting you until later tonight." She jumped to her feet and backed away from him. "How was your weekend with your new friend?"

Skye blinked. Was Simon's new friend a woman? Her stomach clenched, but she made herself relax. Simon having a girlfriend would be a good thing, right? She wanted him to find someone to love, didn't she?

"You must be tired from the long drive." Bunny turned toward the bar. "Let me get you a glass of wine."

"Mother." Simon's tone was firm. "It's only three in the afternoon. I don't want a drink. I want to know what the hell is going on around here."

CHAPTER 7

Let the Cat Out of the Bag

Not wanting to be present while Bunny attempted to explain the weekend events to her son, Skye jumped to her feet. She glanced at Frannie and Justin, noted their fascinated expressions, and grabbed each of them by the hand. As she hustled the reluctant pair toward the bowling alley door, she enticed them with promises of coffee drinks and yummy pastries at Tales and Treats.

The combination bookstore and café had opened last fall to mixed reviews. While many Scumble Riverites were happy to see a new business in town, an equal number resented the change that the shop represented. After protest marches, petitions, and a tragic murder, now, six months later, the controversy had finally died down. And when Skye walked into the store a few minutes later, it was bustling with customers carrying stacks of paperbacks.

Risé Vaughn, one of the co-owners, stood at the front counter talking to a customer and gesturing to the cage that held the store's pet chinchillas. Skye waved as she made her way through the main room, which contained the register, gift items associated with reading and writing, and a massive glass-front oak cupboard holding rare and first editions.

Radiating from the central hub was the café and four areas decorated according the genre displayed—mystery, romance, science fiction/fantasy/horror, and literature. Skye was tempted to make a quick stop in the mystery section. She'd heard about a new series set in a small-town dime store, and wanted to grab a copy of the first book before the store sold out. But after a moment's hesitation, she decided she'd better grab a table instead. Because of the wonderful baked goods, the café was often standing room only.

However, when Skye entered the coffee bar, she saw only a few people lingering over their cups, idly turning the pages of magazines or working on their laptops. She'd forgotten it was Sunday. Tales and Treats would be closing in less than half an hour and the pastry selection looked nearly as barren as a plate of goodies in the teachers' lounge five minutes after the lunch bell rang.

After selecting a seat in the rear corner where their conversation wouldn't be overheard, Skye gazed at the one remaining red velvet cupcake in the display case. She was thinking about nabbing it before someone else bought it when Frannie and Justin burst through the door, their voices raised in an argument.

Frannie stalked over to Skye, pulled out a chair,

and plopped down, her lips pressed together in a thin line. Justin slouched into the remaining seat, crossed his arms, and stared over his girlfriend's head at the empty wall behind her.

Skye looked back and forth between them. She decided to let them stew for a while. So, instead of asking what was wrong, she said, "What do you two want to drink and eat? There's not much left."

"Iced chai tea latte," Frannie answered. "And if there's a cinnamon chip scone, I'll have that, please."

"Double shot espresso and the red velvet cupcake." Justin didn't waste any words.

"Okay." Skye hid her disappointment. She'd have to settle for the shortbread cookies and a caffe mocha. "I'll be right back."

Skye chatted with Orlando Erwin, Risé's husband and Tale and Treats' other co-owner, as he prepared their orders. He was the resident baker as well as the rare book scout for the store, and he told her all about a first-edition Sherlock Holmes title he had recently found at a storage facility auction he'd attended in Moline.

Frannie and Justin were still pointedly ignoring each other when Skye set the loaded tray on the table. Since there was no way to overlook their pique, she admitted defeat and asked, "What's up with you two?"

"He's being a jerk." Frannie grabbed her glass and took a gulp.

"And she's being ridiculous." Justin shook his head mockingly. "Just think, if it weren't for girlfriends, guys could go through their whole lives without ever knowing their faults."

"Glad to be of service, because in that case you'd be even lamer than you already are." Frannie narrowed her eyes. "Now, admit that I'm right and you shouldn't have done it."

"I could do that." Justin smirked. "But then we'd both be wrong."

"What did you do?" Skye interrupted—in part to stop the couple's bickering, but mostly because the suspense was killing her.

"I finessed the numbers a little." Justin cradled the tiny espresso cup in his big hands and gazed into the dark liquid. "It's no big deal."

"What numbers?" Before taking her first sip, Skye blew across the top of her mug. She'd burned her tongue once too often by not being cautious. Orlando was famous for his scorching-hot coffee drinks.

"The speed-dating results." Frannie popped a piece of scone into her mouth.

"Why?" Skye eyed the three cookies in front of her before making a selection. She liked to save the one with the most sprinkles for last.

Justin took a huge bite of his cupcake, then mumbled around the mouthful, "'Cause Ms. Hightower wanted to end up with Mr. Quigley."

"But I thought you were upset about your earlier

run-in with Alexis, when she wanted to see the cats' scores before she was supposed to." Skye wrinkled her brow. "Why would you do her a favor after that?"

"He didn't. She bribed him." Frannie glared. "Ms. Hightower paid Justin fifty bucks to make sure she got the guy she wanted."

"Ah, I see. Greed overcame your wounded ego." Skye savored a nibble of her cookie, then asked, "So which woman was supposed to end up with Ivan Quigley?"

"Ms. Irving." Justin stuffed the rest of his cupcake in his mouth.

"Well." Skye gave herself time to formulate the right response by taking a swallow of her caffe mocha and blotting her lips with a napkin. "What Justin did was unethical." She raised a brow at him. "You do realize it was wrong to take a bribe and manipulate the outcome. People paid you to be honest. They trusted you."

"Hey, it is what it is." Justin shrugged, apparently unimpressed with Skye's admonishment.

"Maybe," Skye countered. "But *it* becomes what your choices make it."

"No harm, no foul." Justin twitched his shoulders again. "It all worked out fine. I made some money, Ms. Hightower got what she wanted, and Mr. Quigley got a much hotter chick. A happy ending for us all."

"Except that's not true." Frannie swatted her

boyfriend's arm. "As I explained to you in the car, someone ended up getting hurt."

"Alexis?" Skye squeaked. She sure hoped that Justin's actions hadn't set off a sequence of events that resulted in the woman's murder.

"Not her." Frannie shook her head. "Ms. Irving and Mr. Quigley."

"Because they might have actually made a love match?" Skye asked, and when Frannie nodded, she continued, "I understand what you mean. However, it's extremely doubtful that a ten-minute speed date could actually predict a romantic connection or end up in a true relationship."

"But I overheard Ms. Irving talking to Mr. Quigley last night at the bowler disco party," Frannie protested. "And she was real upset. She was crying and asking him why he hadn't put her as his first choice after promising her he would. She nearly fainted."

"What did he say?" Skye glanced at Justin, but his expression was unreadable.

Frannie answered, "Mr. Quigley said he had put her name down in his number-one position, and he wanted to know why Miss Irving hadn't put him as her first choice." Frannie shredded her paper napkin. "It was so sad. Neither believed the other and they both walked away mad."

"Did you know then that Justin had altered the results?" Skye asked.

"No." Frannie bit her lip. "I was telling him

79

about Mr. Quigley and Ms. Irving on the way here and that's when he told me."

"I'm not psychic." Justin refused to meet either Skye's or Frannie's gaze. "How was I supposed to know that something like that would happen? I never meant for anyone to get all jacked up."

"It's not your intentions that people judge you by." Skye barely kept the disappointment out of her voice. "You may have a heart of gold, but so does a hard-boiled egg. And look how often an egg gets cracked."

Justin stared at Skye as if she was speaking Elvish, and she swallowed a sigh. She knew it was no use chastising him. Justin was an immature nineteen-year-old, still more a boy than a man. He would learn over time that every action had a consequence. She just hoped he would also acquire the ability to empathize. It was a skill she'd been working on with him since he was in eighth grade. Apparently the training hadn't been a success.

Although Skye managed to keep the conversation going while they all finished their snacks, she noticed that Frannie and Justin rarely spoke to each other. And when they did, their remarks were cutting.

At five to four, just before the café closed, Frannie turned to Skye and said, "Can you give me a ride home?" She glowered at her boyfriend. "I refuse to be in the same car as Justin until he admits he was wrong to change the speed-dating outcome."

"Whatever." Justin jumped to his feet and slammed out of the store, muttering uncomplimentary remarks about spoiled daddy's girls and Frannie not understanding what it was like to be poor.

After a quick stop to buy the mystery book Skye wanted, she and Frannie left the shop. As they got into the Bel Air, Skye said, "Don't forget to buckle up."

"We're only five minutes from my house." Frannie dug through her purse. "Just go."

"Come on," Skye coaxed. "Put it on. The seat belt makes it more difficult for the Martians to suck you out of the car," she teased.

Frannie heaved a put-upon sigh, then complied with Skye's request, but she was silent on the way to her house, and leaped out of the Chevy as soon as it stopped. Shouting her thanks for the ride, she ran in the front door.

Skye was backing out of Frannie's driveway when her cell phone rang, so she pulled over to the curb to answer it. So few people had her cell number, any call was usually an important one.

"Hey, sugar." Wally's warm voice greeted her. "I hear you all had some excitement while I was gone. Are you and Bingo okay?"

"We're fine." Skye knew that Quirk had been trying to reach Wally, but cell phones weren't allowed in the testing room. "Although Mr. Cat was extremely upset with me over the indignities he had to suffer. At least until I gave him a few treats."

"Bingo has his priorities straight. His stomach always wins over his pride." Wally chuckled, then turned serious. "Quirk tells me you and the three masterminds behind the weekend extravaganza were going to come up with the names of individuals who attended the bowler disco party and suspects. Are you finished with that?"

"Sort of. We couldn't think of anyone who might have persuaded Alexis to meet them in the basement or stay behind after the party." Skye touched the pages sticking out of her tote bag. "But I do have the list of people with motives right here. Do you want me to bring it to the PD?" She assumed that was either where he already was or where he was headed.

"That would be best. I just crossed into the city limits—" Wally's voice cut out; cell phone reception in Scumble River was unreliable at best. Finally, she heard him say, "—in five minutes."

Frannie lived only a couple of streets over from the police station, so Skye arrived before Wally did. The redbrick building housing the PD, the city hall, and the library took up the entire corner of Maryland and Kinsman. Usually on a late Sunday afternoon the parking lot would be nearly empty, but because of the murder, several vehicles were huddled together. Skye parked her Bel Air between a rusted-out pickup truck and a bright blue Prius, then went inside.

Through the bulletproof glass, she could see Zelda Martinez sitting at the dispatcher's desk drumming her fingers on her thigh and frowning. When she spotted Skye, her expression brightened and she jumped to her feet. Holding her index finger to her lips, Zelda motioned Skye to the locked entry separating the waiting area from the rest of the station.

She disappeared for a second, then opened the door for Skye, and as Skye stepped over the threshold Zelda said, "Can I speak to you in private?"

"Of course." Skye wondered what the young woman wanted. "Where?"

Zelda gestured for Skye to follow her down the narrow hallway that went past the interrogation/coffee room. As always, the female officer's dark brown hair was drawn tightly back and fastened in a bun at the nape of her neck, and her face was bare of makeup. However, her usually perfectly manicured nails were bitten to the quick, and Skye could see tiny specks of the bright red polish on Zelda's teeth. Clearly, she was extremely upset.

When they reached the door of the women's bathroom, Zelda looked over her shoulder and whispered, "In here." Once they were inside, she leaned against the wall and bit at her thumbnail before finally saying, "I think I might be in trouble. I lied to Sarge."

"About what?" Skye tried not to imagine Quirk's reaction to one of his rookies being dishonest with him. Even though he hadn't been entirely candid about his own involvement in a case a couple of years ago, he didn't tolerate deceit.

"He asked me if I was related to one of the people at the cat show—Lola Martinez—and I said no." Zelda worried a button on her uniform shirt. "But she's my second cousin. Her grandfather is my uncle. We're not close and I haven't talked to her in ages."

"So, why didn't you tell Quirk that?" Skye asked, glancing discreetly at her watch. Wally would be wondering where she was.

"I didn't want him to take me off the case." Zelda's dark eyes glowed with fervid sincerity. "Several of the more senior officers are on vacation, so this is my chance to do something on a murder investigation other than crowd control and background checks." A crease formed between her brows. "If I can't work the investigation, Zuchowski will get a leg up on me. He already lords it over me because he started a week before I did."

"I see." Skye couldn't remember ever seeing the other rookie, although she'd heard Wally mention him from time to time. He'd been hired last summer when she'd been preoccupied planning her cousin's wedding, and he had flown under her radar since then.

Skye waited for Zelda to continue, and when she didn't, Skye finally asked, "I assume you're telling me this because you'd like me to intervene in some way?" She knew she sounded overly formal, but being engaged to the chief put her in an awkward position. "What are you hoping I can do?"

"I hate to ask." The young woman frowned. "But I don't know who else to turn to."

Zelda's expression reminded Skye of a puppy who had made a puddle in the middle of the living room carpet—remorseful, but with no idea how to solve the problem.

"I could speak with Quirk," Skye offered, then cautioned, "But I think he'd respect you more if you went to him yourself and told him exactly what you just told me. Maybe explain he caught you off guard."

"But he'll be mad."

"Probably." Skye nodded. "At least at first. But I think he'll understand your motives." She resolved that if the sergeant gave Zelda too hard a time, she'd remind him of his own indiscretion. "Do you want me to come with you when you tell him?"

"No." Zelda took a deep breath. "I see now that I need to do this on my own."

The women parted, Zelda in search of Quirk and Skye seeking Wally. She found him upstairs in his office. The decor never changed, although Skye did notice he had a new photograph of the two of them on his desktop. The previous picture had been a formal portrait of Skye taken when she was the maid of honor at her cousin's over-the-top wedding. She was glad he had replaced it, since in that photo she was wearing a Pepto-Bismol pink dress that did nothing for either her complexion or her figure.

After a quick hug, Wally cupped her chin and examined the injury to her cheek. Frowning, he shook his head and threatened, "I should arrest Bunny Reid for assaulting you with a deadly grooming tool."

"It wasn't her fault," Skye explained. "I should have known better than to leap into the situation without considering the consequences."

"Well . . ." Wally's tone was grudging. "They do look as if they're healing pretty quickly."

"See." Skye smiled. "I told you I didn't have to see a doctor."

"Hmm." Wally made a noncommittal noise before gently kissing Skye's wounded cheek and returning to the chair behind his desk.

As he settled into his seat, Skye took a moment to appreciate her good fortune in being engaged to someone as wonderful and handsome as Wally. He had turned forty-three a couple of weeks ago, but the silver in his black hair and the slight lines around his mouth did nothing to mar his rugged good looks.

Silently, she thanked God that they had finally ended up together. She'd had a crush on him since she was a teenager and he was a twenty-two-year-old rookie on the Scumble River police force, but up until a couple of years ago, something had always kept them apart.

Wally interrupted her reverie. "I've got Quirk's report here." He flipped open the manila file in front of him and scanned the contents. "There's not much to go on. According to his notes you found the body, called nine-one-one, and when the police arrived, the only people present in the bowling alley were you and Bunny."

"That about sums it up." Skye tried to think if she had anything to add. "The front door was unlocked, although Bunny swears she locked it."

"I see that." Wally lifted a brow. "But how reliable is Bunny?"

"On this matter, I would say ninety-nine percent. She's a surprisingly good businesswoman."

"According to the crime scene techs, there were no fingerprints on the weapon." Wally made a wry face. "They'll get back to us with anything else, although since it's a public place, I'm not holding out much hope."

"And I probably messed up any prints on the utility closet door." Skye shook her head regretfully. "If only I hadn't been juggling a smelly cat, I might have been more observant and not disturbed the scene."

"Or the body might not have been discovered until it started to decompose," Wally said in an attempt to reassure her. "If the weapon was wiped clean, you can bet that the knob and everything else was, too."

"That's true." Skye brightened, then said, "Oh, before I forget, here's the list of people with motives for killing Alexis. And there's one more possibility. Ivan Quigley, the guy she was matched with during the speed-dating event." Skye explained what she had learned from Frannie and Justin at the café.

"Let me take a look at the others." Wally flipped through the paper-clipped pages. "Geez! The vic was sure disliked by a lot of people." He added, "This confirms Quirk's impression from what everyone was saying at the brunch. No one had a kind word for Alexis."

"Ah." Skye crossed her legs. "I was sort of wondering why Quirk allowed Bunny to continue with the awards ceremony." She swung her foot. "Now, I'm guessing he had his officers mingle to overhear the gossip."

"That, and to see if anyone who was supposed to be there didn't show up."

"Right." Skye let her loafer dangle from her toe. "Anyone AWOL?"

"Elijah Jacobsen."

"Shoot. Considering his altercation with Alexis yesterday, his absence doesn't look good." Skye was strangely fond of Elijah, but she had been afraid the odd man might turn out to be the killer. "Maybe his cat didn't make it into the final round and that's why he didn't bother to come to the brunch."

A knock on the door distracted Wally before he could respond to Skye's suggestion, and he shouted, "Come in."

Quirk flung the door open and announced, "I sent a couple of officers to the address Bunny gave me for Jacobsen. The ex-doc has flown the coop."

CHAPTER 8

Crazier Than
John Smith's Cat

"How do you know Jacobsen's gone?" Wally stood up and strode over to the sergeant. "Is it possible he's just not home?"

"His sister lives with him," Quirk reported. "She said he wasn't there when she got up this morning, but he left her a message."

Shoot! Skye held her breath. Elijah's disappearance made him a prime suspect. Could there be any other explanation, except the obvious one, for his abrupt departure? She stared at Quirk, waiting for him to reveal the contents of the note.

Finally, after handing a piece of paper sealed in an evidence bag to Wally, the sergeant summarized what it said. "He tells his sister to take care of Princess and the other cats. God told him that in order to cleanse his soul, he should go into the wilderness for forty days. If he survives, he'll be back then."

"Son of a—" Wally glanced at Skye and cut himself off, then turned to Quirk. "Put an all-points bulletin out on Jacobsen, get a warrant to search his house, and bring his sister in for questioning."

"Yes, sir." Quirk touched his forehead in a half

salute. "I'm on it." He spun on his heel and hurried out of the office.

Once the sergeant was gone, Skye asked, "Does Elijah live in Scumble River?"

"No. He lives within the Brooklyn city limits." Wally handed Skye the evidence-bagged note, then sat back down behind his desk. "Why?"

"I was wondering about jurisdictional issues," Skye explained as she examined the letter.

"As long as the judge who issues a warrant presides over the county in which it's executed, we can conduct the search." Wally laced his fingers behind his neck. "As a matter of courtesy we'll notify the local authorities and we usually request that a county deputy accompany our officers."

"I see." Skye nodded, then said, "Although Elijah's message sounds damning, I can't see Alexis ever being willing to go somewhere alone with him. Or meet him in the basement and hide out with him until the bowling alley closed."

Wally rubbed a hand across his eyes. "But you and the others couldn't come up with *anyone* she *would* agree to meet in the basement." He pursed his lips. "And the medical examiner said that the body wasn't moved. She was killed where you found her. Using liver temp, the ME puts the time of death between eleven thirty and twelve thirty last night."

"Great." Skye tucked an escaped curl back

91

behind her headband. "People won't be able to remember if a particular person was present when everyone was getting their coats on and leaving. That means a lot of our suspects won't have verifiable alibis."

"True," Wally agreed. "But right now I'm more interested in Jacobsen. From what I've read, he sounds Looney Tunes. What's your impression of the guy?"

"He's a damaged soul who seems to have found a refuge in his cats. Bunny said he told her that he applied to her dating site to find a woman who was like him." Skye shifted in her seat.

"Like him in what way?" Wally dragged a legal pad toward him.

"My guess is he meant someone who finds it hard to cope with everyday life." Skye struggled to express her thoughts. "Someone who loves cats for their serenity."

"That makes sense." Wally nodded. "Nothing like petting a cat to lower your blood pressure and calm you down."

"Exactly." Skye leaned forward. "So when Alexis both dissed his favorite cat and let Princess escape, it was as if she was attacking his best friend." Skye considered all she had witnessed and overheard. "Then, to top it off, Alexis taunted Elijah about his past. She really seemed to enjoy making people squirm."

"Hmm." Wally clicked his pen and made a note,

then asked, "After the initial altercation in which he assaulted Alexis, did you witness any other incidents between them?"

"No." Skye reran yesterday's events in her mind. "I never saw them together again, and the few times I ran into Elijah he seemed fine." She closed her eyes, trying to remember. There had been something unusual she'd noticed about the ex-doc's behavior, but what was it? *Shoot!* Nope, she couldn't dredge it up to the surface.

Wally interrupted her concentration. "Can you think of anything more about him? Anything that might explain his weird behavior?"

"While Frannie and I were doing the dishes after the dinner last night, she said that Elijah told her that twenty years ago, he was an extremely successful surgeon, but he was in an auto accident that resulted in his fiancée's death and in which he suffered a traumatic head injury. It ended his career."

"Why's that?" Wally looked up; he'd been taking down all Skye said. "Did it mess up his fine-motor skills or vision or what?"

"I didn't notice any of those concerns." Skye shook her head. "But significant brain trauma can impair cognitive functioning."

"In what way?"

"Memory, reasoning, problem solving, speed of mental processing, concentration, organizational ability, decision making, judgment." She shrugged.

"Pretty much every skill needed to be a good doctor can be compromised."

"Could a head injury cause behavioral issues?" Wally gazed intently at Skye.

"Definitely." She nodded vigorously. "It's very common to see difficulties in socializing, and with self-control, mood swings, irritability, dangerous actions, and physical outbursts."

Wally narrowed his eyes. "Like attacking someone and killing them?"

"In the heat of the moment, yes," Skye agreed. "But I can't see how someone with Elijah's disabilities could have planned a murder that involved luring someone to a place that person wouldn't normally go, then having the fore-thought to bring a weapon—since it certainly wasn't in the utility closet to begin with. And how did he get away without anyone noticing him?"

"It could have been just one of those perfect storm kinds of situations," Wally argued. "The vic could have forgotten something in the basement— you did say the room she'd been judging in was down there."

"Uh-huh."

"Maybe Jacobsen was still ticked at her from that morning, so he followed her to demand an apology," Wally continued. "She said something to set him off, and he just happened to have the wire cat toy in his pocket."

"Shoot!" Skye bit her lip. "That's a plausible

scenario, but having that cat toy in his pocket would have been really awkward since the handle was so long. And something just doesn't feel right to me about Elijah being the murderer."

"Because you liked the guy and felt sorry for him?" Wally suggested.

"Maybe," Skye admitted. "But how about all the other people who disliked Alexis?"

"None of them ran away to cleanse their souls," Wally pointed out.

"How do you know?" Skye asked. "Just because they showed up for the final judging and awards ceremony doesn't mean they're still around." Her voice rose excitedly as an idea popped into her head. "They might have thought that the body wouldn't have been found yet and reasoned that it would look funny if they didn't attend the brunch."

"That's true." Wally stood. "And I never intended to stop the investigation, but like it or not, Jacobsen is our prime suspect."

"I understand." Skye watched Wally step from behind his desk. "What's next?"

"Three of my full-timer officers aren't around—one's on vacation, one's sick, and one had a death in the family—so that leaves Quirk, Martinez, Zuchowski and the two part-timers." Wally pulled the other visitor's chair closer to Skye and took her hand. "Quirk called all of them in, and, as we speak, they're phoning the list of participants that Bunny provided to see who has an alibi."

"Good." Skye smiled in relief. "If Elijah killed Alexis, I want him brought to justice. However, I don't want the fact that he's peculiar to convince you it's him before he's had a fair trial." She leaned forward and kissed Wally. "But I know you'd never do that."

"Thanks, darlin'. " Wally scooped her into his lap and stole another kiss.

"Anytime."

"Now, I need to give my officers your list of possible suspects, so they can make locating those individuals their priority." Wally nudged Skye to her feet, then stood up. "Any of them who don't have alibis that check out, we'll interview in person."

Skye started toward the door, paused, and said, "I know Quirk is aware of the vendors." She explained about Zelda's cousin. "But did Bunny include their names on the list she gave him?"

"I don't know." Wally put a hand on the small of her back and guided her out of the office. "I'll have him check that out."

"Good." Skye started down the stairs. "Because it just occurred to me that Kyle O'Brien, the photographer who was supposed to meet me this morning to take pictures of Bingo, never did show up."

"Hmm." Wally led the way toward the cubicles the officers were using. "I'll be interested in hearing his excuse."

"Me, too." Skye trailed him down the narrow hallway. "And the three other vendors all had a beef with Alexis—they're among the names we gave you. But to be fair, two of them are tiny eighty-year-old twins who I doubt would have the strength to strangle someone as tall and strong as Alexis."

"You'd be surprised what someone intent on murder is capable of doing," Wally commented, then turned his attention to briefing the officers manning the phones regarding the top persons of interest on their calling list. Once he was finished, Wally turned to Skye and said, "You might as well go home. Who knows how long I'll be here, but there's nothing more you can do tonight."

"If you're sure . . ." Skye trailed off. She hated to leave if she could help, but she was bone-tired and tomorrow was a school day.

"I'm positive." He took her hand and tugged her toward the exit. "Can you come in after work tomorrow and help with the witness interviews?"

"Absolutely." Skye allowed herself to be led outside and walked to her car. "I don't have any after-hours meetings scheduled, so I should be able to make it here no later than four."

"That'll be perfect." Wally opened the Bel Air's door. "Right now, I'll go find Frannie, Justin, and Bunny." Once Skye was seated, he leaned in and kissed her good-bye. "I need to talk to the three musketeers in order to get a better picture of the weekend's activities."

"Good luck with that." Skye waved, slammed the door, and drove off. She didn't envy Wally's trying to make sense of all that had gone on during the cat show/speed dating/bowler disco party.

After placing a reassuring call to her mother—she knew May would have heard about the murder the minute she got back from her gambling weekend—Skye spent the evening worrying about Elijah and fussing over Bingo. The cat still stared at her suspiciously every time she approached him. She half expected Wally to call or drop over, but when he hadn't done either by ten o'clock, she gave up and went to bed.

Monday morning should have been the first day of spring break, which the Scumble River School District usually took during the last week of March. However, this year a February flu epidemic had shut down the district for ten days. So, in order to avoid extending attendance into the middle of June when the weather might be too hot—two of the three buildings were not air-conditioned—the board had canceled the vacation, and classes were in session.

Skye feared the students' attitudes would be ugly, and the faculty's dispositions might be worse. What could she do to lighten everyone's mood?

As she parked and walked into the high school, Skye was pleased that the weather had improved and the temperatures were even warmer than yesterday. She wondered if she could persuade Homer Knapik, the principal, to allow her to do something special for everyone during the lunch period.

Maybe she could decorate the cafeteria with some of the props left over from the school's performance of *South Pacific*, have the lunch ladies make nonalcoholic piña coladas for everyone, and hold a hula contest.

Unfortunately, as soon as Skye walked in the door, she saw Homer in his attack position by the teachers' mailboxes, and an alarm went off in her head. Clearly, palm trees and leis were not in her future. Maybe erupting volcanoes, but not a luau.

Classes started at seven fifty, and teachers were required to be in the building half an hour earlier, but Homer hardly ever arrived before eight. The fact that he was not only present but also out of his office did not bode well for anyone, especially Skye.

Before she could figure out a way to sneak past the hovering principal, he saw her and yelled across the lobby, "Get your butt over here." He turned, not bothering to see if Skye heard him. "You won't believe what our little darlings did over the weekend."

Skye followed him down the narrow hall that led from the front counter to his office. Part of her was relieved that the principal's fury wasn't caused by her discovery of yet another murder victim. He hated her involvement in criminal investigations, and loved to remind her that she seemed to be a magnet for dead bodies.

She hid a smile as she entered Homer's lair. Good thing he didn't know about Mrs. Griggs's ghost—a truly dead body that actually did seem to be drawn to Skye—or he'd really be upset. She had barely cleared the threshold when Homer slammed the door. Ignoring her, he marched over to the coffee machine on the credenza beneath the window and poured himself a cup. The big leather swivel chair behind his desk groaned in protest when he flopped into its seat.

Skye studied the principal as he cradled his mug in one large hand, blowing on the dark liquid before taking a cautious sip. He looked like a manatee wearing a fur coat. Hair protruded from his ears, nose, and above his loosened tie. She grimaced when he idly stroked the tuft of fur sticking out between the gaping buttons of his shirt. For as long as she'd known him, Homer had needed a wax job in the worst way.

After taking several gulps of coffee, he acknowledged Skye and grunted, "Are you waiting for a royal invitation? Have a seat, for crying out loud, before I get a crick in my neck."

Skye complied, then dug out a pen and legal pad from her tote. She sat at attention, waiting for further instructions. Homer hated to be rushed, and he didn't encourage initiative in his employees.

"Care to take a guess what a dozen or so of our senior girls decided to do for fun?" Homer tapped a folder on his desk. "You know, those dumbasses you keep insisting are America's future."

Skye was silent. She refused to answer him when he belittled the students. And even though Homer was one of the rare individuals who responded neither to positive nor to negative reinforcement, she hadn't given up trying to get him to be more respectful.

Her lack of response seemed to irritate him and he barked, "Are you deaf?"

She raised an eyebrow, but still didn't speak. Minutes ticked by and she bit her tongue, resisting the urge to fill the empty air.

"Fine." Homer's face had turned a mottled red and he blew out a raspberry. "I suppose I'll have to tell you, since you obviously have no idea what your precious students are up to. What's the matter? Aren't they talking to you anymore? Have you lost your coolness?"

Skye squirmed. Homer had homed in on her weakness like Winnie the Pooh on a honeycomb. For some reason she hadn't been able to get as close to this year's group of kids. Even the ones

101

on the school newspaper didn't confide in her as they had in the past.

"While you were busy playing Nancy Drew—" Homer pointed a hairy finger at her, and when she flinched, he nodded. "Yes, I heard you discovered yet another stiff, but I'm not even going there."

"Thank goodness," Skye muttered under her breath, then asked aloud, "So, what happened?" She supposed someone had gotten drunk and stupid.

"Bitsy Kessler had a slumber party, or whatever in the hell they call them nowadays." Homer pushed the file he'd been toying with across his desktop to Skye, then leaned back and stared at her.

"And?" she asked, flipping the folder open and seeing a single sheet of paper containing a list of names, most of which she recognized as belonging to the popular crowd or to girls who were on the fringes.

"*And* sometime during the night," Homer's two oversize front teeth gnawed on his bottom lip, "they decide to play a game."

"Strip Poker? Truth or Dare?" Skye had a sinking feel that none of the pastimes she could name had been the one the girls had chosen.

"I wish." Homer shook his head from side to side like a mournful bull.

"Just tell me, for heaven's sake," Skye pleaded, unable to stand the suspense.

"Some tomfool thing called Pass Out. I thought it was a drinking game, but Mrs. Kessler explained to me, in detail, that it isn't."

"That's a self-strangulation game!" Skye's voice rose in alarm. "I remember reading about it in one of the psych journals. Kids have died from playing it."

Homer folded his hands across his paunch. "Who thinks up this crazy shit?"

Skye didn't have an answer, but she had a question of her own. "Are the girls all right?"

"Yeah." Homer glowered. "Mrs. Kessler caught them before it went too far."

"Thank God." Skye sank back against her chair, her heart still racing. "That poor woman. Bitsy is her oldest child."

"Yeah." Homer twitched his shoulders. "A lot of times the first pancake turns out the worst."

"Seriously?" Skye rolled her eyes. Where did Homer come up with sayings like that?

"What I want to know," Homer said, gazing at the ceiling as if seeking an answer from the cracked plaster, "is why in blue blazes would anyone want to strangle themselves? Are they suicidal?"

"Hmm." Skye paused to gather her thoughts.

"Come on," Homer prodded. "You're the expert. Are they trying to off themselves or what?"

"According to what I've read, depriving yourself of oxygen induces a kind of euphoric sensation."

Skye might have been flattered that Homer thought of her as an authority, but she knew that his definition of an expert was the person who was the least ignorant about the subject. "This game is nothing new, but cell phones and online videos are spreading it."

"Parents need to keep those kids off the Internet." Homer's tone was exasperated. "Don't those girls realize they could die?"

"That's part of the thrill." Skye took a deep breath, then clarified. "For one thing, adolescents don't have a firm grasp of their own mortality. Then there's the whole peer pressure factor."

Homer grunted, clearly not understanding.

"And topping it all off, today's teenagers have seen so much outrageous behavior from actors and singers and athletes, they think they need to push the envelope themselves in order to be 'with it.' "

"I've been getting calls since yesterday morning wanting to know what the school is going to do about this matter." Homer lumbered to his feet. "Once again, the parents expect us to do their job."

"That's not fair," Skye objected. "Parenting is difficult."

"Parenting is easy." Homer shook his head. "It's the freaking kids that make it hard."

Skye rolled her eyes. Homer's lack of compassion was astounding, but she tried to explain. "Frequently moms and dads have no idea how to handle an issue like this." She added, "I'm glad they're letting us know it's a problem and asking for our help."

"Since you're so thrilled to be included, you can contact all the parents on this list, tell them you'll be taking charge of this matter, and present the results of your intervention to the school board."

Great! Skye knew she was the logical person to deal with the situation, and in fact she wanted to, but she was also the logical person to handle hundreds of other issues. Where would she find the time for everything?

CHAPTER 9

Look What the Cat Dragged In

Skye eighty-sixed her plans to begin Zach Van Stee's reevaluation and instead spent the rest of the morning on the phone contacting parents. Their reactions were mixed. Most were happy to have Skye talk to their daughters about the dangers of games such as Pass Out, but a couple of them took quite a bit of persuasion. And Ashley Yates's folks refused even to consider the matter.

Troy Yates Sr. was president of the First National Bank and thus accustomed to being the one in charge. Furthermore, he was still angry with the school, and with Skye in particular, for an unflattering article about Ashley that had run in the school newspaper a few semesters ago. All that, along with the fact that Ashley was a fifth-year senior, having failed several courses when she was a junior, and there was no changing Mr. Yates's mind.

It was nearly noon by the time Skye finished the last call, and she was due at the grade school at twelve thirty. With the clock ticking, she hurriedly filled out the counseling permission slips for the eleven girls whose parents *had* agreed to let her see their daughters, rushed out of her office and down the hall.

Since Skye didn't have time to hand out the documents herself, she was asking Opal Hill, the school secretary, to make sure the girls received the consent forms before they went home that afternoon when Trixie approached the front counter.

"Where have you been?" Trixie asked Skye. She had recently decided to write a mystery novel in hopes of becoming the twenty-first-century Agatha Christie, so her next question made sense to Skye: "And why didn't you call me after you found that body yesterday? It sounds like a great plot for my book."

"I'm sorry." Skye crossed her fingers. "After I got done at the police station, I was just too exhausted to talk about it all again." In truth, she hadn't even thought to phone Trixie. She'd been too worried about Elijah, and too upset about the whole situation to discuss it—even with her BFF.

"Come, tell me now." Trixie grabbed Skye's hand and tried to tug her down the hall. Which, considering that Trixie was five inches shorter and quite a bit lighter, wasn't very effective.

"I can't." Skye refused to budge, freeing her hand and heading toward the front door. "I'm due at the elementary school in fifteen minutes."

"Can't you be a tiny bit late?" Trixie called after

her. "I made chocolate cupcakes over the weekend, and I brought you one," she coaxed. "It has lots of your favorite buttercream vanilla icing on top."

"Well . . ." Skye hesitated. She was starving, and had forgotten to pack a lunch. "Maybe a couple of minutes. I really should fill you in on an issue that concerns your cheerleaders."

"Is there a problem?" Trixie immediately sobered. As cheerleading coach, she usually knew any mischief her girls were up to. "I haven't heard anything." She ran her hands through her short faun-colored hair, making it stick up like peaks of meringue. "Are they okay?"

Skye filled her in as they walked toward the library, then added, "So I'm talking to all the girls tomorrow, with the exception of Ashley, whose parents refused to give their consent. Maybe you can get her to bring up the subject, and since you're not a psychologist you don't need permission, which means it wouldn't be a problem if you two had a chat."

"Sure." The two women entered the library's storeroom and climbed on stools pulled up to the worktable. "She's my student aide second hour."

Trixie pulled a square Tupperware container toward her, pried off the lid, and offered it to Skye. "So, tell me everything about the murder."

Skye summarized the weekend's events around bites of cupcake, ending with, "Then I went into the basement's utility closet to clean Bingo up, and there was Alexis lying dead on the floor."

"From what you've said"—Trixie swallowed the last crumb of her cupcake, and reached for another—"she was nearly universally disliked."

"So it seems." Skye licked icing off her fingers, grabbed her tote, and stood up.

"Do you think the murderer is that peculiar ex-doctor?" Trixie asked.

"I hope not." Skye edged toward the door, checking her watch. If she hurried, there was a chance that Caroline Greer, the grade school principal, wouldn't notice that she was late. "At least five others had good reasons that I know about to dislike Alexis."

"The guy from speed dating, the jewelry maker, the twins, and the cat breeder," Trixie ticked off, following Skye through the library.

"Uh-huh." Skye hurried down the hall toward the lobby. "And there's a good chance there are others I'm not aware of."

"True." Trixie trotted after Skye. "She sure sounds like a mean girl who never changed, so it could even be someone from her past."

"Probably not." Skye pushed through the front door. "Bunny had bouncers at the entrance so no one but cat show and speed-dating participants could attend the bowler disco party."

"This is almost like a locked-room mystery," Trixie called after Skye. "They're the best kind."

• • •

Skye had been able to sneak into the elementary school without running into the principal. And Caroline didn't mention her tardiness when they met for the special education intake conference later that afternoon, so it appeared Skye was in the clear.

Classes ended at three thirty, but the staff was required to stay an additional twenty minutes. Typically Skye was among the last to leave, but today she beat everyone out the door—even the teacher who was retiring in two months and was usually the first to pull out of the parking lot.

As Skye stepped across the PD's threshold into the lobby, she noticed a young woman sitting on the bench, and stopped in midstride. "Spike Yamaguchi! When did you get into town?"

"About an hour ago." Spike stood and smoothed her trouser-cut jeans.

Spike was Simon's half sister—a sibling he hadn't known existed until she was sixteen and contacted him after her adoptive parents were killed in a car crash. Simon had been shocked to discover that Bunny, who had left him and his father in order to pursue her dream of becoming a dancer, had had a secret baby.

Spike gave Skye a hug. "Sorry I didn't e-mail you that I was coming."

"That's okay," Skye assured her. "It's great to see you."

Their friendship had had a shaky start. When they first met, Skye was convinced that Spike and Simon were having an affair. It hadn't helped matters that that mistaken belief had exposed other problems in Skye and Simon's relationship, which had in turn ended it. Still, despite everything, once Spike's true relationship with Simon was fully explained, Skye and Spike had become good friends.

"Are you here to visit your mom?" Skye asked.

"Yes and no. Remember I told you about the gig at the TV station in Chicago?" Spike was an investigative reporter for a newspaper in California, but she had been actively pursuing a television career.

"Of course." Skye had respected Spike's request to keep the possibility of her relocation to Illinois from Bunny and Simon. "I've had my fingers crossed for you."

"Thanks." Spike's delicate features, a blend of Asian and European, relaxed into a smile. "Anyway, I found out Thursday afternoon that I got the job! But the catch was they wanted me on the air by the weekend. So I threw a few things in a suitcase and flew into O'Hare the next day. Grandfather will follow once I get settled."

"Wow!" Skye shook her head in awe. "You really travel fast and light."

"Yep." Spike sat back down, then continued, "On Saturday when I was going through my predecessor's desk, I found a tip about government corruption in an Illinois small town. He'd scribbled a note that said no one was interested in a downstate scandal and shoved it in a drawer." Spike made a face. "I disagreed, and when I showed it to my new boss, she concurred. Which is why I'm here."

"What town are you investigating?" Skye asked as she sat next to Spike on the bench.

Spike didn't answer right away, and Skye held her breath. If it was Scumble River, her family was in for a hard time. Skye's uncle was the mayor, which pretty much put her whole family smack-dab in the middle of every new controversy in town.

"Not here, but that's all I can say." Spike's voice had sharpened. "I can't risk being scooped. This could be a big story for me."

"No problem. As long as it isn't my hometown, I'm happy." Skye gave her a thumbs-up. "Are you at the PD to ask questions for your story?"

"No." Spike shook her head and her straight black hair swung back and forth. "I'm waiting for Bunny to get done. The chief is interviewing her about Saturday's murder."

Skye frowned. "I thought he was going to talk to her last night."

"I gather he couldn't find her." Spike raised a feathery brow.

"Oh?"

"Bunny pulled into her garage just as I got out of my rental car this afternoon," Spike explained. "Apparently, since the bowling alley was closed yesterday and she didn't have to work, she didn't spend the night at home. From what I overheard when the chief arrived a few minutes later, Bunny had her cell phone turned off as well."

"Ah." Skye tilted her head, thinking. Was Bunny with the man Skye had seen her join after the speed-dating event? She had forgotten to mention him to Wally. "When did you and she get to the station?"

"About forty-five minutes ago." Spike crossed her legs, swinging her foot impatiently.

Skye looked at her watch. It was three fifty-seven, and Wally was expecting her at four. She'd better let him know she had arrived.

"Can you check on how much longer Bunny will be?" Spike asked.

"Sure, I can do that." Skye stood, patted Spike on the shoulder, then walked toward the inner door. "Let me go see what's happening."

Using her key to enter the restricted area of the PD, Skye stepped into the narrow hallway. To her immediate right was the dispatcher's office, and she stuck her head around the open doorway. She had thought it odd that her mother hadn't greeted her at the counter when she walked into the lobby, but now she saw why. May held two phones to her ears, and she was talking on both.

Skye waved to her mother, who raised her eyebrows questioningly and pointed to her daughter's cheek.

Mouthing the words "cleaning accident," Skye crossed her fingers. Housework was the one activity her mother would think justified sustaining an injury.

May raised her chin in acknowledgment, then refocused on her dual conversations. The scowl on her face made Skye wonder if May was dealing with the press. Skye didn't think the murder of a cat show judge would bring out the media, but if it was a slow news day, anything was possible.

When Skye reached the coffee/interrogation room, she knocked on the partially open door and Wally motioned her inside. Bunny, engaged in a battle to the death with the soda machine, ignored her.

Silently, Skye took a seat next to Wally at the table, and they both stared wordlessly at the redhead, who was feverishly pushing buttons and cursing. Each time a can didn't appear in the dispenser, Bunny stabbed the buttons harder and swore louder.

Today she was wearing a black and gold satin halter dress with a smocked bodice and a mid-thigh-length handkerchief hem. Suddenly Bunny stamped her gold four-inch-high stilettos, and Skye flinched as she heard something snap. She hoped it was the heel and not the redhead's ankle.

Finally, Bunny wrestled a can of Jolt from the

recalcitrant machine and joined Skye and Wally. She slumped into a chair and immediately popped the top, breaking one of her fuchsia-tipped nails. She swore, bit off the remainder of the nail, then shrugged and took a long gulp of the highly caffeinated soda. After a couple more hits of caffeine, she leaned back and closed her eyes.

Wally waited a beat, then said, "Are you ready to continue now?"

"I've told you everything I know," Bunny whined. "I have a splitting headache and I feel like barfing. Why won't you leave me alone?"

"Bunny, this attitude of yours is going to get you into trouble," Wally warned.

"I don't have a bad attitude." Bunny fluffed her hair. "I just have a personality you can't handle."

"At your age you should know better than to talk back to the police."

"Hey, buddy! Watch it." Bunny glared. "I'm not a day over fabulous."

"Right." Wally gritted his teeth. "I have only a couple more questions. Concentrate," he ordered. "Is there any way into the bowling alley besides the front doors?"

"Let's see." Bunny rummaged through the contents of her purse until she found a nail file. "There's the door in the back where the deliveries come in and the window exit from the basement." She paused, then nodded. "And the outside door to my apartment."

"So someone could have gotten in any one of those ways?" Wally asked.

"No." Bunny shook her head, then winced in pain. "Those first two are wired, so if they're opened when the alarm is set, a buzzer goes off. I keep the inside door to my apartment locked at all times, and since I already told you the outer door to my apartment is wired, that entrance is doubly protected."

"How about the alley's front entrance?" Wally looked up from his notebook.

"It's on a different security system that's right next to the door."

"And during the party, that first system was activated?" Wally asked. "You're sure?"

"Yes." Bunny finished repairing her manicure and put away the file. "I have a checklist that I follow before I open the bowling alley, and making sure the alarm is set on the other entrances is item number one."

"Okay." Wally rubbed the back of his neck. "Tell me one more time—who, besides the paying customers, was present at the bowler disco party?"

"The three judges, the four vendors, the deejay, the bouncer, the bartender, and three waitresses." Bunny sighed and rubbed her temples.

"That's all?" Wally persisted. "You're not forgetting anyone."

"Yes, that's all." Bunny rested her elbows on the table and her head in her hands. "Unless the

116

bouncer let in someone that I didn't notice."

"We interviewed him and he says no one other than the people on the list you gave him got in." Wally drummed his fingers on the table. "Did you set the front entrance alarm once the cleaning crew left?"

"Yes," Bunny snapped, then hesitated. "Shit! Sonny Boy insisted that I change the code when we fired a waitress last week, and I couldn't remember it." She slumped. "I was too tired to run all the way upstairs to get it. And no, it's not my age, it's the damn mileage."

"So someone inside could have used that door to leave, which is why it was unlocked even though you thought you locked it." Wally flipped his notebook shut.

"I guess." Bunny rolled the cold soda can across her forehead. "Can I go now?"

"I have a question," Skye said, noting how bloodshot Bunny's eyes were.

"What?" The redhead's voice was a mixture of querulousness and caution.

"How about the guy that you slipped out of the bar with after the speed-dating event?" Considering how Bunny normally dressed it was hard to tell, but the wrinkles in her outfit suggested that she might still be wearing the same clothes from last night's date. Especially since Spike had said she and her mother arrived at Bunny's apartment at the same time that afternoon. Which meant the headache was probably really a hangover. "Was he at the party?"

"What guy?" Bunny squealed, jerking upright. "I told you the man you saw just wanted me to show him the bathroom."

"I don't believe you." Skye met the redhead's gaze straight on. "I saw him kiss you."

"You're mistaken." Bunny looked away. "He was just one of the men from the cat show who didn't participate in the speed dating."

"Then why didn't he know where the bathroom was?" Skye asked. "Didn't he need it during the day?"

"Do I look like I monitor people's toilet habits?" Bunny demanded.

"Fine." Skye gritted her teeth. "Then who were you with last night?"

"That's none of your business. Since you've chosen not to be my daughter-in-law, I suggest you butt out." Bunny rose from her chair and stormed out of the room.

"Well, that sure wasn't like the Bunny we've all come to know and love," Wally commented.

"No, it wasn't." Skye bit her lip. "Bunny usually tries to flirt her way out of trouble."

"Instead she got mad."

"I can't put my finger on exactly why, but she seemed more frightened than angry to me." Skye wrinkled her brow. "I've never seen Bunny scared before."

CHAPTER 10

Morals of an Alley Cat
and Scruples of a Snake

After advising May that he was leaving, and instructing her to call him on his cell with anything concerning the murder, Wally hustled Skye out of the police station and into his squad car.

"Where are we going?" Skye asked as she fastened her seat belt.

"To visit Lola Martinez." Wally pressed a button clipped to the sun visor and the PD's metal garage door rolled up. "Considering she's Officer Martinez's cousin, I thought it best that you and I question her."

"That makes sense." Skye turned to face Wally. "How did Quirk react to Zelda admitting she had lied to him about being related to Lola?"

"Let's just say it's a good thing the Scumble River Police Department doesn't have KP duty, or Martinez would be peeling a lot of potatoes."

Skye grinned. "I hope he doesn't give her too hard a time."

"Nah." Wally eased the robin's-egg blue Caprice out of the building and made a left onto Kinsman Street. "I talked to him, and we agree it was a rookie mistake. But it was a good thing she fessed up when she did, or she could have really messed up the investigation."

"Which would have been a lot harder for either of you to forgive."

"Exactly." Wally lowered the volume on the police radio to a less earsplitting level. "As long as I'm aware of her relationship with one of the suspects, I can make sure she isn't involved in any aspect of the case where she could be accused of bias."

"Good. By the way, any news on Elijah?" Skye tried to keep her voice casual. "Has anyone come forward with any info about his location?"

"Unfortunately not." Wally stopped at the light on the corner of Maryland and Basin streets. It was the only traffic signal in town and it always seemed to be red. "There's been nothing from the APB and no one has reported seeing his car anywhere."

"Did you find out anything when you interviewed his sister?"

"Her description of the problems caused by Jacobsen's head injury jibed with what you told me." Wally tapped his fingers against his thigh. "And she says she has no idea where he might be."

"How about the search of Elijah's house?" Skye had wondered what they would look for. Since the murder weapon was a cat toy, it wasn't as if there would be a gun or knife they could match to the wound. Maybe they were hoping for a map with a wilderness location circled in red or a journal with his written confession.

"Except for the feline paraphernalia and his music collection, the guy lives like a monk." Wally twitched his shoulders. "His room contained a single bed, a chest of drawers, an elaborate stereo system, and about a million records, tapes, and CDs."

"I guess Elijah thought what Albert Schweitzer said was true. Music and cats are the only two real means of refuge from the miseries of life," Skye commented absently, then paused. Something was niggling at the back of her mind. She concentrated until she dredged it up. "What about his cell?" She remembered seeing Elijah preoccupied with the phone during the cat show.

"He must have taken it." The light turned green and Wally stepped on the gas. "I've asked the county crime techs to try to track the phone's signal."

"Can they do that?"

"Only if he turns it on." Wally frowned. "So far, he's been too smart to use it."

"Maybe the battery's dead." Skye twisted a curl around her finger. "Elijah doesn't seem to have the ability to think far enough ahead to figure out that the police might use his phone signal to find him."

Wally shot her a worried glance. "I know you

121

like him, or feel sorry for him or something, but he's probably guilty, so try not to be too disillusioned when we find him and he admits he did it."

"I'm not denying there's a lot of circumstantial evidence stacked up against him." Skye gnawed at her thumbnail. "It's just that my gut says he didn't do it, and my instincts are usually pretty good."

"As long as they don't blind you to the facts, that's fine."

They rode in silence until Skye asked, "Did Frannie and Justin have anything to add to what I told you?"

"Nothing."

"That's what I figured. I was pretty sure I'd gotten the whole story from them," Skye said, then asked, "Were they still fighting?"

"Considering they refused to be in the same room together, I'd have to say yes." Wally looked at her. "Why, are you planning an intervention?"

"No. It's a shame, because they seem like a good pair, but I'm not getting involved." Skye pursed her lips. "They need to work this one out on their own." She was silent, lost in her thoughts, until another question occurred to her. "Where does Lola live?"

"Just outside Clay Center's city limits. And the photographer lives a few minutes from her, so we'll see him once we finish with her."

"I take it neither Lola nor Kyle has an alibi," Skye deduced.

"No, they don't." Wally slowed the cruiser as he approached a rough railroad crossing. "They both claim that they parted from their speed dates right after the bowler disco party and went home alone."

"Since the party ended at midnight, and the ME said that Alexis was killed between eleven thirty and twelve thirty, that leaves both Kyle and Lola a half an hour to have killed Alexis." Skye gazed down at I-55 as they drove across the overpass, and shook her head at the snarled traffic. Even this far south of Chicago, a steady stream of vehicles clogged the highway. "What was Kyle's excuse for missing his appointment with me?"

"His alarm didn't go off." Wally turned left onto County Line Road. "But since he was sleeping alone, there's no way to prove it."

"Who else doesn't have an alibi?" Skye watched the fields go by on either side of the squad car. At this time of year, before the ground was plowed and planted, the dark weed-covered land always depressed her.

"Sandy and Sonia Sechrest say they were together, but sisters often lie for each other." Wally pulled into a long driveway that led to an old farmhouse. "Fawn Irving claims she was at her house, but since she was by herself there's no way to prove it."

"How about Ivan Quigley?"

"He has a live-in housekeeper," Wally answered, then added, "At first she said she didn't know what time Quigley got home, but later she conveniently remembered that it was around eleven."

"Hmm. So his alibi might not stand up," she mused, rubbing her temples. "How about the others, the ones not on my list?"

"It looks as if we might have gotten a break with them." Wally parked, got out of the car, and came around to Skye's side to open her door. "During the bowler disco, the pairs stuck together, and they all alibi each other up until midnight. The longest anyone was alone was a five-minute bathroom break. Then after Bunny shut down that party, a group of thirty-six of them went over to the Brown Bag to continue the festivities. They closed the place at two a.m."

"But with such a big crowd, couldn't someone have slipped away?"

"Several shutterbugs took pictures all night long." Wally rested his hand on the small of her back. "I've got Anthony checking the photos and time stamps to see if we can confirm that none of them snuck out a back exit between twelve and twelve thirty."

"Which is the remaining half hour in the timeline the ME gave for the murder?" Skye clarified for herself.

"Yes."

"Let's see." As she and Wally walked over to the steps leading to the front door, Skye visualized the bowling alley bar setup. "Forty people took part in the speed dating."

"Right."

"The Sechrest twins didn't participate, but Alexis, Lola, Kyle, and the other two judges did, which leaves thirty-five cat show competitors who were also speed daters."

"Uh-huh."

"Kyle and Lola didn't go to the after party. Did their dates?"

"Yes. As it happens, Kyle's and Lola's dates got together and went as a couple."

"Of course Alexis didn't go. And Ivan Quigley left early and said he went straight home, as did Fawn Irving. Did Elijah go to the Brown Bag?"

Wally shook his head.

"And I assume the bartender, deejay, bouncer, and servers didn't go, either, which leaves thirty-four." She paused to check her math, then asked, "Who were the other two that went to the bar?"

"A couple of the breeders made a love connection during the show, so opted out of the speed-dating event," Wally explained as he rang the doorbell. "But they did attend the party and go to the Brown Bag with the rest of the group." He punched the bell again.

A second later, the door was flung open and

Lola Martinez yelled, "I told you to leave me alone!" She blinked as her gaze settled on Skye and Wally. "Oops! Sorry. I thought you were my ex."

"Ex-husband?" Skye asked.

"No." Lola shook her head. "Ex-boyfriend. Ever since that slut he left me for dumped him, he's been trying to get me back. He's been calling me all afternoon."

"May we come in, Ms. Martinez?" Wally interjected. "I'm Chief Boyd from the Scumble River Police. I believe you talked to Sergeant Quirk earlier, and you already know Skye, who's the department's psychological consultant. We have a few questions to ask you about this past weekend." When Lola hesitated, he added, "It's important and I promise we won't take up too much of your time."

"Sure." She smoothed the stained blue chambray shirt she was wearing. "I was working on a new design. Just let me turn off my soldering iron." She moved over to a drafting table.

Skye and Wally stepped into a large area that clearly was meant to be the house's living room, but most of the space was taken up with jewelry-making equipment. Shelves holding pieces in various stages of completion lined three of the four walls and a massive painting of Lola stretched out semi-nude on a bed hung on the fourth.

Lola motioned them to the sofa facing the portrait, then dragged the leather swivel chair from behind her desk over to where they sat.

Sinking into the seat, she looked at Skye and asked, "Is this the man who bought you that gorgeous engagement ring?"

"Yes, it is." Skye twisted the diamond on her finger. "Wally's my fiancé."

"You didn't mention he was the chief of police or that he was so handsome."

"Uh." Skye felt the color creep up her cheeks. "It didn't come up."

"It's a good thing Alexis never met him." Lola's tone was teasing. "She would have sunk her claws in faster than a cat at a scratching post."

"I'm sure she would have tried." Skye glanced at Wally, who seemed disconcerted by the jewelry maker's bluntness. "But she never would have succeeded."

"That's what I thought, too." The light in Lola's dark eyes dimmed.

"Was Alexis the woman who came between you and your boyfriend?" Wally asked.

"Yes." Lola turned her attention to him. "I thought she and I were friends."

"But?" Wally prompted.

"But a woman like her doesn't have any real friends." Lola sighed.

"A woman like her?" Skye asked.

"Alexis constantly had to be reassured that she

was smart and wonderful and beautiful. An extra pound, a gray hair, or a zit would send her into a deep depression," Lola explained. "And she was overemotional—everything was a crisis, not to mention her mood swings." Lola scowled. "But what should have warned me off was how seductive she was around men, especially at totally inappropriate times. I saw her come on to a grieving widower at his wife's funeral." Lola shook her head. "How could I have been so naïve?"

"So why did she pretend to be your friend?" Wally asked.

"Alexis liked pretty things, and she thought everyone should just hand over whatever she decided she wanted. She . . ." Lola paused as an enormous cat with a pushed-in face strolled into the room.

The feline ignored Skye and Wally, sauntering over to Lola and rubbing against her blue jeans–clad leg. The jewelry maker stroked the cat's white fur. It purred loudly and jumped into her lap, where it curled up and started to knead her thigh.

Once the animal was settled, Lola continued. "Alexis wanted a piece of jewelry I'd had made. A very expensive necklace. I offered it to her at cost, but she insisted that I give it to her as a gift. She said she'd act as a model for my jewelry and send customers my way." Lola shook her head. "But I couldn't afford to do that."

"What happened?" Skye was pretty sure she knew, considering Lola's warning to her after she'd faced off with Alexis on Saturday afternoon.

"I overheard her telling people that my jewelry was overpriced because the gold was an overlay and the stones weren't genuine." Lola's mouth thinned. "I confronted her and we had a huge shouting match. Next thing I knew, I caught Kyle in bed with her."

"Your ex is Kyle O'Brien?" Wally asked, flipping open his notebook. "The photographer?"

Lola nodded. "I call him the Rat." She pointed to the cat. "Jabba the Fluff was a gift from him. He's a Persian, which is an extremely loyal breed. Too bad Kyle wasn't."

Skye pointed at the portrait. "Is Kyle the artist?" It was clear that the painter had loved his subject. And now that Skye studied the canvas, she notice a white cat curled at the foot of the bed.

"Yes." Lola's voice broke and she cleared her throat before adding, "In our happier days, I was his favorite subject. He really is very talented. I think he's an even better painter than a photographer." She made a droll face. "But you know what they say, right? Behind every successful man is a woman. And behind the fall of every successful man is usually the other woman."

"So Alexis stole Kyle from you, then dropped him?" Skye asked, wanting to make sure she completely understood the situation.

"Yep." Lola's tone dripped with satisfaction. "Kyle makes a nice living as a photographer, but nowhere near the amount of money Alexis required to keep her in the style to which she wanted to become accustomed."

"Was O'Brien upset when Alexis broke up with him?" Wally asked. He leaned forward, his pen poised. "Did he threaten her or make a scene?"

"Not that I heard about." Lola stroked Jabba. "He told me he was relieved."

"Relieved?" Skye asked. "That's an odd reaction. Did he say why?"

"He said it had felt as if Alexis had cast a spell over him, and once she dumped him, he could finally see what she was really like." Lola shrugged. "Needless to say, I didn't believe him and told him to take a hike."

"Is that why you both participated in the speed-dating event last night?" Skye asked. "Do you think Kyle was hoping you two would be paired up, and, if you were, that you'd give him another chance?"

"I can only answer for myself." Lola took a wire brush from an end table and started to comb the purring feline in her lap. "I was hoping to meet Mr. Right, but instead I met Mr. Right For Somebody Else." She sighed. "It seems I have lousy taste in men."

"The guy you were matched with didn't work out?" Wally asked, raising a brow.

"That's an understatement." Lola sighed again. "Turns out the guy was really into blondes and hit on Kyle's date all night."

Wally and Skye spent another half hour with Lola. No matter how they phrased their questions, Lola's answers remained the same, and finally she glanced pointedly at her watch.

Skye shot Wally an inquiring look.

He nodded slightly, then stood up. "Thank you for your cooperation."

"No problem." Lola led the way to the door. "I hope I was helpful."

Wally and Skye followed her. Skye said good-bye, then stepped onto the outside landing.

Before Wally joined Skye, he said to Lola, "If you think of anything else, call me. Oh, and if you plan to leave the area, let me know."

"Will do, Chief." Lola saluted. Before she closed the door, she said, "I didn't kill Alexis. Someone with a bigger grudge than mine did that."

Once Wally and Skye were back in the squad car, Wally turned to her and asked, "What's your take on Lola's description of Alexis?"

"It jibes with everything other people have said about her." Skye settled into the cruiser's seat. "But hearing it all together like that makes me wonder if Alexis had a hysterical personality disorder." Skye ticked the symptoms off on her fingers. "Constantly seeks praise, overly concerned with physical attractiveness, overemotional, rapid mood swings, and inappropriately sexually seductive."

"In other words, a woman who in a relatively short amount of time would alienate everyone she came in contact with?" Wally asked.

"Exactly. And her disorder would explain why she worked as a temp. There is no way a woman like that could keep a job for very long."

"How about a position where she worked alone?" Wally asked, starting up the Caprice's engine. "Would she be okay in that type of situation?"

"I doubt it." Skye fastened her seat belt. "It's not only the personal interaction that would be a problem. Someone like that would lie, cheat, and steal without any remorse because she would feel entitled to whatever she wanted."

"Interesting." Wally put the car in gear. "Did you believe Lola's account of what happened between her, Alexis, and Kyle?"

"It's hard to say." Skye leaned her head against the seat back and thought about the past hour. "Did everything take place as she said? Perhaps. Is she still holding a grudge against Kyle and Alexis? Yes. Did she kill the woman who stole her man? Possibly."

"Hmm." Wally concentrated on backing out of the long, narrow lane. "If Lola offered Alexis a free piece of jewelry, Alexis would probably agree to meet her in the basement. Greed and power seem to be two of the major forces that motivated her."

"And Lola is strong enough to overpower Alexis if she caught Alexis by surprise." Skye dug in her tote for her lipstick. "You couldn't see her upper arms today, but Lola had a strapless dress on Saturday night and her biceps are impressive. No saggy flesh on her."

"That gives her motive, means, and opportunity." Wally turned the car toward town. "Now it's time to hear O'Brien's version of the story."

CHAPTER 11

The Catbird Seat

O'Brien Photography was located on Clay Center's main street. The studio shared a building with a financial advisor's office and a Mexican restaurant called Los Tres Caballeros. It was a little past six when Wally pulled the cruiser into a spot in front of the three businesses, and only the restaurant still had an OPEN sign on its door.

"Shoot!" Wally hit the steering wheel. "We could have come here first if I'd thought to ask Chief Leery about O'Brien's hours." At Skye's questioning look, he explained, "I phoned Clay Center's chief this afternoon to let him know we'd be questioning suspects in his jurisdiction."

"I wondered about that." Skye stared at the photography studio's darkened window, where large pictures of cats, children, and brides were prominently displayed. "Why did you particularly want to talk to Kyle at his studio?"

"I like catching people on the job. They're usually embarrassed to be questioned by the police in front of their customers or coworkers, and that throws them off balance. It's a lot harder to think of a lie when you don't feel in control."

"I can see how that would be an advantage."

Skye looked at the nearly deserted sidewalks. "Most people are just finishing up dinner, so Kyle's probably at home. Are we going to try him there?"

"Absolutely." Wally threw the cruiser into reverse. "Having the cops show up on your doorstep is almost as disquieting as having them invade your workplace."

"I should think so."

"Let's go see if we can rile him up enough to get the truth out of him." Wally checked his notebook. "He only lives a few roads over."

The photographer's home was a modest bungalow on a tree-lined street in a typical small-town neighborhood. A blue MINI Cooper was parked by the curb in front, and a white panel van with O'BRIEN PHOTOGRAPHY stenciled on both sides was sitting in the driveway.

As Wally and Skye walked past the van, she shivered and turned her head.

"Are you cold?" Wally put an arm around her, tucking her against his side to shelter her from the wind that had kicked up since they'd left Lola's place. "Do you want me to get your jacket from the cruiser?"

"No. I'm fine." Skye leaned against Wally for a second. Then, feeling a little foolish, she explained, "It's just that Kyle's van freaks me out a little. It seems as if every news bulletin of an abducted child or snatched woman always reports that the bad guy is driving a white panel van. I guess because it doesn't have side windows it's the perfect transportation for criminals."

"I suppose it is." Wally hugged her. "But it's also perfect for florists, plumbers, and anyone who has to haul a lot of equipment. Like a photographer who needs to cart around lighting paraphernalia and props and large framed portraits."

"Of course." Skye kissed Wally's cheek. "I'm just being silly."

"Never." Wally's expression was somber. "Believe me, I trust your instincts."

"Thank you, sweetie." Skye enjoyed one last cuddle, then headed toward the tiny porch. "One of the things I love about you is that you take me seriously and never patronize me or my ideas."

"Your hunches have been right too many times for me to ever dismiss one." Wally rang the bell. "It would be stupid of me to underestimate you."

When no came to the door, Wally pressed the button again. After waiting a couple of minutes, he knocked. Still no response from inside.

"Looks like he's not home." Skye turned to Wally. "What do you want to do?"

"I'll come back tomorrow." Wally turned away and started back to the squad car. "I guess I'll catch him at his studio after all."

Skye followed, but skidded to a stop. "Hey, did you hear that?"

"What?" Wally retraced his steps and cocked his head toward the house.

"I could have sworn I heard a thump." Skye moved over to the front window. "I think I see a shadow moving in the wall mirror."

Wally joined her and cupped his face to the glass. He whispered, "I see it, too." Then in a loud voice he said, "I don't see anything. Obviously, O'Brien's not home. We might as well leave."

Wally took Skye's arm and guided her toward the Caprice. Once they were inside, he started the motor, revved it a couple of times, then drove away.

"What's the plan?" Skye knew there was no way Wally was giving up.

"I'm going to turn down the next street and circle back, which will give us a view of the house." Wally winked. "With any luck my shouting and the engine noise convinced O'Brien that we left, and while we wait to see what happens, I'll call in the license number on that MINI Cooper. I have a feeling it isn't his."

A few seconds after Wally made his request, May's voice crackled from the radio. "The plate is registered to Alexis Hightower."

"Ten-nine," Wally demanded.

"Repeat, plate is registered to Alexis Hightower." May paused. "Do you copy?"

"Ten-sixty-nine. Boyd out."

"What is Kyle doing with Alexis's car?" Skye asked.

"Good question." Wally reached for his cell.

"Let's see if its presence is enough to get a warrant to search O'Brien's house."

After assigning Quirk the responsibility of tracking down a judge, no easy task in a small county with as few of them as Stanley, Wally said to Skye, "I'm going to run you back to the PD. This could take several hours."

Skye quirked her right brow. "I take it I'm not invited to the search party?"

"Too dangerous." Wally punched a number into his cell. "Leery, it's Wally Boyd."

Skye couldn't hear the other side of the conversation so she stared at the O'Brien house while Wally explained the situation to the Clay Center chief. She saw no signs of movement.

She tuned back in to what Wally was saying when she heard, "So if you could send an officer to sit on the place until my sergeant gets here, I'd be much obliged." Wally listened, then laughed. "You drive a hard bargain, but I'm sure something can be arranged." Still chuckling, Wally flipped his cell phone shut.

When he didn't immediately fill her in, Skye asked, "What did Chief Leery want in exchange for his help?"

"To come to our wedding." Wally's voice held a hint of amusement.

"Why?" Skye didn't see what was so funny about someone wanting an invitation.

"Leery's wife is a Clay Center dispatcher, and it

seems your mother has been talking to her about how wonderful our wedding is going to be. Now Mrs. Leery wants to attend."

"Mom was talking about *our* wedding?" Skye wasn't sure she had heard correctly.

May had always disapproved of Wally for her daughter on the grounds that he was too old, too divorced, and too not Catholic. She had also steadfastly refused to accept that Skye and Simon would never reunite, wed, and produce a houseful of grandkids.

"Yes." Wally nodded, smiling broadly. "Isn't that mighty interesting?"

"Hmm. I guess Mom is finally accepting the fact that I'm marrying you." Skye felt a profound sense of relief. "What did you do to win her over?"

"Nothing." Wally shrugged, but there was a gleam in his eye.

"Spill it."

"Okay. One day, while things were slow at the station, I saw her making a baby afghan and I commented that I'd never seen her knitting before."

"Yeah." Skye shook her head. "It's a relatively recent interest for Mom, but she's approaching it the same way she does everything else."

"Like a competitive sport?" Wally suggested.

"Exactly."

"Anyway, we chatted a little about her new

139

hobby; then since she seemed to be in a mellow mood, I may have mentioned that now that the annulment is in the final stages, and we can start planning the wedding, I was considering turning Catholic."

"And?"

"Well, I almost told her that there had been an error on my birth certificate and I was really thirty-nine instead of forty-three, but instead I said that my granddad fathered a child when he was in his seventies."

"That was a mistake." Skye *tsk*ed. "Not only will Mom be feeding you pomegranates and pumpkin seeds, she'll be picking out baby names."

"Actually, she swears by oysters." Wally waved at the Clay Center officer who had pulled his cruiser next to their car. "And she likes 'Marie' for a girl and 'Ernest' for a boy."

"Speaking of children . . ." Skye bit her lip. She'd been putting off having this conversation, but it was time. "How do you feel about fatherhood?"

"As long as you're their mother, I'd love to have a couple of kids." Wally took her hand. "But if you'd rather not, I'm okay with that, too."

"Then let's keep our options open." Skye leaned over and kissed him.

By the time Wally dropped Skye off at the PD to pick up her car, it was after seven. Having missed lunch and dinner, she was famished, and too tired to cook. The Feed Bag, Scumble River's only sit-down restaurant, was closed, which left McDonald's or the deli counter at Walter's Supermarket. The drive-through window tipped the odds in favor of Mickey D's, and after picking up supper, Skye drove home.

Clutching the white paper sack of fragrant fried goodies, she stepped across her threshold and nearly fell over Bingo. The black cat sat squarely in the middle of the small braided rug in front of the door and glared at her out of slitted green eyes. His body language conveyed quivering outrage at having been left to starve.

After taking care of Bingo's need for food and a clean litter box, Skye took her dinner into the sunroom and curled up on the white wicker love seat. As she ate, she read through her ghost-buster file.

Her plan was to give Mrs. Griggs another chance to prove she could behave herself when Wally and Skye got affectionate. However, if the apparition interfered with their love life one more time, Skye fully intended to banish the former owner's spirit—even if that meant calling Father Burns in to perform an official exorcism.

Several hours later, Skye woke herself with a scream. She felt as if she was being smothered and had to fight her way to consciousness. She'd been having a nightmare in which human-size cats pursued her around the bowling alley carrying fishing poles from which stuffed mice dangled. Standing on the sidelines watching the chase were other humanoid felines, who were texting on their cell phones.

It took her a few seconds, but Skye finally realized that the cause of her breathing problem was Bingo. The feline was curled up on her chest with his tail over her mouth and nose. After removing him, she looked at her watch. It was nearly three in the morning.

Stretching, she got to her feet and rubbed the crick in her neck—the love seat was way too short to sleep on. As she passed through the kitchen on her way to bed, she checked her answering machine. The little red zero glowed steadily, which meant Wally hadn't phoned.

She dug her cell out of her tote bag, but there were no messages on it, either. She knew that the search of Kyle O'Brien's home would have taken several hours, and if the police had found the photographer hiding inside, the interrogation would also be a lengthy process. Still, she had hoped for an update on the situation.

As she climbed the stairs to her bedroom, Skye wondered what had been found at Kyle's residence. More important, how would he explain Alexis's car being parked in front of his house?

Tuesday morning Skye was scheduled to attend the junior high's Pupil Personnel Services meetings at eleven thirty. Homer had thrown a hissy fit when Skye had informed him she wouldn't be able to talk to the girls who had been caught playing the Pass Out game until that afternoon.

All the principals that Skye worked for felt that their problems should take priority, and they jealously fought for her time. Since the girls weren't in any imminent danger, and their parents were fully aware of the situation, Skye couldn't justify missing her regular hours at the junior high.

She spent the time before the PPS meeting evaluating a sixth grader who had moved to Scumble River the week before. His mother had presented Skye with paperwork indicating that a case study was in progress. Although the boy had left his old school before the psychologist could complete the required testing and observation, the clock was still ticking toward the sixty-day deadline for the case study's completion.

Finishing up with five minutes to spare, Skye sent the student back to his class, gathered up her appointment book and legal pad, and hurried to the PPS meeting. It was being held in the art room, which was free during the first thirty-minute lunch period but was used as a study hall for B lunch.

The purpose of PPS meetings was to discuss kids who were experiencing learning or behavioral problems. The committee was composed of the principal, the special ed teacher, the speech therapist, the school psychologist, and the nurse. In addition, any regular ed teacher with a student on the agenda was required to attend.

As the others trailed in, Skye studied the names of the three kids on today's list. They'd have ten minutes per child. Unless, of course, there was an emergency add-on.

As was her habit, Neva Llewellyn, the junior high principal, arrived precisely on time. Skye often wondered if the woman waited just out of sight until the second hand clicked on the twelve.

Neva took her seat, looked around, and asked, "Is everyone here?"

Skye struggled to maintain an attentive expression and to keep a giggle from escaping. Did the principal really think a missing team member would speak up? Neva ran a tight ship, but even she couldn't force her employees to respond when they weren't physically present.

"Good." Neva was a tall, lean woman in her forties who wore expensive suits and expected everyone to be as perfectly groomed and as good at their jobs as she was. "Let's get to our first student."

Before she could begin, a banshee-like whooping came from the hallway.

As the group turned toward the strident sound, a

small red ball with a burning green wick sailed through the art room's open transom.

Everyone stared as if mesmerized until Skye jumped to her feet and yelled, "Holy crap!"

From behind the door came a noise that might have been laughter, or a cat hacking up a hairball. A split second later a bright flash and a resounding boom echoed through the room.

CHAPTER 12

The Cat Will Meow

S kye stood in the middle of the art room and looked around. The others still sat, stunned. Luckily, the cherry bomb had landed near the door, which was in the back, and the women had been sitting at two long tables near the front, so no one appeared to be hurt. And with the exception of a small scattering of red paper and the lingering smell of the flash powder, there was no visible damage to the classroom.

After making sure that everyone was all right, Skye pulled Neva aside and told the principal that she had a good idea of the identity of the cherry bomber. She also revealed her strategy to apprehend him. Once Neva agreed to Skye's plan, albeit a bit reluctantly, and said she'd call the student's parents, Skye rushed from the room in pursuit of her quarry.

That distinctive asthmatic hyena laugh could belong to only one boy, so after briefly considering her options, Skye headed left. The art room was just a few feet from the cafeteria/gymnasium, and students on their way to lunch passed right in front of its door.

She entered the room at a trot, but once inside she slowed to scan the cavernous space. Rows of picnic-style tables were set up on the gym's floor, and nearly two hundred seventh and eighth graders were talking in strident adolescent voices. The sound was nearly as deafening as her brother's band when they had played acid rock under the name Pink Elephant.

Skye and her target spotted each other at precisely the same moment. He swiveled his head in search of an exit. There were only three choices—through the kitchen where the lunch ladies would grab him; over the stage and into the PE teacher's office, which was a dead end; or through the main entrance, where Skye stood waiting.

Shrugging, he remained seated, glaring at Skye as she walked toward him and ordered him to his feet. He waited several heartbeats before complying. Although Skye's expression didn't show it, she had been worried that he would refuse and the situation would escalate.

Even though the boy walked docilely down the hall beside her, Skye didn't relax until they reached her office. The windowless room was painted road-stripe yellow and was only slightly larger than a refrigerator box or a port-a-potty. Crisp white curtains hung over a travel poster scene of the Rocky Mountains did little to lessen the claustrophobic feel of the space. Having originally been used to store cleaning supplies, the place gave off a faint, lingering smell of ammonia no matter what air freshener Skye tried.

Still, she was grateful for the private office. It was a blessing many school psychologists would give up their laptops and next raise to possess, especially in a situation such as this one. Dealing with a recalcitrant teenager was always better without an audience.

Once Skye had settled in the seat behind her desk and the boy was sitting across from her, she demanded, "Junior Doozier, what in the world were you thinking of?"

"About what?" He folded his arms, tipped his metal chair onto its two back legs, and stared at the brown marks on the white ceiling tiles.

Skye considered asking what he saw in those blots. Would his responses tell her anything about his personality? Or did he just see stains?

It took longer than with most kids—usually students couldn't stand the silence and hurried to fill it—but finally Junior said, "It weren't only a cherry bomb, Miz Denison." He wrinkled his heavily freckled nose. "Nothing but flash powder inside a paper cup. No reason at all for you to get so worked up."

"You could have blown off a finger." Skye narrowed her eyes. "Not to mention injured me or one of the others in the room."

"I didn't know you was going to be there." Junior's milk white complexion became paler. "Honest. I'd never hurt you. Pa would kill me."

Junior's father, Earl Doozier, was the king of the

infamous Red Ragger clan, which made Junior the crown prince. The Red Raggers were difficult to explain to anyone who hadn't grown up in, or at least lived many, many years in, Scumble River. Their version of reality rarely matched other people's. And their sense of right and wrong never did.

Like feral cats, the Red Raggers were untamed predators who stalked anyone more vulnerable than themselves. And they survived despite local law enforcement's attempts to either domesticate or eradicate them.

For some reason Earl considered Skye a part of his family. Perhaps he thought of her as his liaison between the kingdom of Doozierland and the rest of the world. She certainly hoped it wasn't anything more personal than that. The last thing Skye needed was Earl's wife getting jealous and plotting her demise.

"Fireworks are dangerous." She lectured Junior, knowing she was wasting her breath but unable to stop herself. "What if you'd blinded yourself?"

"Look, Miz Denison." Junior ran grubby fingers through his unevenly cut red hair. "From the time you light the fuse, youse have about three, four seconds afore the cherry bomb goes off. Evens a girl can throw it by then."

"Let's put the safety issue aside." Skye blew out a frustrated breath. "Why did you throw an explosive into the art room?"

"She disrespected me." Junior's large ears vibrated with indignation.

"Who?"

"Miz Wormwood."

"The art teacher?" Skye wondered what the woman had done. She was new this year, straight out of college and still learning how to control her class. "She wasn't even there."

"Well, how was I suppose to know that?" Junior huffed. "It's her golldurn room, ain't it?" He crossed his arms. "I heard someone that sounded like her talkin' and figured, hey, here's my chance."

"I see." Skye hadn't realized that Neva and the art teacher had similar-sounding voices, but now that she thought about it, both *were* originally from Boston. "So what did Ms. Wormwood do to you, anyway?"

"You wouldn't understand." Junior frowned. "You'll take her side."

"Look, we have maybe ten more minutes before your folks get here." Skye decided to lay it on the line. Counseling techniques didn't seem to work with the Doozier family. "And our school district has a strict policy about weapons. You could be expelled."

"It weren't no weapon." Junior bristled. "An AK-47 is a weapon."

"Junior!"

"Fine." He slumped back in his chair. "Our assignment was to draw a comic strip. And I'm good at drawin' so's I did it. And it was on time and everything."

Skye nodded. Turning in homework when it was due was a major accomplishment for Junior.

"But she says, 'This is unacceptable, young man.'" His voice sound eerily like the teacher's.

"Why?"

"My comic hero was a dude called Moonshine Man." Junior grinned. "He can outrun any police car, handle hot copper tubing with his bare hands, and is stronger than a liquored-up redneck."

"Ah." Skye was beginning to understand. "So what happened?"

"She scrunched it up right in front of everyone and told me not to try to be smart."

Oh, oh. Skye was willing to bet her engagement ring that Junior had not taken that comment the way the art teacher had meant it.

"I knows I ain't the smartest one in the class, but she don't have no call to say I'm stupid." Junior blinked his muddy brown eyes.

Skye nodded again, more sympathetically. Junior had a severe learning disability, which made reading extremely difficult for him, but his IQ was above average. Skye knew this for a fact since she had tested him twice in the past six years.

"That was a good drawin'." Junior sat forward, his expression earnest. "So I says to her, 'I ain't the dumbass. You is.'"

"And?"

151

"And she sent me to the principal's office." Junior slumped back in his chair, clearly defeated by a system he didn't understand. "But Miz Llewellyn weren't there, so's Mrs. Nelson told me to come back after lunch."

"And on your way to the cafeteria you thought you heard Ms. Wormwood, who had insulted you, so you retaliated by throwing a cherry bomb," Skye recapped, wanting to make sure she was clear on the sequence of events. "Do you always carry one around in your pocket?"

"Yep." Junior nodded. "Ya never know when a fella might need a little distraction."

"Okay." Skye stood up and motioned Junior out of his seat. "Let's go see if your folks have arrived, and what we can do about this mess."

As she and Junior walked toward the principal's office, Skye tried to formulate an argument that would dissuade Neva from kicking the boy out of school. She had a bad feeling that if Junior was expelled, they'd have a hard time getting him to come back.

Neva surprised Skye. The principal was sympathetic to Junior's plight, and promised to speak to the art teacher about how she had handled the situation. And because of the extenuating circumstance, Neva suspended Junior for only three days rather than expelling him for the rest of the year or longer.

Once Earl and his wife had taken their son home, promising the boy wouldn't sit in front of the TV or play video games all day, Skye headed to the high school. She was running more than an hour late, but still hoped to see the Pass Out game girls before the end of the day.

While she crossed the expanse of grass separating the schools, Skye mentally thanked Neva for not making her bring up Junior's disability in order to save him from expulsion. She definitely didn't want to have to go through the Manifestation Determination process.

The procedure to determine if a student's behavior was or was not due to the student's handicapping condition involved a long, drawn-out, often excruciating course of meetings, paperwork, and more meetings, requiring time that everyone involved could put to better use.

Skye sprinted into the high school. Seventh period started in ten minutes, so she grabbed the stack of papers from her mailbox and dashed to her office. As she raced down the hallway, she shuffled through the pages, counting the consent forms.

Shoot! Only eight of the girls' documents were present. Now she'd have to call the other parents and ask why their daughters' permission slips were missing. Which meant she'd have to put off talking to the girls until tomorrow. Homer would not be happy.

• • •

What with the crisis at the junior high and having to track down the moms and dads of the last three Pass Out game girls, Skye didn't have a chance to call Wally. By the time she got off work, she was dying to know what had happened with the Kyle O'Brien situation.

As she slid into her car, she was already digging through her tote bag for her phone. While she waited for it to power up—cell phones had to be switched off while in the school building—she fastened her seat belt, started the Bel Air, and turned on the heat. The temperature had dropped again and her new spring trench coat, while cute, wasn't lined.

Wally didn't answer his private line and his cell went straight to voice mail. Frustrated, Skye dialed the PD's nonemergency number.

After several rings, Thea Jones, the daytime dispatcher, answered, "Scumble River police, fire, and emergency. How can I help you?"

Skye identified herself, then spent a few minutes exchanging pleasantries with Thea before asking, "Is the chief around?"

"No." The dispatcher paused, and Skye heard her say to someone else, "Hold your horses. I'll be with you in a minute." Thea turned her attention back to Skye. "Sorry, hon. People just don't have any manners nowadays. They see you're busy and think it's still okay to butt in."

"Well, I don't want to keep you." Skye didn't want to get involved in whatever squabbling was going on at the police station. "I just wondered if you knew why Wally isn't answering his cell."

"He's probably in a dead zone." Thea dropped her voice. "About half an hour ago, we got a tip regarding Elijah Jacobsen's whereabouts. The chief and Quirk and Martinez lit out of here quicker than a squirrel crossing a road in front of a semi."

"Oh." Skye's chest tightened. She hoped that Elijah would come in peacefully and no one would get hurt. "Thanks for your help."

Now what? Surely, she had better things to do with her time than hanging around the PD waiting for Wally and the others to return. She'd already left him two messages, so she knew he would call when he had a chance. She certainly didn't want to seem like a pathetic loser who had no life or interests outside of her fiancé.

She could go visit someone. But who? Just before the final bell had rung, Trixie had stopped by Skye's office for a quick chat and had mentioned that she and her husband, Owen, were going out to dinner and then to a movie in Joliet. So Skye's best friend was out.

Too bad her mom would be reporting for her four o'clock shift in a few minutes. Now that it seemed as if May was okay with the idea of Wally and Skye getting married, Skye really needed to talk to her about the wedding plans before May rented Buckingham Palace for the reception and hired the Chicago Symphony Orchestra to play at the church.

There was her brother, Vince. They used to hang out together a lot, and even though his new bride was Skye's friend and sorority sister, dropping in on the newlyweds unannounced seemed tacky.

Oh, well. Skye shrugged and put the Bel Air in reverse. Bingo would be glad to see her, if only because he'd get an early supper.

Five minutes later Skye pulled into her driveway and skidded to a stop behind a shiny red antique pickup that was blocking the way to her garage. As she got out of her car, Sonia and Sandy Sechrest climbed down from the truck's cab and headed toward her.

Today the twins were dressed in identical jeans, blue plaid blouses, and denim jackets. Skye could tell them apart only by their cowboy boots. As she had previously noticed, Sandy's had a higher heel than her sister's.

"See, I told you if we waited a little bit, she'd come home," Sonia scolded her sister. "But you're always so impatient."

"And I told you we should have called first," Sandy admonished. "But you always think everyone will be at your beck and call."

"Ladies." Skye raised her voice. "Ladies." Clearly, the twins had spent a lifetime quarreling with each other, so she talked over them. "What a cool classic truck. Who restored it for you?"

"No one." Sonia's expression was puzzled. "Horatio's never been in a wreck."

"We're very careful drivers," Sandy added, patting the pickup's side as if it were a pony. "We've kept Horatio in tiptop condition ever since Papa gave him to us on our sixteenth birthday."

"Wow." Skye was momentarily speechless at the idea of a vehicle that still looked brand-new after sixty-four years of use. Finally, she realized the twins were staring at her, and she asked quickly, "What brings you out to my neck of the woods today?"

"We're delivering the cat condo you ordered," Sonia announced, pointing to the back of the pickup. "Don't you remember me telling you it would be ready today?" She added in a concerned tone, "I hope we haven't ruined the surprise for Bingo."

"No." Skye shook her head. "I told him about it." She noticed Sandy's mouth form a pout. "When I gave him the toy on Saturday, I mentioned that he had another present coming on Tuesday."

"Good. Let's get the condo in the house." Sonia lowered the truck's tailgate. "I can't wait to meet Bingo and show him his new kingdom."

"Here." Skye hurried over. "Let me get that." She lifted the four-foot-high cat tree from the pickup's bed, wrestled the multilevel shag-carpeted object into her arms, and wheezed, "Follow me."

Once they were inside, and the sisters had been properly introduced to Bingo, Skye seated them and offered them something to drink. Sandy asked for wine and Sonia wanted a beer. Skye was glad she hadn't offered them tea. Clearly, they weren't anything like stereotypical old ladies.

After pouring the sisters' preferred refreshments into glasses, Skye put them along with her own Caffeine Free Diet Coke on a tray and carried it into the front parlor. She expected the conversation to focus on the murder, but instead Sonia explained in detail how she had constructed the condo, the best way to take care of the structure, and how to lure Bingo onto the tree if he was reluctant. It seemed a sprinkling of catnip on each level usually did the trick.

When Sonia paused to take a breath, Sandy leaped in and talked about next season's cat toys. Skye kept her expression interested while she listened to Sandy describe her entire summer catalog.

Finally the sisters wound down, and Skye stood. "Would you like another drink?"

The twins shook their heads.

"I don't want to keep you ladies." Skye stepped toward the parlor's archway. "If you have other deliveries, I completely understand."

"Uh, well . . ." Sandy hesitated. "You work with the police. Right?"

"Yes." Skye sat back down, realizing the sisters were about to tell her the real reason for their visit. "I'm the psychological consultant."

"The thing is—," Sandy started.

"Oh, for crying out loud," Sonia broke in. "Just tell her, for heaven's sake."

"You tell her." Sandy frowned at her sister. "You're the one who thinks we should."

"And you're the one who told me." Sonia crossed her arms. "So it would be hearsay if I told her. And that kind of testimony isn't legal."

"You watch too much *Law and Order*." Sandy crossed her arms, too.

"I do not." Sonia's lower lip started to quiver. "You watch as much as I do."

"Ladies." Skye was getting a headache. This was worse than playground duty. "Sandy, you start and Sonia can fill in anything you forget."

"Do the police know about Fawn Irving?" Sandy fiddled with the buttons on her blouse.

"What about her?" Skye asked, leaning forward in her chair.

"You know she and Alexis didn't get along?" Sandy waited for Skye's nod, then added, "Not that many people did get along with that witch."

"Right." Skye allowed the elderly women to tell their story at their own pace.

"Do the police know that Fawn was in the hospital?" Sandy asked.

"I'm not sure." Frannie had mentioned the woman's recent hospitalization, but Skye couldn't remember if she had told Wally or not. Probably not, as it hadn't seemed relevant. "Is that fact important?"

"Maybe." Sandy stared at her twin, who made an encouraging sound. "The thing is, she wasn't in the hospital for a physical problem."

"The problem was a psychiatric one?" Skye asked, wishing she had a notepad and pen but not wanting to interrupt.

"Yes." Sandy nodded. "I volunteer at the Laurel Hospital, and I was there when they brought her in. She had tried to hurt herself."

"Oh." Skye felt awful for the fragile woman. This new revelation made Alexis's bullying seem even worse than Skye had originally thought.

"Once she was stable, they transferred her to St. Joe's in Joliet," Sandy explained, "but I heard people saying that her suicide attempt was because of her husband's disappearance."

"How awful."

"The really awful part is that everyone thinks Fawn might have killed him."

CHAPTER 13

A Cat Has Nine Lives

Placing a rolled-up towel behind her neck, Skye lay back in the bathtub. Lit votive candles on the vanity were the only illumination in the darkened room, and Nat King Cole was singing "Unforgettable" on the CD player.

A few minutes later, just as she started to doze off, the overhead light was suddenly switched on. Skye's eyes popped open and she sat up, squealing and splashing water and bubbles everywhere.

Still breathless, she gasped, "Wally, you scared me to death!"

"Sorry, darlin'. It's not even seven fifteen; I didn't think you'd be sleeping." He flipped the light back off, knelt beside her, and gave her a slow, drugging kiss. "I yelled that I was here when I walked in, but you must not have heard me over the music."

"Oh." Skye moaned as his lips seared a path down her neck to her shoulders. "My!" Shivers of delight followed his caresses and she felt transported away from Scumble River and all its problems.

Wally's hands slipped below the bubbles and Skye felt a delicious warmth radiate throughout her body. She ached for another of his kisses.

Tangling her fingers in his dark hair, she brought his mouth back to hers, angling her neck until they fit together perfectly.

Raising his lips a fraction of an inch from hers, his voice was a rasping whisper as he asked, "Are you getting out or am I coming in?"

"Hmm." She arched her back and stretched. "I did order the extra-large tub when I had the bathroom remodeled, so there's plenty of room."

Skye's pulse quickened as she watched Wally kick off his shoes and shed his uniform. His powerful, well-built body moved with an easy grace as he deftly removed each piece of clothing. She purred, admiring the glowing bronze skin that covered every visible inch. How did he maintain a year-round tan? She knew for a fact that he didn't sunbathe or make use of a tanning bed.

He stepped into the water and eased down beside her. Gathering her into his arms, he tucked her close to his side. His body exuded an enticing heat that made her want to cuddle closer to his flame.

Even after two and a half years of dating him and ten months of being engaged to him, Skye still found Wally's vitality captivating. There was some intangible bond between them that had lasted since they had first met when she was sixteen and he was twenty-two. He projected a strength and power that she found impossible to resist.

Wally's heart pounded against her ear as he trailed a finger down her side, tracing an imaginary pattern on her hip. Skye crooned encouragement while stroking the length of his back.

His hands and lips explored the soft curves of her body. She felt bound in a honeyed web of growing desire and gasped in pleasure at the sensation of her breasts being crushed against his chest.

Skin to skin, just as they were about to become one, a cacophonous ringing erupted from the bedroom phone. It jarred Skye from the moment, and she stiffened at the intrusion.

Wally kissed her until she relaxed again, then said huskily, "Ignore it."

Before Skye could respond, "Hail to the Chief" began to play at an incredibly loud volume. Now it was Wally's turn to freeze.

Both of them lay suspended, trying to disregard their phones when suddenly the doorbell started to buzz. And continued and continued, as if someone was leaning against the button. Between the ringing, the music, and the drone of the doorbell, the racket was intolerable.

Swearing, Wally heaved himself to his feet, then gave Skye a hand out of the tub. While he was searching his pants pocket for his cell, she threw on her robe and ran downstairs. Sliding on the throw rug at the bottom of the steps, she barely managed to right herself as she skidded toward the door.

Out of breath, she pushed aside the front window curtains, and peered out. Instantly, the doorbell became silent, as did the music from the cell and the ringing of the telephone. What the heck was going on? There was no one on the porch, and she couldn't see any vehicle other than Wally's squad car in the driveway.

To get a better view, she opened the door a few inches and poked her head through the gap, but there was no one anywhere around her house. She ran to the kitchen window and looked out. The backyard was empty as well. She retraced her steps and checked the front once more. Not even a bird was flying overhead. Clearly, no corporeal being had been pressing the doorbell.

Trudging back to the master bath, Skye narrowed her eyes and muttered under her breath, "Mrs. Griggs, this had better not be your doing or so help me—" She broke off as she met Wally on the landing, and asked, "Was there an emergency at the station? Who was calling?"

"No one." Wally's expression was puzzled. "There wasn't a voice mail or even a number from a missed call." He looked toward Skye's bedroom. "And it sounds as if your phone stopped, too."

"Isn't that odd?" Once she and Wally had gotten engaged, Skye decided that since she wanted them to live in her house after they were married, it was best if she didn't mention to Wally the possibility that Mrs. Griggs was haunting them. "No one was at the door, either."

"Maybe I should check with the PD." Wally fingered his cell phone.

"Might as well." Skye sighed. "The mood is completely shattered."

"I'm sure we could recapture it." Wally raised a brow and reached for her.

"Sorry." She evaded him, not wanting to stir up the resident ghost again. "I don't think I can." Seeing him slump, she felt bad. None of this was his fault. "Let me get dressed and I'll rustle up something for supper. I bet you haven't eaten."

"You must be psychic." Wally smiled. "I came over here as soon I got back from the manhunt."

"What—" Skye stopped herself. "Wait. You make your call to the PD, I'll throw on some clothes, and you can tell me everything while we eat."

Twenty minutes later, clad in black leggings, a zebra-striped tunic, and her bunny slippers, Skye set a platter of scrambled eggs, bacon, and toast on the kitchen table and took her seat.

Wally had put on a pair of sweatpants and a T-shirt from the stash of clothes he kept at Skye's place, then joined her in the kitchen. While she was cooking, he'd poured her a glass of white merlot and opened a bottle of Sam Adams for himself. Then when the food was nearly done, he'd set out the dishes and silverware.

Skye ate in silence until Wally finished his first helping and reached for seconds. Then she asked, "So, did you find Elijah?"

"Just his car." Wally took a swig of beer. "It was parked inside the rec club, which is why no one spotted it earlier. The groundskeeper found it this afternoon when he went in to do his weekly rounds."

The Scumble River Recreational Club had been established on the property of an abandoned coal mine that was worked from the 1900s until the 1950s. It consisted of a beach, several lakes, a large picnic area, and woods for hunting. March was usually too cold to swim or picnic and most hunting took place in the fall, so the club was generally not used at this time of year.

"Was there anything inside Elijah's car?" Skye asked before eating her last bite of toast.

"Nothing I could see." Wally pushed his plate away. "On the surface, the vehicle's interior looked clean enough to do surgery, but the county crime techs had it towed to their garage and are going over it."

"How did he get inside the gate?" Skye asked. "Was he a member?"

"Yep. We found a key lying in the dirt near the entrance, and since all keys are numbered, we were able to trace it back to him."

"Did you search the grounds?" Skye asked. If they did, she wondered how they had done it so fast. The club covered nearly five hundred acres.

"Uh-huh." Wally got up and started to clear the table. "Both the state police and the county sheriff's department sent officers and dogs to help. Unless Jacobsen drowned himself in one of the lakes—and there was no evidence of that—he's still in the wind."

"In the wind?"

"On the run. Hiding from the police."

"Oh." Skye followed him to the sink and turned on the water. "It's too bad he wasn't at the rec club. It could certainly be the wilderness he mentioned in his note."

"Maybe that's what he wanted us to think." Wally took the dishcloth from where it lay draped over the faucet and wiped down the tabletop. "He's probably across the border in Mexico by now."

"I doubt it." Skye shook her head. "If he had retained that kind of organization and planning ability, he'd still be a surgeon."

Once the kitchen was cleaned up and the dishes were done and put away, Skye and Wally moved into the sunroom. Because it was more comfortable than the formal parlor, it was their usual choice. As they settled in on the wicker love seat, Bingo, who was curled on the floral cushion of the matching chair, opened one eye, twitched his tail, and went back to sleep.

Wally reached for the TV remote, but Skye plucked it from his fingers. "Oh, no, you don't. First, tell me what happened at Kyle's."

"But I want to catch the ten o'clock news," Wally protested.

"Then talk fast." Skye clutched the black plastic oblong to her chest.

"Sometimes you're a spoiled brat." Wally pretended to try to wrestle the remote from her, but allowed her to keep possession of the device and stole a kiss instead. "Good thing I'm a patient man."

"Yeah. Right." Skye stuck out her tongue. "Now tell me everything."

"As you and I thought, O'Brien was hiding in the house." Wally laced his hands behind his head and put his bare feet up on the coffee table. "So, while Quirk searched the place, I interviewed the photographer. He claimed he didn't hear us at the door because he was in his art studio in the back, engrossed in painting."

"Did you believe him?"

"It could be true." Wally shrugged. "There was a fresh canvas."

"Did Quirk find anything incriminating?" Skye put her slippered feet next to Wally's bare toes. "How did Kyle explain Alexis's car?"

"Nothing that implicated O'Brien in the murder

was found in his residence." Wally twitched a shoulder. "And he claimed he had no idea that the car out front was Alexis's because she drove an old Chevrolet Impala when they were dating. He said he figured the MINI Cooper belonged to one of his neighbors' kids home from college for spring break."

"Was what he said about Alexis driving a Chevy true?" Skye asked.

"Unfortunately." Wally's face revealed his frustration. "According to the DMV, the vic only owned the MINI Cooper for a few weeks."

"Shoot!"

"Yeah." Wally shifted, plainly exasperated. "And the only prints in the car were Alexis's. The steering wheel and door handle had been wiped clean. Which means whoever dumped the car in front of O'Brien's had to know about their past relationship and was trying to make him look guilty."

"Again, not something you'd expect from a man with Elijah's disabilities."

"So you keep saying." Wally's voice was impatient. "Did you ever think maybe he got better, and has been fooling people for years?"

"Recovery to that extent would be highly unlikely." Skye bit her lip. "And why would he pretend to be disabled if he wasn't?"

Wally shrugged and clicked on the TV. As they watched the news, Skye noticed his eyelids drooping more and more. At the end of the local weather forecast, she switched off the television, tugged Wally to his feet, and led him upstairs. She had barely pulled back the covers when he sank into the mattress, and he was fast asleep as soon as his head touched the pillow.

Skye changed into her nightshirt, brushed her teeth, and moisturized her face before joining him. Her last thought before drifting off was that at least Mrs. Griggs allowed them to share a bed.

The next morning when they were sitting down to breakfast it occurred to Skye that she hadn't told Wally about the twins' visit the day before. What else had she forgotten to share with him?

She scrunched up her forehead, trying to remember what she had and hadn't communicated. *Shoot!* Had she mentioned Spike's story?

Before she could gather her thoughts, Wally asked, "Are you okay?"

"I'm fine." Skye smiled at the concern in Wally's voice. He really was the sweetest guy. "But I just realized that I haven't mentioned a couple of things."

"Like?"

"First, I don't think I ever told you what Bunny's daughter, Spike, is doing in Illinois."

"Then I take it she wasn't in Scumble River just to visit her mother?"

"In Scumble River, yes, but she's in the area investigating a story." Skye took a sip of tea, relishing the smooth Earl Grey, then explained Spike's new job and the local government corruption lead she was following. Skye ended with, "So thank God it isn't Uncle Dante who's embezzling." She paused and twisted her lips to one side. "At least as far as we know."

"You said a couple of things," Wally reminded her. "Is there something else?"

Skye played with her spoon. "The Sechrest sisters visited me yesterday afternoon."

"What did they want?" Wally's tone was curious. "They're both so tiny and elderly, after their initial interview I pretty much crossed them off my suspect list. Was that a mistake?"

"Probably not. I doubt they killed Alexis over an insult, even one about a cat." She ate a spoonful of Special K, then said, "But they did have an interesting bit of information about Fawn Irving."

"Oh?" Wally poured Cap'n Crunch into a bowl and added milk.

Skye hid her grin. He had recently confided his love for the sugary corn and oat squares and she now kept a supply for him, but she still found it funny that a macho guy like Wally ate a kid's cereal.

"Did you know that not too long ago Fawn's husband disappeared?"

"No." He put down his spoon and frowned. "When did that happen?"

171

"I'm not sure. But shortly afterward, Fawn attempted suicide." Skye's expression grew sad. She hated hearing that anyone had been so despondent that they felt their only option was to end their life. "I don't have the exact dates, but Fawn was on the psychiatric floor of Saint Joe's up until a little while before the cat show."

"She certainly didn't volunteer that information." Wally poured a cup of coffee for himself, then sat down. "And neither did anyone else."

"I'm not surprised." Skye drank her cranberry juice. "Probably very few people are familiar with the whole story. Bunny and Frannie were aware that Fawn had been recently hospitalized, but I don't think they knew why." Skye explained how Sandy had come to hear about it, adding, "There really is no privacy anymore. Even though the medical personnel respect confidentiality, the volunteers can't be held to the same standards."

"I won't be able to see the records of her stay, but I will reinterview her." Wally cradled his mug, his expression thoughtful. "Actually, considering the circumstances of her hospitalization, I think the department's psych consultant should be present, too."

"Before we talk to her, you might want to check with the Laurel Police Department," Skye cautioned. "According to the rumor mill, a lot of folks seem to think Fawn might have killed her husband."

"Son of a B!" Wally nearly spewed the gulp of coffee he had just taken. "Every time I think we've eliminated a suspect we add two more. If we could just find Jacobsen, maybe we could wrap this case up."

"Maybe." Raising an eyebrow, Skye took a delicate sip of her tea. "But I wouldn't count on it."

CHAPTER 14

Busier Than a One-eyed Cat Watching Two Mouse Holes

Skye wasn't scheduled to be at the high school at all on Wednesdays or Thursdays—a fact that Homer tended to conveniently overlook. When things were running smoothly, he resented giving up any space or budget for her needs. But the minute a tricky situation reared its ugly head, he felt that she should devote all her time and energy to his school.

Unfortunately, as a school psychologist assigned to multiple schools, Skye was often put in the awkward position of reminding all the principals that she wasn't their full-time employee. And as she stepped over the threshold of the elementary school's office Wednesday morning, she sensed that today would be one of those days when she was needed everywhere at once, with everyone thinking his or her crisis was the most pressing.

Caroline Greer was standing between Mrs. Canetti and Mrs. Hinich, the mothers of two of Skye's social-skills group counselees. The principal was trying to keep the two women apart, while they were engrossed in a heated discussion involving loud voices, mean faces, and wild gesticulations.

As soon as Caroline spotted Skye, she abandoned her arbitration attempts and hurried over to her. The office was crowded with teachers signing in, chatting with each other, and watching Mrs. Canetti and Mrs. Hinich argue, but the principal pulled Skye to a semi-secluded area.

Once out of earshot, Caroline said in a low voice, "Help me get these parents into my office." She glanced worriedly back at the two antagonists. "I don't want to do this in public."

"What's up?" Skye kept a wary eye on the women, who continued their bickering.

"We have a major problem," Caroline said over her shoulder as she darted over to Mrs. Canetti, who was jabbing her finger in Mrs. Hinich's chest. The principal gripped the woman's arm just above the elbow, and motioned with her chin for Skye to take charge of the other mother.

Skye moved into place and waited for instructions.

"Ladies, let's sit down in private, have some coffee, and talk this over," Caroline suggested, tugging on Mrs. Canetti's arm until the much larger woman gave in and began to move. "I'm sure we can come to an agreement that will be in the best interest of both children."

Shooing Mrs. Hinich toward the principal's office, Skye passed Fern Otte, the school secretary, who handed her a sheaf of small pink pieces of paper. Fern was a small-boned woman who dressed in shades of brown and flapped her arms as if she was about to fly away. That, along with her tendency to sound as if she were cheeping when she spoke, had earned her the nickname Tweets. Not that anyone was cruel enough to call the fragile woman that to her face, but sometimes it was hard not to slip up.

While Caroline poured coffee for everyone, Skye glanced through the while-you-were-out memos. Most of them were from Homer, each succeeding one more agitated than the last. In short, he commanded her to drop everything and report to the high school immediately to deal with the Pass Out game girls.

From Homer's increasingly more detailed messages, Skye gathered that the gossip mill had been busy grinding out bigger and more exaggerated accounts of what had happened Saturday night at the infamous slumber party. Now parents whose kids had not even been involved were calling the high school principal in a state of panic, demanding information about what he and the district were going to do about the situation. And Homer, being Homer, in turn ordered Skye to handle the whole mess ASAP.

Neva had left the remaining message. She had called Earl Doozier to come pick up the classroom material for the instruction Junior would be missing due to his suspension. However, Earl had claimed his car wasn't working. Since Neva didn't want him and his brood trooping into her school anyway, she had promised that Skye would deliver the homework—Skye being the only one from the school that Earl allowed on his property.

Skye glanced up from her perusal of the pink slips and saw Caroline fussing with white foam cups, sugar, and creamer. If Fern reminded Skye of a wren, Caroline made her think of a partridge. The elementary principal was short, round, and had a monobosom. She had poufy white hair, black-framed glasses, and a reddish nose.

Once everyone had been supplied with coffee, Caroline settled behind her desk and said, "Let's start with a clear picture of what occurred yesterday." She clasped her hands. "Mrs. Canetti, for Ms. Denison's benefit will you please explain what happened?"

The muscular blonde frowned, but began. "Alvin Hinich bit my Duncan during afternoon recess." Her short platinum hair bristled as she continued. "Now Duncan is convinced he has rabies."

Duncan Canetti was germophobic. Duncan— or, as the kids called him, Mr. Clean—liked everything to be perfectly orderly and hygienic. So much so that he had persuaded his mother to allow him to have his head shaved in order to avoid ever having a hair out of place. He carried a can of Lysol with him wherever he went.

Skye knew that Duncan couldn't stand being

touched, so she could certainly see how having someone's mouth and saliva on his bare arm would upset the boy. Something like that could easily push him over the edge.

"Alvin didn't even break the skin," Mrs. Hinich pointed out, her tone exasperated. "How in the world can Mr. Clean think he has rabies if there isn't a puncture?" She huffed and sat back in her seat.

"Duncan"—Mrs. Canetti emphasized her son's name—"thought he was foaming at the mouth when he brushed his teeth this morning." She glared at the other woman. "He freaked out and has already taken three showers since then. He's rubbing his arm raw."

"And Alvin is traumatized by how his teacher treated him after the incident." Mrs. Hinich fingered her dark brown braid. "He'd been getting so much better lately." Her voice broke and she slumped. "Now he only growls and barks at me when I try to talk to him."

Skye knew that Alvin insisted he was a beagle named Spot. However, Skye had been making some headway with both boys. Now, hearing how Alvin and Duncan had regressed, she almost sobbed in frustration. It looked as if all the progress they had made was gone. She made a mental note to check on Clifford, the third member of the social-skills group she'd been conducting for the past six months.

"You need to stop indulging that child," Mrs. Canetti said with a sniff. "If my son acted like some kind of hound, I'd serve him dog food and make him sleep on the floor until he snapped out of it."

"Sure you would. Because you have such great parenting skills." Mrs. Hinich scoffed and folded her arms across her chest. "Is that why you allowed your son to go bald?" She shook her head. "And for heaven's sake, just take away that damn Lysol can. The reason Alvin bit him was because Duncan sprayed it in his eyes."

"Ladies!" Caroline leaned forward and addressed the two mothers. "I can understand your concerns, but both of you know that your children have difficult issues and special needs. Which is why I'm sure you can sympathize with each other's challenges."

The women refused to meet Caroline's gaze. Neither one seemed willing or able to empathize with the other's tribulations.

While the principal's statement had been diplomatic, it hadn't gotten them anywhere, so Skye decided to try a more direct approach. "Mrs. Canetti, I assume that if Duncan got over his rabies paranoia that would satisfy you. You'd drop the matter."

"Yes." The blonde nodded. "If he comes out of the bathroom and stops scrubbing himself bloody, I'm willing to overlook the assault."

"And Mrs. Hinich, I assume that if Alvin stops growling and starts talking, that would satisfy you."

"Yes."

"Great." Skye took a deep breath. What she was about to suggest was most certainly not recommended in the school psychology best practices manual. However, since no other immediate solution came to mind—therapy certainly did not produce rapid results—she said, "Mrs. Canetti, stop at the drugstore and pick up a tube of antibiotic ointment—a brand Duncan has never seen before. Then ask the pharmacist to paste a label on the box reading RABIES VACCINE."

"Will he do that?" Mrs. Canetti asked. "Isn't that illegal or something?"

"I think if you explain the problem, the pharmacist will be willing to help you out." Skye shrugged. "If he isn't able to, then you can create a label on your computer, print it out, and stick it on the package yourself."

"Okay." Mrs. Canetti sound uncertain, but she took a breath and nodded.

"Once you have the carton fixed up, show your son the medicine, then apply it to his arm and tell him he'll be cured in half an hour."

"But—"

Skye cut off Mrs. Canetti's protest and turned her attention to the other mother. "Mrs. Hinich, you need to rent a DVD of *Cats and Dogs*."

"What—?"

Skye interrupted her. "Watch the movie with Alvin and point out that the star is a beagle who talks. Emphasize throughout the film that the dog doesn't just growl." She bit her lip. She hated reinforcing the boy's fantasy, but she would deal with the fallout from that shortcut later, during group. "Make sure you stress that the dog communicates using words."

"Well . . ." The brunette paused, then twitched her shoulders. "It's worth a try." She shook her head. "If he's not talking by the time his father gets home, my husband will smack him with a rolled-up newspaper."

Skye did a double take and barely stopped herself from commenting. That one sentence explained so much about Alvin's behavior. Why had his mother never mentioned it before? Did she honestly not realize that her husband's conduct might be influencing her son's actions?

Realizing she'd been lost in thought, Skye recovered and asked, "How about you, Mrs. Canetti? Are you willing to take my suggestion?"

"Sure." The blonde picked up her purse from the floor and stood. "A tube of antibiotic ointment is a heck of a lot cheaper than a visit to the doctor, which is about my only other option."

Once the women had departed, Skye explained to Caroline about Homer's problem and requested permission to leave the elementary school as soon as she checked on Clifford. Caroline agreed. Pausing at the secretary's desk on her way out, Skye asked Fern if she could use the phone.

Having decided that Neva's issue was the least urgent, Skye called her and wheedled permission to make the Doozier delivery tomorrow. Normally, she would have offered to take the homework to Junior after work, but she figured that Wally might want her to accompany him to interview Fawn that afternoon.

Neva granted Skye's request to spend the afternoon at the high school. However, she wasn't pleased that Skye would miss her regular stint at the junior high, and told Skye to inform Homer that she expected reciprocal consideration the next time she needed Skye's presence on a day the psychologist was supposed to be at his school.

Skye considered it best to speak to the Pass Out game girls as a group, so when she arrived at the high school and found out she was still lacking one consent form, she pacified Homer about the delayed intervention by proposing that she write a letter that he could send to all parents that afternoon via their students.

She promised Homer that in the note she would clarify what had happened during the slumber party, offer recommendations as to what to look for if they were worried their kids might be participating in the game, and include a list of ways to discuss the dangerous pastime with their teenagers. She also swore she would conclude the document with a paragraph assuring the parents that the school was aware of the situation and was dealing with the students involved.

It took Skye the rest of the day to do the research and write the letter—then rewrite it again and again until Homer approved. Just before quitting time, she finally reached the mother of the one girl who still had not turned in her counseling consent form. The woman promised to drop off the permission slip herself the next morning since her daughter kept "forgetting" to bring it to school.

Feeling as if she'd been on a supersonic bullet train all day, Skye was so relieved to drive out of the high school parking lot that she forgot that Wally had asked her to call him when she got off work. Ordinarily she would just stop by the station, but he'd explained that it was best for her to phone, since he wasn't sure where he'd be or what they'd need to do regarding the investigation.

Pulling over to the side of the road, Skye turned on her cell. As soon as the device powered up, she saw that there was a voice mail from Wally.

After pressing multiple buttons, she finally persuaded her phone to play Wally's message. "Sugar, I have to go to Laurel to talk to the chief there about Fawn Irving. I'll be in touch as soon as I get back, which should be before six."

Skye smiled to herself. That meant she finally

had time to visit her parents. She hadn't had a chance to see them since Wally had told her about May's change of heart regarding their marriage, and she wanted to talk to her mom before May planned the whole wedding without her.

Normally Skye's mother worked afternoons at the PD, which meant May was usually just starting her shift when Skye was leaving school. However, she knew her mom had taken Wednesday off this week to attend a special meeting of her knitting group that night.

Since Skye didn't knit, she had no idea why a special meeting would be needed—maybe a new way to purl had been discovered—and she didn't care. As long as it meant May would be home, it was all good.

Skye's parents lived a few miles east of town, off a two-lane blacktop. In the spring, summer, and fall it was a pleasant drive, but during the winter, the trip could be a terrifying experience. After a snowstorm, cars slid into the ditch like pucks across an air hockey table.

Skye had a December birthday, and the first time she drove down that road after getting her license, she managed to flip her cousin's old Volkswagen. When she and her cousin had crawled out of the passenger-side window, the Beetle had looked like an upside-down turtle. It was a miracle that neither of them was injured.

The sound of her tires crunching the white pea

gravel on her parents' well-tended driveway interrupted Skye's journey down memory lane. Her father's old blue pickup was missing from its normal place in front of the garage, which meant Jed was probably still working somewhere on the farm.

Considering the cold, rainy weather they'd had this March, he wouldn't be in the field planting yet, so he was probably in the machine shed getting the tractors ready for the season. Either that or doing one of the hundred other chores that comprised a farmer's life.

Skye gazed over the acre of property that was her parents' pride and joy. During the spring and summer, Jed kept the lawn in better shape than a lot of golf course putting greens, but today the only signs of life were a row of bright yellow daffodils under the picture window and the purple crocuses around the miniature windmill.

As Skye got out of the Bel Air and walked toward the back patio, she noticed that her mother's concrete goose was dressed in a diaper and bib, with a blue ruffled cap on its head, a pacifier held in one wing and a baby bottle in the other. *Shoot!* The fowl's attire reflected May's desires, and Skye had been hoping for an Easter Bunny costume. She would have settled for a wedding gown.

Trust her mother to skip the wedding and zero in on the grandchild she so desperately wanted. Skye frowned, then mentally slapped herself. The whole world did not revolve around her. The bird's costume was probably intended as a hint for her newly married brother and his wife.

Still, Skye girded herself for battle as she opened the back door of the redbrick house. It was always difficult to predict her mother's frame of mind, and Skye liked to be prepared for the worst.

Entering the large kitchen, which was bisected by a counter edged with two stools, Skye noticed that, as always, the taupe floor tiles were pristine, the dark brown granite countertop was spotless, and the white sink and chrome faucet sparkled as if they were brand-new. Dirt and grime didn't stand a chance against May's elbow grease. And dust bunnies quaked in terror of her vacuum.

Pots were bubbling on the stove, but Skye spotted her mother standing by the opposite wall talking on the phone. May gestured that she'd be only a minute, and Skye opened the refrigerator. She made a moue of distaste. Her mom's preference for Pepsi products over Coke never ceased to amaze her. Still, she was thirsty, so she grabbed a bottle of soda from the shelf, poured some into a tumbler, added ice, and took a seat at the round glass table in the dinette.

May hung up the receiver and said, "That was your brother." She opened the oven and slid a cookie sheet of dinner rolls onto the wire rack. "Vince is such a good boy. He calls me every afternoon before I go to work to see how Dad and I are and to tell me what he wants for lunch the next day."

"How are he and Loretta doing?" Skye had long ago accepted that Vince could do no wrong in her mother's eyes, but the fact that May didn't bring Skye her lunch still hurt a little. "I haven't seen them since Dad's birthday."

"They're fine." May closed the oven door and set the timer. "They've decided to build since they couldn't find a house they like."

"That's nice." Skye had wondered if that would happen. It was a sacrifice for Loretta to move from Chicago to Scumble River, and she knew Vince would do whatever it took to make her happy there. "Have they found the property they want yet?"

"Dad's giving them an acre of that farmland he bought a couple years ago."

"Great." Skye got up and leaned against the counter. "That will save them a bundle."

"When you're ready to build, you can have an acre out there, too." May added salt to the contents of one of the simmering pots. "Wally told me his annulment should be finished in a month or so, and I know he doesn't want to live in that old place of yours. Something is always blowing up, catching on fire, or flooding in that house."

CHAPTER 15

There's More Than One Way to Pet a Cat

S kye felt stunned by her mother's declaration, but knew May well enough to make her clarify her assertion. "Did Wally actually say he didn't want to move in to my place, or are you assuming he doesn't want to live there because you don't like old houses?"

Skye had been hoping that Wally was unaware of, or at least not bothered by, Mrs. Griggs's antics, but she might have been deceiving herself. He'd always seemed more amused than upset when each new catastrophe occurred. Could he have fooled her into thinking he wasn't perturbed by the ghost's tricks?

"I don't assume." May drew herself up until her five-foot-two frame seemed to tower over her much taller daughter. "He said, and I quote, 'Skye's poured so much money and energy into that house, I'd like to build her a new one that has everything she's ever wanted.'"

"That's really sweet of him." Skye ran Wally's words through her mind, then smiled. May's understanding of what Wally had said wasn't the only way to interpret his statement. Since he didn't believe that the previous owner was haunting them, maybe he thought the house was in worse shape than it really was.

"He's a practical guy," May commented, her lips pressed into a thin line. "He's learned the hard way that an unhappy wife is a recipe for disaster, and he won't make that mistake again."

"That's one way of looking at it," Skye admitted. "However, I think what he meant is that he wants me to be happy—and I love my house."

"Maybe." May wiped an imaginary spot off the countertop next to the stove. "But you should still let him build you your dream house."

"Why?" Skye took a swig of soda. "We can finish fixing up my place for half of what new construction would cost. I already did the roof and shingles, as well as the plumbing and electrical work. And I just finished remodeling the kitchen and master bath. Those projects were the most expensive renovations."

"Wally can afford to give you the best." May took the makings for a tossed salad from the fridge and started peeling carrots, ignoring Skye's arguments.

"How do you—" Skye stopped herself just in time and changed what she had been about to say to, "How do you get the carrot shreds so thin?"

While May explained her culinary technique, questions raced through Skye's mind. Had her mother found out that Wally was the son of a Texas oil multimillionaire—which would explain her sudden second thoughts regarding his suitability as Skye's groom?

Or did she mean that as the chief of police he made a good salary? Having grown up poor, then lived the life of a farm wife for the past forty years, May would consider Wally's income a lot of money.

As far as Skye knew, she was the only one in town that Wally had told about his father's wealth. However, his ex-wife had known, and she'd visited Scumble River a few months ago. Could Darleen have told May? The two women weren't exactly buddies, but . . .

No. If her mother had had any inkling of Wally's family's wealth, she would have blurted it out long ago. May wasn't the subtle type.

Having decided that there had to be another explanation for her mother's sudden about-face regarding Wally, Skye brought the conversation around to the real purpose of her visit. "So, Mom, since you and Dad are now offering us land to build a house, I guess you've changed your mind about my fiancé."

"Well." May looked over Skye's shoulder, refusing to meet her daughter's eyes.

It was a well-known fact that May hated admitting that she might have made a mistake. Actually, now they she thought about it, Skye couldn't remember hearing her mother say the words "I was wrong"—ever.

"Yes?" Skye was not about to let this opportunity pass. May had put both her and Wally through too much hell the past two and a half years for Skye to allow her mother to pretend it had never happened. "So, what made you decide it was okay for me to marry Wally?"

"For heaven's sake," May huffed, "I don't know why you have to make such a big deal out of everything." She sneaked a peek at her daughter. "It's not as if I disowned you when you got engaged to him."

"No." Skye raised a brow. "You only pretended it was a phase I was going through, and kept throwing Simon in my face any chance you got."

"I just wanted to make sure you picked the right guy." May arranged the lettuce, carrots, and cherry tomatoes in three salad bowls, concentrating on the task as if she were about to enter her creations in an art show. "Simon seemed more your type. You always liked boys who could discuss books and stuff with you."

"Wally's intelligent," Skye objected. Granted, his taste in reading was questionable since he was into techno thrillers, which bored her to tears. But she'd been luring him over to the light side, and he was now reading humorous mysteries as well. "He's a college graduate, and no one runs a police department for long if they're stupid."

"I'm not saying Wally isn't smart," May protested. "What I meant is that he seems more macho and small town, and you always went for the smooth, cultured guys. The kind who liked to go into the city."

"True." Skye frowned. Her mother was right about the type of man she'd been attracted to in the past, although Wally had always been the exception. "I guess my tastes have matured." When had her preferences changed? Probably about the time she had decided she liked living in Scumble River and was no longer counting the days until she could move away again. "I don't think many people know what they really want in their teens and twenties."

"Humph." May sniffed, clearly unconvinced.

"Wally's a lot more sophisticated than you might think." Skye swallowed a grin. What would her mother think if she knew that Wally had regularly summered in Europe the first twenty years of his life? And he hadn't traveled via cattle class on some commercial airliner, but on one of the many private jets owned by his father's company.

"Uh-huh."

"Anyway, Wally's intelligence and refinement are not the question." Skye refocused the conversation. There wasn't enough vodka in Russia to distract her from the real issue. "The question is why did you change your mind about the suitability of him as my husband?"

"Fine." May quit fussing with dinner. "Since it

obviously makes you feel good to torment your mother, I'll make you happy and explain."

Skye's only response was to narrow her eyes and cross her arms.

"It turns out"—May ran her fingers through her short salt-and-pepper hair, a sure sign she was agitated since she hated it when her waves weren't perfectly arranged—"that I sort of lost sight for a little while that Wally is a really good man."

"Yes, he is." A warm glow washed over Skye at hearing May finally admit it. Until that moment, Skye hadn't realized how hurt she'd been by her mother's disapproval.

"And seeing how he treats you like a princess, and obviously loves you to death . . ." May struggled for words. "So . . ."

"So?" Skye smirked. Finally she had her mother on the spot rather than the other way around. "The fact that he went along with the annulment process, has offered to turn Catholic, and has stated that late-in-life fertility runs in his family had nothing to do with it?"

"That's right." May turned back to her cooking. "Now let's talk about something more interesting, like planning your wedding."

Skye and her mother were discussing the wedding date when Jed pushed through the swinging doors that led from the utility room into the kitchen. He took off his blue-and-white polka-dotted cap, revealing a steel gray crew cut, faded brown eyes, and a tanned, leathery face, and asked, "When's supper, Ma?"

"Ten minutes." May examined her husband's dirty jeans and sweaty flannel shirt. "Hurry and get washed up before everything gets cold. Clean clothes are on the bed and I put a new bar of Lava in the shower."

Skye stared at her father's hands. The scars, ragged nails, and embedded oil were a badge of honor for a life spent fixing machinery and making a living for his family. She knew that Lava was the only thing her mother had found that cleaned the engine grease from Jed's skin. He didn't seem to mind that the pumice-based soap felt like a Brillo pad against his flesh. But then, he was used to hardship, and often stated that he wouldn't have it any other way.

Dipping his head in acknowledgment of May's instructions, Jed backed out of the kitchen. He was a man of few words, which was just as well, since his wife had enough to say for both of them.

Skye heard the door of the bathroom off the utility room click shut, then went over to the cupboard, took out a stack of dishes, and started to set the table. It went without saying that Skye would stay for dinner. If you were in May's house when mealtime rolled around, she fed you. And no one left her kitchen hungry.

Not that Skye minded. Her mother was a fabulous cook and had a plaque from a culinary contest to prove it. She also had a trophy, but Skye's name was engraved on it instead of hers. How her daughter instead of May had won top honors was a topic neither woman was inclined to discuss.

When Skye grabbed the butter dish from the fridge, her mother said, "Put that by your dad's plate. You and I need to use this new Smart Balance spread I found. It only has forty-five calories."

"No." Skye shook her head. "In the case of butter or margarine, I always pick butter. I trust cows—chemists who make fake food, not so much."

May opened her mouth to argue, but a burst of music made her pause. As soon as Skye recognized the tune "When You're in Love" from *Seven Brides for Seven Brothers*, she rushed into the utility room. It had taken her over an hour and much reading and rereading of the instruction book, but she had finally managed to program that song into her cell as Wally's ringtone.

Skye grabbed her purse from where she had dropped it on top of the clothes dryer and dug through it until she found her phone near the bottom next to a Tic Tac, a broken pencil, and a grocery receipt from two weeks ago. Wanting to catch the call before it went to voice mail, she quickly flipped it open.

Wally's voice greeted her. "Hi, darlin'. I'm back in town."

"Hi, sweetie. Can you hold on a minute?" Skye walked into the kitchen, covered the cell's microphone with her hand, and asked her mother, "It's Wally. Is it all right if I invite him to supper?"

"Of course," May answered, then asked, "How fast can he get here? Your dad's not going to want to wait more than five or ten minutes."

"It shouldn't take him long." Skye uncovered the phone and said, "Sorry for making you wait. I'm at my parents' and we're about to sit down to dinner. Want to join us?"

"If you're sure it's okay with your mother." Wally's voice was cautious.

"Don't worry. I checked before asking you," Skye assured him.

"I'm on my way."

Skye propped open the utility room's swinging doors so she could keep an eye on the driveway while she finished setting the table. As soon as she saw Wally's squad car pull in, she hurried outdoors and met him as he strode onto the patio.

After a quick hug and kiss, she asked, "Did the Laurel chief have anything interesting to say about Fawn Irving?"

"Let's talk about that later." Wally glanced uneasily at the door. "I don't want to get on your parents' bad sides by holding up dinner."

"Okay." Skye understood his concern. She was a little anxious herself.

As they stepped into the kitchen, May looked up

196

from the counter where she was pouring water into four glasses. Skye held her breath. This would be the true test. Had her mother really accepted Wally as her future son-in-law, or would she remain aloof toward him? A long heartbeat went by, then May put down the pitcher, turned to Wally, and opened her arms.

Wally leaned down—he was a foot taller than May—and enveloped her in a hug. Skye saw her mother whisper something in Wally's ear, kiss his cheek, and pat his back, then move away.

Skye let out a huge sigh of relief. Before she could ask Wally what her mother had said, Jed strolled through the kitchen wearing nothing but his undershorts.

As Skye's dad disappeared down the hall, Wally put his arm around her, cocked his head in the direction Jed had taken, and murmured, "Was that for me? Is your dad marking his territory?"

"Nope. We're just between him and his clothes." Skye raised her hands palms up and rolled her eyes. "I bought him a robe for his birthday, but Dad's not one to stand on ceremony. He figures Mom and I have seen him in his Jockeys before, and if you're going to be part of the family, you might as well get used to the sight, too."

Once Jed was dressed, he returned to the kitchen and took his seat at the head of the table. Skye subtly steered Wally to the place across from hers;

all they needed was for him to take May's chair by mistake. As soon as Wally was settled, Skye brought her dad a can of Budweiser. Since Wally was in uniform, she knew he wouldn't want a beer.

May put a platter of crispy fried veal cutlets in the center of the table. Bowls of homegrown sweet corn that May had frozen last August, creamy mashed potatoes, silky gravy, and a basket of hot dinner rolls were then arranged around the main course. Individual tossed salads were already set to the right of everyone's plate, and a bottle of Thousand Island dressing, Jed's favorite, and French, May's choice, were next to the salt and pepper.

Once they had helped themselves, May said to Wally, "I think you and Skye should get married at the end of September. Skye mentioned June, but six months is the minimum we'll need to plan the wedding."

"Uh." Wally took a quick bite of veal, indicated that he couldn't talk with his mouth full, then shot a questioning glance at Skye.

"Mom, as I explained, the wedding needs to be this summer. Otherwise we'll have to wait until a year from June." Skye blew out an impatient breath. "You know I'm not allowed to take extra days off during the school year."

"We are not waiting another fifteen months. And that's nonnegotiable." Wally's voice was firm.

Skye, Wally, and May continued to argue about dates—Skye adamant that she could not take off work during the school year, Wally unwilling to delay their marriage until next summer, and May determined to put on the big wedding she'd always dreamed of for her daughter.

While the others continued to debate the issue, Jed ate in silence. Finally, between mouthfuls, he grunted, "Christmas vacation."

"That's a great compromise!" Wally beamed at his future father-in-law. "We can get married the Saturday after Christmas." He took out his wallet and slipped a pocket calendar from one of the slots. "That would be December thirtieth." He turned to Skye. "I remember you saying that you have a full sixteen days off for winter break this year, so you'd have the week before the wedding to get ready and we'd have the week after for our honeymoon."

"But Skye already hates having a birthday so close to Christmas," May protested. "Now she'll have an anniversary then, too." She was not fond of settling for anything less than getting her own way.

"True." Skye considered her options, then smiled. "However, if we get married on December thirtieth, we can celebrate our anniversary by going somewhere warm and tropical every winter." She turned to her father. "You're a genius, Dad."

"Yep." Jed nodded and spooned another mound of potatoes onto his plate.

Once Father Burns had been called and confirmed that the church was available on the date they'd agreed upon, the four of them discussed Jed and May's recent weekend getaway. A half hour later, as her mother cleared the table, Skye started to put the scraped and rinsed plates into the dishwasher.

May noticed what she was doing and screeched, "Wait! Those aren't clean enough."

Skye had thought it odd that, considering her mother's fanaticism about spotlessness, May had agreed to the dishwasher when Vince and Loretta had had it installed for her a couple of weeks ago.

"You know, Mom," she said, raising a brow, "I think there may be a support group for women like you."

"What are you talking about?"

"You know, people who feel the need to wash their plates before putting them into the dishwasher to be washed."

May *tsk*ed, clearly not amused by her daughter's foolishness.

Once the kitchen was returned to its usual spotless state, May walked Skye and Wally to the door.

As they reached the threshold May said, "Did I tell you that I got your dad to play mini golf?"

"No." Skye stopped dead. "How in the world

did you get him to do that?" Jed's idea of a great vacation was sitting in either a bar or a casino, not taking part in what he would consider a silly game.

"Well, we went with Maggie and her husband," May explained. "And they had a certificate for four free rounds of miniature golf."

"Dad loves a freebie," Skye told Wally, then turned to her mom. "So it was you who bought the gift certificate for Maggie in the first place?"

"Of course."

Wally and Skye were still chuckling when they got outside and headed to their cars.

"I need to stop at the station for a second, and then I'll meet you at your house," Wally said, getting into the Caprice. "If it's okay with you, I was thinking we'd go talk to Fawn Irving about her husband's disappearance."

"Sure. See you in a few minutes." Skye waved as she slid into her Bel Air and backed out of the driveway. She was giggling again, thinking about her mother's maneuverings and her father playing mini golf, when a wisp of memory flitted across her mind. She straightened her spine and turned off the radio, trying to lure the elusive thought back, but it was gone.

Frustrated, Skye hit the steering wheel. What was it about miniature golf that had triggered an idea about Alexis's murder?

CHAPTER 16

Nervous as a Cat

A few minutes later, when Skye arrived home, she was still thinking about mini golf and murder, but Bingo's demands for supper, fresh water, and a clean litter box pushed the notion to the back of her mind. When the cat was taken care of and Wally still hadn't arrived, Skye made a quick call to her Grandma Denison to tell her that a date had finally been set for the wedding.

By the time she finished talking to her grandmother and went back outside, Wally was pulling up to the front walkway. He stopped the squad car, leaned across, and opened the passenger door.

As Skye slid into the seat, she demanded, "So tell me what you found out about Fawn and her husband."

"As we thought, the Laurel police are well aware of those two." Wally put the Caprice in gear. "They had suspected for quite a while that Fawn's husband was abusing her, but they could never get any evidence. Although Fawn was frequently seen around town with cuts and bruises, she always claimed that she was just clumsy."

"Which is fairly typical for a battered woman,"

Skye commented, buckling her seat belt. "As I understand it, they're either too ashamed or too terrified to admit that they're being assaulted."

Wally turned out of the driveway and onto the blacktop. "The problem is that even though the police are able to press charges when the victim won't, they have to have more than just a gut feeling in order to get a case to stick." He wrinkled his forehead in disgust. "And no one ever saw Irving raise a hand to his wife."

"Isn't that how it always is?" Skye said. She was having trouble concentrating on the conversation because her dad playing mini golf had popped back into her brain. "It's the same way when I file a report with Children and Family Services. There's not much DCFS can do if the child denies the abuse. And, naturally, there are never any witnesses willing to come forward."

"Of course." Wally took Skye's hand. "Very few people are willing to put themselves at risk to try to help someone else." He kissed her palm, then turned his attention back to the deserted country road. "The fact that you always do is one of the things I love the most." He grinned. "Well, that and everything else."

"Ah." Skye traced a finger down Wally's cheek. "You are so sweet."

"Guys do not want to be thought of as sweet." Wally made a face.

"Why?" Skye frowned, remembering that Simon

had also objected to that description. She'd never understood why he hated it. "It's a compliment," she assured Wally. "Women love sweet men."

"No, they don't." Wally shook his head. "They say they do, but if they're telling the truth, why do they always go for the guys they think are hot instead of the ones who treat them well?"

"Unlike men?" Skye cocked an eyebrow. "I believe the expression 'trophy wife' was in existence long before the term 'boy toy' was coined."

"All that proves is that both genders want someone sexy rather than nice." Wally eased up on the accelerator as he expertly guided the squad car through a series of sharp curves. "Which is why *sweet* is not how I want you to think of me."

"Well, you're definitely hot." Skye licked her lips suggestively, then winked. "Believe me, you have no worries on that front." She leaned back, sighing contentedly. "And in only nine months you're finally going to be my husband."

"Or we could fly to Vegas the day after school gets out for the summer. Then we'd only have to wait ten weeks rather than nine months."

"My mother would kill us both." Skye cringed. "After Vince and Loretta eloped, Mom made me swear on a stack of her favorite cookbooks that I'd have a big wedding." Skye crossed her arms. "And I made her promise that she wouldn't turn it into a three-ring circus, like my cousin Riley's over-the-top platinum spectacle."

"Thank God!" Wally shuddered. "That extravaganza was plain ridiculous."

"And that was *before* the body turned up." Skye shook off that awful memory, and getting back to the matter at hand, asked, "What did the Laurel chief say about Mr. Irving's disappearance?"

"Well, here's the deal." Wally's ears turned red, which told Skye he didn't approve of his fellow chief's actions. "Since Irving was a pain in the as—uh—butt, no one is too concerned that he's not around anymore." Wally twitched his shoulders. "Fawn reported him missing, the police filled out all the paperwork and put him in the system, but no one is actively looking for him."

"How about his employer?" Skye asked, then lost her train of thought when an image of a demented killer running around a miniature golf course distracted her.

"Irving didn't have a job."

"Oh." What was her subconscious trying to tell her about the murder? Since she had no idea, she tried to concentrate on the topic they were currently discussing. "What were the circumstances of his unemployment?"

"Irving had worked on an IDOT road crew." Wally tightened his grip on the steering wheel as he turned down a rutted gravel road. "Supposedly, he hurt his back when he slipped on some ice last winter. But the Laurel police say he was just bone-idle." Wally pressed his lips together in disapproval, then added, "Either way, Irving's been on disability for the past year or so."

"How about his parents or siblings?" Skye found it hard to believe a man could vanish and no one cared. Even one who seemed as thoroughly disliked as Mr. Irving. "Did he and Fawn have any children?"

"No kids." Wally guided the squad car around a series of potholes. "And when the police talked to Irving's parents and sister they essentially said, 'Good riddance to bad rubbish.'"

"Ouch." Skye shook her head. "Who was this guy, Attila the Hun?"

"Yep." Wally grimaced. "Or maybe his meaner younger brother."

"Again, ouch." Skye wondered about the man's backstory. In her experience as a psychologist, she had found that few people were born evil. Generally, something in their history pushed them in that direction. Still, that was no excuse if Mr. Irving had been abusing his wife.

For the next few miles the only sound in the squad car was the crackle of the police radio. Eventually, after several minutes of deep breathing, Skye was able to push her obsessive thoughts about miniature golf to the back of her mind. Maybe if she ignored it, the answer would materialize—sort of like when you stopped watching the toaster and the Pop-Tarts finally came up.

Entirely focused for the first time since Wally had picked her up, Skye said, "You know what I keep forgetting to ask you?" Wally shook his head, and she continued, "Has Alexis's body been released? Has the funeral been scheduled? Does her family live in the area?"

"No, no, and we haven't found her next of kin yet." Wally turned down a dirt road, this one even more rutted than the last. "Both of the vic's parents are dead and she was an only child."

"So who *is* her next of kin?" Skye asked. "Did her folks have siblings? Doesn't she have uncles, aunts, cousins?" Skye's extended family was so enormous, it was hard for her to imagine anyone not having a lot of relatives—even if they didn't live close by.

"Each parent had one sibling, but the mother's sister died several years ago, and Alexis didn't keep in touch with her father's brother, so we're having some trouble tracking him down."

"I guess that means there's not much of a chance that a family member killed her?" Skye asked, still hoping for a better suspect than Elijah.

"Probably not." Wally swung the Caprice into a long tree-lined lane. "According to the vic's neighbor and self-proclaimed best friend, Alexis has had no contact with any relatives for as long as the BFF knew her. And the last address we found for the uncle was New Zealand. He's some kind of merchant seaman."

"How about Alexis's bestie?" Skye asked. "Maybe she killed her."

"The neighbor has an ironclad alibi." Wally chuckled. "She spent the night in jail on an indecent exposure charge. Turns out she got a little drunk at some party and mooned the mayor of Clay Center."

"Shoot." Skye tilted her head. "If she has to have an alibi, the least she could have done was flash Scumble River's head honcho." She snickered. "I'd pay good money to see Uncle Dante's face if that happened."

Wally chuckled as he stopped the squad car on a gravel-covered rectangle to the side of the farmhouse. The area was illuminated by a halogen pole lamp—the kind that came on at dusk and turned off at sunrise—and it was clear to Skye that it had been a long time since any of the buildings had seen a paintbrush. Apparently, Mr. Irving hadn't spent his time off work keeping up his property.

Wally got out of the cruiser and walked around to open Skye's door. As she was exiting the Caprice, Fawn Irving emerged from the barn. She was carrying a carton of canning jars and didn't notice her visitors until she was nearly on top of them. Then her hands flew up and the box crashed to the ground.

Recoiling at the clattering of breaking glass, Skye yelped, then took a breath and said, "Fawn, I'm so sorry we startled you."

"It's my fault." Fawn's cheeks turned scarlet, and she hid her face by squatting down and inspecting the contents of the smashed carton. "My husband, Lee Harvey, always said I was clumsier than a goat on stilts."

"I'm sure he didn't mean it." Skye shot Wally a look. He hadn't mentioned that Mr. Irving shared a first name with a famous assassin. What in the world had his parents been thinking?

"Oh, I'm sure he did mean it," Fawn said, "since Lee Harvey said it nearly every day for the past thirty-some years." Fawn picked up the box and straightened. Facing them, she said, "Now, I bet you aren't here to discuss my klutziness, so . . ." She trailed off, her brief show of spunkiness evaporating like an August raindrop on a tin roof.

"Do you remember me? I'm Skye Denison from the cat show?" Skye waited for the other woman to nod, then touched Wally's forearm and said, "This is Chief Boyd, from the Scumble River Police Department. I believe you talked to Sergeant Quirk earlier."

Fawn nodded again, but remained silent. Her blue eyes were wide and her shoulders were tense. She stood flinching, as if expecting a blow.

"We need to ask you a few more questions." Wally took the carton from Fawn and said,

"Would it be okay if we talked inside? It's too cold to stand around out here."

Fawn bit her lip, and it was clear from her posture that she wanted to refuse, but suddenly she sagged and led them to the back door and into the kitchen. She flipped on the light and pointed to a couple of wooden chairs pulled up to an old walnut table.

Grabbing the kettle from the stove, she asked, "Would you like a cup of tea?"

"No, thank you." Wally took a seat and fished his notebook from the inside pocket of his jacket. "I've been drinking coffee all day, so I'm already sloshing."

"I'd love a cup." Skye smiled. "It's always nice to meet another tea drinker. What's your favorite kind? I like Earl Grey."

"Lipton." Fawn's tone was dry. "Lee Harvey didn't hold with spending money on anything fancy." She opened a cupboard and took down two thick white mugs. "He said there was no difference between the expensive stuff and what you could buy at Aldi for half the cost."

Aldi was a discount grocery chain that offered a nice selection of mostly generic and low-end products. The prices were good, but the store's system of metal gates and turnstiles, as well as the charge for shopping bags and the cash-and-debit-card-only policy kept some people away. Still, the supermarket was a boon to families on a budget.

"Aldi is great," Skye agreed. "I like a lot of their products, but I do indulge myself when it comes to tea and chocolate."

Fawn didn't comment, instead asking, "Do you take sugar or lemon?"

"Sweet'N Low if you have it, otherwise sugar is fine." Skye paused, thinking of Fawn's display at the cat show, which had indicated she bred Oriental Shorthairs. Finally Skye said, "Pardon me for asking, but if your husband didn't like you to spend money on fancy stuff, what did he think of your cat-breeding business?"

"He wasn't happy when I first started, and he never let me enter a show." Fawn rubbed her left wrist with her right hand as if remembering an injury. "But once I sold my first litter, he tolerated my babies." She nodded to herself, a thoughtful expression on her face. "I made sure to keep them out of his way, just like I kept out of his way, and everything was fine."

"Oh." Skye bit her lip, hating that this fragile woman might have felt so hopeless she'd had to resort to violence to survive. "Well, you certainly don't have to worry about neighbors complaining since your house is the only one on this stretch of the road."

"Lee Harvey liked being out here on our own, but I sure wish that housing development they keep talking about would go in," Fawn said, looking off into space. Then she abruptly changed the subject, asking, "Would you like to see my cattery?"

Skye glanced at Wally, and when he gave a slight nod and pointed to himself, then down, indicating Skye should go with Fawn and he would stay where he was, she said, "I'd love to. How many cats do you have?"

"Eight." Fawn turned the kettle down to simmer, then motioned Skye to follow her. "You met Miss Pearl and Miss Opal at the show." Fawn led the way down a series of hallways to the back of the house. "In addition, I have a stud and another queen. I just sold the last kitten from Miss Topaz's litter yesterday."

Fawn ushered Skye into a large room with multiple windows. From the well-used appearance of the furniture and the old computer in the corner, it was clear that this was where Fawn spent most of her time. When she began dispersing treats, the cats that had been lounging on kitty condos, chairs, and the back of the sofa came running. She introduced Skye to each one, and indicated which liked to be petted and which didn't tolerate strangers.

Skye wondered who had taken care of the animals while Fawn was in the hospital, but she didn't ask, since she wasn't sure how Wally wanted to handle their knowledge of her hospitalization. Instead, for the next fifteen minutes she petted and admired the beautiful cats.

Finally Skye looked at her watch. From Wally's gestures, she had deduced that he wanted to look around the house without the owner's knowledge. Had he had time? She couldn't keep Fawn here much longer.

The cat breeder noticed Skye checking the time and said, "I suppose we'd better get back to the kitchen. Chief Boyd will be getting bored."

Skye agreed, and with a final stroke for each of the felines that had allowed themselves to be petted, she left the cattery.

Once she and Fawn were in the hallway, Skye said loudly, "Thank you so much for allowing me to see your cats. They are really gorgeous." She walked slowly, hoping Wally had heard her warning.

Apparently he had, because he was sitting where they had left him. Skye noticed that he was slightly out of breath, and as soon as Fawn turned her back to finish making the tea, Skye raised her eyebrows.

Wally nodded, then asked, "Did you enjoy seeing all the cats?"

"Definitely." Skye smiled. "Bingo would be so jealous if he saw all their toys."

Fawn placed a sugar bowl, a teaspoon, and a steaming mug in front of Skye, then fetched her own cup. She joined Skye and Wally at the table, and the three sat in silence while the two women spooned sugar into their tea and stirred.

After a long moment, Fawn blew on her tea and took a sip. She swallowed; then, as if making up her mind about something, she said, "I didn't kill Lee Harvey and I didn't kill Alexis Hightower either, Chief."

"Oh?"

Fawn looked Wally in the eye, her gaze unwavering. "Both of them were awful excuses for human beings. And it's certainly better to have loved and lost than to put up with that horrible man for the rest of my life. But I decided a long time ago that who lives and who dies is up to the Lord, not me."

Skye was surprised to hear Fawn admit that her husband hadn't been a good man. According to the local gossip and the Laurel police, the woman had never acknowledged Lee Harvey was anything but wonderful.

"That's a good way of thinking," Wally said without inflection. "Unfortunately, at least in the case of Ms. Hightower, I need more than just your word that you aren't the murderer."

"I checked my e-mail when I got home from the disco bowler party and sent a reply around midnight," Fawn said. "I forgot about that when Sergeant Quirk asked me about an alibi, but you can check that sort of thing, right?"

"Yes, I believe we can. I'll have the county crime techs look into it." Wally made a note. "Who did you e-mail that night?"

"A man who was interested in buying a kitten." Fawn ran her finger along the rim of her mug. "I let him know that I only had one left, and asked him for some information if he was interested."

"Information?" Wally asked.

"About his home, how many people lived there, and why he wanted to buy a purebred instead of just adopting a shelter cat," Fawn answered. "I always make sure that my babies are going to good homes before I agree to sell them." Her smile was fierce. "That used to drive Lee Harvey crazy." She rubbed her wrist again. "But I protected them."

Wally asked a few more questions, then said, "Thank you for your time." He got to his feet and waited for Skye to stand. Then as they walked toward the door, he said to Fawn, "Until we can verify your alibi, please don't leave town without letting me know."

"Don't you worry, Chief." Fawn crossed her arms. "I'm not going anywhere. This farm has been in my family for a hundred years, and if I didn't let Lee Harvey run me off, nothing will make me leave."

CHAPTER 17

While the Cat's Away

Once Skye and Wally had gotten into the squad car, she asked, "Did you find anything suspicious or useful when you were looking around the house?"

"Nothing obvious." Wally rubbed the back of his neck. "In fact, the only thing that was the least bit out of the ordinary was that there are still men's clothes in the closet and drawers in the master bedroom. So if he left voluntarily, he didn't take his belongings."

"On the other hand, if Fawn killed her husband, she'd know he wasn't coming back and would have gotten rid of his stuff." Skye bit her lip. "I think she's afraid that if he does come back and his possessions are gone, he'll be angry."

"That's one way to look at it." Wally stretched. "Or she's putting on a good show in case his body turns up and the police search her house."

"I guess that could be true." Skye shrugged, then said, "Regarding Alexis's murder, the ME puts the time of death between eleven thirty and twelve thirty, right?"

Wally nodded.

"So if Fawn really sent an e-mail at midnight there's no way she could have killed Alexis." Skye paused, calculating distances and road conditions on Saturday night. "At the very least, it would take Fawn forty-five minutes to drive from Scumble River to her house, probably closer to an hour if she went the speed limit."

"I agree." Wally pulled his cell off his belt. "Fawn will be in the clear—at least for our case— if the county crime techs are able to confirm she sent the e-mail at the time she said and from her home computer."

"I saw her PC. It's about a hundred years old and money seems tight, so I doubt she has a laptop."

"We'll see." Wally punched a series of numbers into his phone. "I'm going to call the techs right now and ask if they have the ability to determine when, and from where, an e-mail was sent."

While Wally talked on the phone, Skye freshened up her lipstick. Vince had informed her at her last hair appointment that she was getting too old to go around with bare lips. At the time, she had resented his comment, but later, looking in the mirror, she had to agree that she looked better with some color on her mouth.

"Good news." Wally closed his phone and turned to her. "The tech says their computer guy can confirm the e-mail info."

"Great." Skye smiled. She liked Fawn and wanted to clear her of suspicion—at least for Alexis's murder. Having been married to a man like Lee Harvey, the poor woman must have suffered enough punishment for two lifetimes. "So that leaves Kyle O'Brien, Lola Martinez, and Ivan Quigley as suspects."

"Don't forget Jacobsen," Wally cautioned as he headed the Caprice back to Scumble River. "Although I know you would like us to overlook him."

"Did you interview Ivan yourself?" Skye asked, ignoring Wally's comment about Elijah. "I know you said his housekeeper alibied him, but you also said she changed her statement, which seems pretty fishy to me."

"He's on my list, but not anywhere near the top of the page." Wally concentrated on the road. It was a little after nine p.m. and since it was a moonless night, the countryside was completely dark. "Quigley's motive is one of the weakest of the bunch. Interfering with his chance to have Fawn for his speed date is pretty minor when he can just pick up a phone and ask her out some other time."

"True." Skye nodded. "But it did happen within a couple of hours of Alexis being killed, and as far as we know, she didn't have an altercation with anyone else between then and her death."

"I see your point. We can talk to Quigley together tomorrow." Wally's agreement was good-natured. "But he'll probably call his lawyer and clam up, so it might be a wasted trip. He has a lot of influence in this area and he didn't get as rich as he is by being stupid."

"Well." Skye blew out a frustrated breath. "It's worth a try."

"Sure." Wally braked for a deer crossing the road, then waited as two more followed. "Sometimes guys like that are so used to being deferred to, they're arrogant enough to blurt out something incriminating."

"Who else do we have to interview?" Skye watched the graceful animals disappear into the woods, hoping they wouldn't become one of her cousins' hunting trophies or fill one of their freezers.

"No one I can think of," Wally admitted. "We've interviewed everyone from the cat show, a few of them twice. Alexis had no family to speak of and her only friend seems to be the neighbor who is taking care of her cats. The woman with the airtight alibi."

"How about the servers, bartender, deejay, and bouncer?" Skye asked, remembering that Wally hadn't mentioned the staff. "Do they have alibis?"

"We spoke to all of them on the phone and they claim to have gone home after work." Wally's expression was discouraged. "A couple of them live alone, but no one reported seeing any interaction between the vic and the workers. Heck, the only one Alexis seems to have spoken to was a waitress who brought her a couple of drinks."

"Darn. I suppose that makes the staff unlikely suspects." Skye chewed on her thumbnail. "Unless—was she mean to that waitress?"

"Nope." Wally glanced at Skye, who was frowning, and assured her, "Martinez and Zuchowski are checking around to see if there are any connections between the employees and Alexis. But Bunny's recordkeeping leaves a lot to be desired. She hires a lot of employees off the books, and her only means of contacting them is their phone numbers, which are often pay-as-you-go cells. Which means it's hard to tell if the staff has ever crossed paths with the vic before."

"I figured you were on top of it." Skye smiled and patted his knee. "I'm so thankful that you don't get all defensive when I make suggestions. A lot of men would have a problem with that."

"Why?" Wally drew his brows together. "I know I'm a good police officer, but no one can think of everything." He put his hand on top of hers and squeezed. "My main concern has always been catching the bad guys. If I was worried about getting my ego bruised, I would never have hired you as the department's psych consultant."

"I know you don't want to be called sweet, so how about awesome?" Skye teased. "Or maybe incredible and amazingly wonderful."

"Awesome works for me." Wally grinned. "And hot and sexy are always good."

For the rest of the drive they discussed wedding

plans. They agreed to have the reception at the Country Mansion in Dwight—the restaurant that had been the site of their first real date. Skye was fairly certain that the Mansion's banquet facility would be available on December thirtieth, since all the Christmas parties would be over and New Year's Eve wasn't until the next day. But if the restaurant was unavailable, there was always the country club, the American Legion, or even the Grand Union of the Mighty Bulls assembly hall.

Skye already knew which three people she would ask to be her attendants, but Wally wasn't sure which friends he'd ask to stand up for him. She suggested his cousin. Although she had never met the man, she knew he worked for Wally's dad in Texas. But Wally seemed less than enthusiastic about that idea, saying they weren't all that close. They were discussing his other possible choices for groomsmen when they pulled into Skye's driveway.

A second later, the police radio crackled into life, and the dispatcher's voice said, "Ten-thirty-three at the First National Bank."

"An alarm is going off." Wally translated for Skye. "Martinez is on duty alone tonight. I'd better go back her up. Sorry."

"No problem." Skye understood Wally's concern for the young rookie.

"It's probably nothing." Wally stopped the

squad car in front of Skye's porch. "Those alarms go off when a butterfly lands on them."

"Sure." Skye leaned over and kissed his cheek, then hopped out of the Caprice and said, "Go ahead."

"Unless it's too late, I'll call you when I'm finished checking things out." Wally waved, put the cruiser in reverse, and took off toward town with his siren blaring and his lights flashing.

Skye was almost relieved that Wally had had to leave. Although she missed him when they spent a night apart, she needed to deal with the Mrs. Griggs situation before he stayed over again. She was fairly sure another instance of coitus interruptus would push him over the edge, making him hate her house, and she'd end up living in new construction when they got married.

It was already quarter to ten when Skye let herself into the house. But no matter how tired she was, tonight she was going to read the ghost-busting file and figure out what she would need to do to get rid of the former owner's spirit once and for all. Mrs. Griggs's shenanigans with the phones ringing and the doorbell buzzing the previous evening had sealed her fate. It was time for the apparition to go toward the light—or wherever ghosts went when they left this mortal plane.

With Bingo on her heels, Skye darted into the kitchen and grabbed the exorcism folder, paper, and a pen. The black cat protested loudly when she didn't dish out a second dinner, then hunkered down by his bowl and glared at her as she sat at the table.

Skye chewed on the end of her Bic as she read the instructions for the "cleansing." According to the clippings she had found on the Internet, the task required a willingness to open one's mind to mystical pathways and a certain level of spirituality.

She could handle that. She definitely had an open mind and she certainly believed that there was more than just what was visible to the eye. As long as the ritual didn't include killing chickens or making some sort of blood sacrifice with a pentagram, she was okay with it.

She was also reassured to read that an exorcism was intended to banish not just demons, but any spirit that was a source of negative energy and adversely affecting your life. The article claimed that the ceremony had its roots in Native American and druid cultures, and that an average person could safely perform the ritual without the help of a priest or minister.

So far, so good. Skye pulled the legal pad toward her and wrote:

ITEMS NEEDED:
THREE OR FOUR DRIED SAGE BRANCHES
YARN OR STRING

SMALL SHOVEL OR TROWEL
ONE POUND OF SMALL-GRANULE SEA SALT
LIGHTER OR MATCHES

She had everything but the sage and the salt. The latter could probably be purchased at the grocery store, but where was she going to get sage branches? She was pretty sure they didn't grow on trees.

The grade school's Pupil Personnel Services meetings were always scheduled for Thursdays at seven thirty a.m. The first item on the agenda was yesterday's situation with Alvin and Duncan. Caroline reported that both students had responded well to Skye's suggestions. Their mothers had assured the principal that the boys would be back in the classroom that morning.

Once again, Skye had to cut her time at the elementary school short because she had promised Neva that she would deliver Junior Doozier's assignments that morning. However, when she arrived at the junior high, there was a message from Junior's father saying the family would be gone all day on an emergency and asking Skye to bring the homework on Friday instead.

As she got back into her car, she debated returning to the grade school, but decided that seeing the Scumble River High's Pass Out game girls was more urgent than finishing Perry

Underwood's reevaluation. The boy had been in special education since he was three, and he was now completing fifth grade. This would be his fourth re-eval, and Skye seriously doubted there had been much change in his intellectual functioning or his processing skills. Perry's deficiencies had always been in the areas of fluid reasoning and working memory, and while children were taught compensatory learning methods, those abilities rarely improved.

So far, Skye's day was going incredibly well. She'd scored a win with the Alvin and Duncan issue, and had been able to delay her trip to Doozierland. Would she be three for three and make it through the lobby at the high school without Homer pouncing on her?

Yes! The principal was nowhere in sight when Skye entered the building. She held her breath as she stopped at the front counter to sign in and grab her mail. Quickly scooping up the contents of her box, she speed-walked down the hall and secured herself behind her office door.

Adding to her sense of well-being, the last permission form from the parents of the Pass Out game girls was among the papers in her box. After getting what she needed from her tote bag and locking it in her desk drawer, Skye turned on her computer and clicked through until she found the student schedules.

Her luck was holding. All eleven girls had

eighth period study hall together. Skye wrote passes for them, dropped them off for Opal to distribute, and left Homer a note explaining her plans.

The bell rang as she walked back to her office, and she checked her watch. It was ten twenty-five, third hour had just ended, and Trixie's planning period was fourth. Deciding, for once, to take the fifteen-minute break she was entitled to according to her contract, Skye headed to the library. It was time to tell her best friend that she had finally set her wedding date, and to ask her to be her matron of honor.

After a detour to the staff lounge to buy a couple of sodas, Skye found Trixie in the library's storeroom sitting on a stool pulled up to the worktable and typing away on her laptop. Several books were piled around her, including *Writing the Modern Mystery*, *Deadly Doses*, and *Self-Editing for Fiction Writers*.

Trixie didn't notice Skye until she cleared her throat. As if coming back from another world, Trixie looked up from the keyboard, and said, "Why haven't I seen you since Monday?" She clicked the SAVE button and demanded, "What's been happening with the murder and with the girls involved in that Pass Out game?"

"Sorry." Skye hugged her friend. "During the day all three schools have had crises for me to deal with, and I've spent most of my evenings interviewing suspects with Wally. Not that we're getting anywhere."

"How about the girls?" Trixie asked, shutting down her computer and twisting to face Skye. "Ashley said it was the first time they had tried the game, and they couldn't quite figure out how to do it since they all panicked when one of them started to lose consciousness. She promised me they wouldn't try it again."

"I'm talking to the other girls this afternoon." Skye took a seat and handed Trixie a can of A&W Root Beer. "Did you believe Ashley?"

"Maybe." Trixie popped the top of the soda and took a long swig. "But I told her if I found out she or any of the cheerleaders were ever involved in something like that again, they were off the squad."

"Good." Skye opened her Diet Coke and sipped. "Hopefully if the cheerleaders don't play, the others won't, either."

"So, nothing on the murder?" Trixie got up and rummaged through a cupboard. "I heard the best suspect has disappeared. What's up with that?"

"First, I'm not convinced Elijah is the killer." Skye took the packet of peanut butter wafers Trixie handed her. "And second, there are still at least two or three other good suspects that don't have an alibi, so I really hope everyone doesn't convict him before he even has a chance to explain himself."

"But since the ex-doc ran away, isn't that almost like a confession?"

"No." Skye tore open the cellophane and selected a cracker. "In fact, the more I think about it, the more I wonder if Elijah witnessed the murder and the real murderer lured him somewhere and killed him."

"That would be a great plot twist." Trixie licked peanut butter from her fingers, picked up her pen, and made a note on a piece of paper. "I think the eighty-year-old twins did it. Alone they'd be too frail, but together they could pull it off and no one would ever suspect such sweet old ladies." Trixie tilted her head. "Hey, that would be a great title, *The Sweet Old Lady Murderers*."

"I think there's already a book out by that name." Skye shook her head. "Although my understanding is that you can't copyright a title. Still, you wouldn't want to use it and have people think they'd already read your book. Although if it's an old—"

"So . . ." Trixie cut her off, clearly losing interest in titles and getting back to a topic she found more interesting. "If you don't think the ex-doctor did it, who do you think is the killer?"

"So far my money is on the photographer, but we're going to talk to the rich business guy tonight, so he may move up on my list."

"Cool." Trixie widened her brown eyes and pleaded, "Any chance I can come along? It would be great research for my novel."

"No." Skye held up her hand at her friend's protests. "Sorry, but if I can distract you from homicide for a second, I do have some other exciting news, and an important question to ask you."

"What?" Trixie perked up.

"Wally's annulment will be finalized in the next month or two, and we've set the date for our wedding. It's December thirtieth." Skye grinned. "And I'd like you to be my matron of honor."

"No!" Trixie let out a howl of anguish.

Skye watched, speechless, as tears rolled down her friend's face.

CHAPTER 18

Playing Cat and Mouse

It took Skye a couple of seconds to process Trixie's refusal and subsequent waterworks. As soon as she could move, Skye hopped off her stool, put her arms around her friend, and asked, "What's wrong?"

"I. Can't. Be. In. Your. Wedding." Trixie sobbed out the words.

"Why not?" Skye tilted her head. "If it's the cost, we can pick out an inexpensive dress, or you can even wear something you already own."

Skye thought that maybe Trixie and her husband might be having a rough time financially. Although Trixie made an okay salary as school librarian, Owen was a farmer, and the crops hadn't been good the last couple of years. He had recently begun to breed exotic animals, but she wasn't sure if that endeavor was making a profit yet.

"It's not that." Trixie hiccuped. "Actually, for once we're doing pretty well." She made a face. "Who knew there was actually money to be made raising llamas and emus?"

"Then what?" Now Skye was really confused. "I thought you liked Wally and wanted me to marry him. Did Simon get to you or something?"

When Skye had first broken up with Simon, he had tried various outlandish ways to win her back, but that had stopped six months ago, and she thought he had given up. Had he taken his efforts to a new level, a sneakier one?

"No." Trixie pulled a tissue from her pocket. "How could you think I'd take Simon's side? Haven't I always said Wally was the man for you?"

"Yes." Skye was stumped. "So why can't you be my matron of honor?"

Trixie blew her nose. "Last night Owen surprised me with tickets for a seven-day Caribbean cruise." She threw away the used Kleenex and stared dejectedly at Skye. "We leave December twenty-fourth and don't get back until the day after your wedding."

"Shit!" Skye put her hand to her mouth. She'd given up swearing for Lent. *Great!* Now she'd have to go to confession before Mass.

"My feelings exactly." Trixie started crying again. "I'm always after Owen to be more romantic. To take vacations. And winter break is the perfect time for a farmer to be away." She wiped her eyes on the back of her hand. "How can I tell him I don't want to go?"

"You can't." Skye sighed. "Unfortunately, I can't change my wedding, either. Negotiating that date was harder than getting the House and the Senate to agree on the national debt."

"How come?" Trixie sniffed, searching her pocket for another tissue and coming up empty. "Was Wally really that difficult?"

"Not Wally." Skye handed Trixie the box of Puffs from the shelves behind them. "Mom." Skye explained May's amazing change of heart, ending with, "So, since my mother is finally on board with me marrying Wally, I don't want to derail her by insisting on a summer wedding when she claims there isn't enough planning time."

"How about next summer?" Trixie suggested. "That would give her over a year."

"Wally doesn't want to wait that long. And truthfully, neither do I."

"Which is totally understandable." Trixie exhaled noisily. "Crap! Crap! Crap! I guess that means I'm going to miss your wedding."

"Wait a minute." Skye narrowed her eyes. "What if I talk to Owen?"

"What good would that do?" Trixie asked, her expression hopeful.

Skye counted on her fingers. "December is nine months away."

"Right."

"So, maybe Owen can switch the cruise for one that leaves December thirty-first," Skye suggested. "You'd have to rush a little, but I'm pretty sure I read that most ships leave in the late afternoon. So you'd have all day Sunday to get to the port."

"That might work." Trixie brightened. "We leave from Fort Lauderdale, and that's only a two-and-a-half- or three-hour flight from here."

"Which means you could catch a morning plane out of O'Hare on Sunday." Skye grinned. "You'll just have to behave yourself at the reception so you can get up early enough to make it to the airport."

"Darn!" Trixie grinned back. "Guess that means only one glass of champagne."

Promising to follow Trixie home after school so she could speak with Owen right away, Skye gave her friend a final hug, grabbed her can of soda and the half-eaten packet of crackers, and headed toward the door. She had three hours until she saw the Pass Out game girls. If she worked straight through, she could score the tests from the psych evaluation she'd completed on a third grader who had somehow fooled everyone into believing he could read. Heck, she might even get a couple of reports written before the girls showed up for their session.

At two forty-five, feeling satisfied with having accomplished so much on her to-do list, Skye greeted the eleven girls with a smile as they trooped into her office. None looked happy to be there, but only a couple seemed out-and-out resentful.

Skye knew the ringleader, Bitsy Kessler, from her co-sponsorship of the school newspaper. Bitsy had been a freshman when the *Scoop* was formed, and had been on its staff for the past four years.

Although Bitsy came across as an airhead, and was by no means the sharpest eyeliner in the makeup case, she had shown a real talent for writing on-target satirical humor. Her contributions had been a consistent hit among both students and staff.

Knowing that she would have such a big group at this counseling session, Skye had had the custodian bring in folding chairs. She was just thankful that her office at the high school could actually accommodate such a large number.

Once the girls were seated in a circle, Skye introduced herself and had them all identify themselves. Regrettably, she knew she probably wouldn't remember all of them, because so many looked alike. Although they claimed to want individuality, they usually adopted similar clothing styles, hair, and makeup. Too bad it would be considered unprofessional and less than therapeutic to ask them to wear name tags.

After the preliminaries, Skye said, "I'm sure you all know we're here to talk about the game you played Saturday night." The girls all nodded. "Can anyone tell me why we're talking about that subject?"

"Like, because our parents are freaked out," a bubbly redhead offered.

"True." Skye's voice was neutral. "Any other

reason you might find yourself in the psychologist's office because of that activity?" She looked around.

"It's dangerous and someone could have gotten hurt," a bored-looking blonde recited in a monotone, her voice holding all the sincerity of a padded bra. "Now that we cleared up that little matter, can we go back to study hall? Some of us have homework to do."

Skye ignored the blonde's request. "I'm glad you realize that it's an extremely risky game. Do you understand that one of you could have *died?*"

The blonde continued to gaze sullenly at Skye, although when Skye emphasized the word *died,* a flicker of comprehension caused the girl's pupils to dilate.

"No senior trip. No prom. No graduation. No college. No career." She checked out the girls' reactions, then stressed, *"No life."*

Their expressions ranged from indifference to skepticism to surprise. One or two drew in a sharp breath and whispered to their neighbors.

"But that's the stuff I figured your folks would have already discussed with you." She leaned forward and made eye contact with each of the girls, one after another. "What I'd like to hear about is your feelings. What were you after when you decided to play the game, and what's been your reaction to what has happened since your actions have become public?"

"We weren't trying to kill ourselves, if that's what you mean," Bitsy protested. "We were just bored. We didn't have a suicide pact or anything. 'Cause that's only for pathetic losers."

"Totally, dude." Murmurs of agreement sounded from the others.

The redhead said, "Like, there's never anything to do around here." She pouted. "And, like, none of our parents will let us drive into Joliet or Kankakee by ourselves, which is, like, so bogus."

Skye held her tongue. The redhead really needed likeosuction to suck that word *like* out of her vocabulary for good, but vocabulary was a matter for her English teacher to handle.

"Heidi read about it on the Internet." Bitsy gestured to a quiet brunette. "So when we got sick of doing each other's hair and nails, she told us about it. We looked it up and it seemed fun."

Skye recognized Heidi from the book discussion group she had led last September, and remembered that the teen had mentioned moving to Scumble River when her dad married a local woman. As Skye recalled, the girl hadn't been very happy with the home situation.

"And was it fun?" Skye asked, trying to inject interest rather than censure into her tone.

"Not really." Bitsy seemed to have appointed herself spokesperson of the group. "If my mom hadn't had a heart attack and gotten all uptight and called everyone's parents, none of this would have happened." Bitsy frowned. "It was, you know, awkward."

"You feel your mother overreacted?" Skye asked. "And all the other parents as well? That you could have handled the situation on your own?"

"Definitely." Bitsy nodded emphatically, her copper ringlets bouncing. "We would have learned a lesson from our experience."

"I see." Skye raised a brow. "Well, experience is an excellent teacher." She paused, then added, "Too bad the homework she gives is so rough."

"Truthfully"—Bitsy sighed—"we couldn't quite figure out how to do it."

"It's my fault." Heidi spoke up. "The others were ready to forget about it when I found a video on the Web. It showed someone using a belt and hanging themselves from the top of their closet door."

"Is that what you used?" Skye asked, wondering how anyone thought something like that would be fun.

"Uh-huh." The blonde still sounded like she would rather be doing calculus than talking to Skye. "I'm the lightest, so I said I'd try it."

"Yeah." Bitsy poked the other girl in the shoulder. "But you panicked when you started to lose consciousness. And when Ashley tried to help you, you kicked her in the stomach."

"Then Ashley screamed," Heidi said, "and Mrs.

Kessler came running in. Once she saw what was going on, she went ballistic and yelled for Mr. Kessler."

"And once Dad got involved"—Bitsy shook her head, a look of disgust on her face—"the whole thing became a freaking nightmare."

Bitsy's statement seemed to open the floodgates for the others, and all the girls began to chime in. Skye sat back, allowing the teenagers to talk, processing the events for themselves. She occasionally clarified or refereed, but mostly observed for the rest of the time.

There were three minutes left in the period when Bitsy whined, "I still say none of this is our fault and we shouldn't be the ones in trouble."

Skye hid her smile. "Why is that?" She'd been watching Bitsy, and it had taken her nearly forty-five minutes, but the girl had finally come up with an excuse. Skye couldn't wait to hear it.

"If that guy at the door to the bowling alley would have let us in to hear the music, we wouldn't have gotten so bored," Bitsy explained.

"The bowler disco party didn't start until ten, though, right?" Skye asked. "What time did you girls decide to play the game?"

"Like, an hour or so after we went back to Bitsy's house," the redhead volunteered. "But, like, I heard that the music sucked. Someone said it was like the guy had never, like, deejayed before. So, like, no loss."

"Totally," the blonde agreed. "The *real* problem was that Bitsy's mom and dad didn't keep their promise to take us to Bolingbrook to play miniature golf and stuff at Wilderness Falls."

"Yeah." Bitsy shrugged. "They had some lame excuse about it being too cold and rainy, but they just didn't want to have to do it."

Before Skye could respond, the final bell rang. As the teenagers filed out of her office, she made sure the girls knew that she was available for an individual counseling session if they felt the need. None of them appeared eager to take her up on her offer.

Once she was alone, Skye closed her door, pulled her chair back around behind her desk, and called Homer. While she was assuring the principal that she was satisfied that the girls appeared to understand the consequences of such an unsafe game, and that their actions had arisen from boredom, not self-destructive tendencies, she quickly typed up a short note to that same effect to be sent to the girls' parents.

Hanging up the phone, she clicked on the PRINT button. As she watched the printer spit out a dozen copies of her letter, it hit her. *That* was why her dad's miniature-golfing adventure had been bugging her. She sagged back in her seat. Was it possible? Could she really have figured out where Elijah Jacobsen was hiding?

CHAPTER 19

Scaredy-cat

As Skye followed Trixie's Civic out of town and into the countryside, she assessed her conclusion regarding Elijah's whereabouts. Her first inclination had been to phone Wally with her idea, but she had hesitated. What if she was wrong? She hated to look stupid, or even worse, to waste everyone's time.

She needed to start at the beginning and carefully think through her conclusion to see if it was logical. Elijah's note had said he was going into the Wilderness—with a capital *W*—for forty days. At the time, she didn't think the uppercase letter was important, but now she speculated that it might be extremely significant. Going into the wilderness was certainly a biblical reference, but going into the *Wilderness* could mean something else, as well.

A week or so ago, Skye had received a Valpak envelope in the mail. Even though the majority of the coupons were usually for businesses miles from Scumble River, she always flipped through them to see if any were local. Like her father, she loved a bargain.

In the packet, she remembered seeing a voucher for Wilderness Falls Family Fun Center. Had

Elijah's household gotten the same coupons? And if so, had the name stuck in his mind?

Before Skye could decide if the notion was brilliant or ridiculous, she turned into the Fraynes' driveway. By the time Skye stopped the Bel Air, Trixie was already out of her Honda and waiting impatiently by the Chevy's door. The decision whether to tell Wally her idea or not would have to wait until after her talk with Owen.

Trixie pulled Skye from the car's front seat. "Owen doesn't usually come inside until five for supper." She nodded at the white two-story home to her left. "You don't want to wait in the house, do you?"

"Not really." Skye tucked the car keys in her tote. "I'm in a little bit of a hurry. I have something to discuss with Wally, and—" She interrupted herself. "Did I mention Wally got called away on an emergency last night?"

Trixie shook her head.

"The bank alarm went off," Skye explained. "And when he phoned to let me know that the problem turned out to be a bird that had flown into the window, he said we'd go talk to Ivan Quigley tonight."

"That rich geezer from Brooklyn?"

"Yeah, I guess so." Skye wrinkled her forehead. "But he's not that old."

"Geezerhood is bestowed on any guy who is

somewhere between not young and not dead." Trixie waved her hand in the direction of the garage, equipment shed, and barn. "Anyway, Owen's probably somewhere around here. Let's find him so you can get going."

"Great." Skye hoisted her bag onto her shoulder. "Which way?"

"We'll start with the barn." Trixie linked arms with Skye and they started walking.

Bales of hay were stacked along one end of the barn and stalls lined either side. Although the odor of the llamas and emus lingered in the air, neither they nor their owner was present.

"If Owen isn't with his precious livestock, he's probably tinkering with his tractors." Trixie led the way to the machine shed.

The shed's only entrance was a towering door that opened by rolling it to the side. Together Trixie and Skye managed to shove the heavy panel open wide enough for them to squeeze through. The interior was a single cavernous room with corrugated-steel walls and a packed-dirt floor. Arranged in irregular rows were tractors, combines, threshers, and a variety of other equipment that Skye didn't recognize, even though she was a farmer's daughter.

They picked their way carefully down the center walkway, peering into the shadows cast by the enormous implements. Trixie called out Owen's name, and a few seconds later he slid out from under a hulking metal machine. It was almost as if the huge tractor was giving birth.

"Hey." He got to his feet and wiped his hands on the red bandana he took from his overall pocket. "Is it suppertime already?"

"Nope." Trixie stood on tippy toes and gingerly kissed her husband's grimy cheek. "But Skye's in a hurry and she has a favor to ask you."

"Sure." He smiled, creating white creases in the dirt on his face. "What can I do for you?"

Skye explained the conflict between her wedding and the Fraynes' cruise.

When she finished, he said, "I think we can fix that problem pretty easily."

"Wonderful." Skye felt as if a huge weight had been lifted from her chest.

"I only took the first date because Trixie always wanted to be away for Christmas and not have to deal with both our families, but I know she wants to be in your wedding more than she wants to avoid the relatives during the holidays." Owen winked at his wife. "The travel agent in town is real accommodating. In fact, she mentioned that she's got a big group going that second week, and we could get an even better rate if we went then."

"Thanks so much." Skye patted Owen's arm and gave him a quick peck on the cheek. "I really appreciate you rescheduling your trip for me. My wedding wouldn't be the same without you guys there."

Ignoring his filthy state, Trixie hugged and kissed her husband soundly.

As Trixie and Skye walked back to the driveway, they talked about the wedding plans. While vetoing her friend's idea of Christmas-themed decorations, Skye dug her cell out of her tote bag and tried to power it on.

"Heck." She frowned at the little silver rectangle. "The battery's dead. I keep forgetting to put it in the charger overnight."

"Oh, well." Trixie smiled. "At least you're somewhere you can use a landline." She beckoned to Skye. "Come on inside and use our phone."

"Thanks." Skye followed her friend into the house, down the hall, and into the kitchen. As she dialed, she said, "I hope Wally doesn't think that what I'm about to tell him is as dumb as it sounds."

Wally answered on the first ring, and listened without interrupting as Skye explained her theory about Elijah's location. After a moment he said, "Don't you think that's sort of a stretch?"

"I do," Skye admitted. "Believe me, I know how silly it sounds, but I figured I'd better let you make the decision whether to look there or not."

"I understand," Wally answered slowly, clearly wanting to think about what Skye had told him before committing himself to a plan of action.

"It's just"—Skye twisted the phone cord around her finger—"I never want you to think that I'm keeping something from you again."

"That's good." Wally cleared his throat. "Because secrets can ruin a marriage."

"I promise I've learned my lesson." Skye knew that the last time she had kept something from Wally it had almost destroyed their relationship.

"Good."

After that single word Wally was silent for so long, Skye thought they'd been disconnected. She waited a little longer, but when he still didn't say anything, she asked, "So, what do you think? Are we going to Bolingbrook?"

"No, *we* aren't." Wally's voice was firm. "Zuchowski and I will go."

"But—"

"No buts." Wally cut off Skye's protest. "If you're right, and Jacobsen is hiding at this Wilderness Falls, he could very well be dangerous when we corner him. I'm not risking your safety."

"But you could use me as the psych consultant to talk him down," Skye pointed out. "He's a big guy and he might be too much for the two of you."

"No buts." Wally repeated himself. "I'll ask the Bolingbrook police to help us," he assured her, then added quickly before disconnecting, "I'll call you as soon as we get back."

"For crying out loud." Skye looked at the receiver in exasperation. "He just came pretty darn close to hanging up on me."

"We could go to Wilderness Falls on our own."

Trixie dangled her car keys enticingly. "I bet I could beat the cops there."

"Never mind." Skye blew out a breath. She had no doubt that Trixie, aka Lead Foot Andretti, could get to Bolingbrook way ahead of the police. However, she also had no doubt that she wouldn't be getting married in December if Wally arrived and found them there. "I have something better to do while Wally's busy."

"What?"

"I'm going to get rid of Mrs. Griggs's ghost." Trixie was the only one she had confided in about her problem with the spirit's refusal to allow Skye and Wally to make love in her house.

"Can I help?"

"Do you happen to have a pound of sea salt handy?" Skye asked, not really expecting an affirmative answer.

"Actually, I do." Trixie hurried into the pantry and returned with a round blue container. "I like sea salt for cooking and it's cheaper if you buy it in bulk."

"Great." Skye decided she might as well ask Trixie about the other ingredient she needed. "I don't suppose you know where I can get some sage branches?"

"As a matter of fact, I probably do." Trixie's voice was smug.

"You're kidding." Skye gaped at her friend. "You've heard of that?"

"Uh-huh." Trixie's eyes sparkled. "A friend of mine is a witch."

"Like Samantha?" Skye wiggled her nose.

"Well, as it happens, her name *is* Samantha." Trixie snickered. "But she's Wiccan, not *Bewitched*. And believe me, she doesn't appreciate the comparison, so if you meet her don't bring it up."

"Sure. Right. Of course not." Skye was disappointed. She had been hoping to meet someone magical. "Does she live close by?"

"Her place is a couple of farms down." Trixie pointed out the window.

"Can you call her and see if she'll sell me a few branches?"

"Sure." Trixie picked up the phone. After a brief conversation with her neighbor, she said to Skye, "Sam said the sage is on her, and she'll drop off the branches on her way to her office in town. She's an attorney and has to meet with a client at six."

"Terrific."

"Why don't you stay for supper? Then we can go get rid of Mrs. Griggs together."

"Great." Skye sniffed. An enticing aroma was coming from a Crock-Pot on the counter behind Trixie. "What are we having?"

"Spareribs." Trixie pointed to the fridge. "You can make the coleslaw while I change clothes, then all I have to do is pop the baked potatoes in the microwave, pour some sauce over the ribs, and stick them under the broiler for a couple more minutes."

During dinner, Trixie and Skye discussed bridesmaids' dresses, the Pass Out game, and ghosts. Owen ignored all three topics of conversation, ate quickly, and disappeared into the living room.

A few seconds later, when Skye heard loud voices as the TV came on and a commentator announced another political scandal in Chicago, she said to Trixie, "How come the news always begins with the words *Good evening,* but then they go on to tell you why it isn't?"

Trixie snickered as she and Skye started to clear the table. They had finished wiping down the stove and the counters and started to do the dishes, when the doorbell rang. Trixie excused herself and was gone several minutes before returning with a small bundle of sage branches in one hand and a piece of paper in the other.

"What's that?" Skye asked, pointing to the yellow notebook page.

"Sam said this is the method she recommends for cleansing a house of an unwanted being." Trixie gave Skye the instruction sheet.

Skye glanced down the page and frowned. "Everything here looks the same as what I got off the Internet, except this says you should do the ritual between the full and new moons. The new moon was just a couple of nights ago, and I can't wait for it to come again."

Trixie looked over Skye's shoulder and pointed out, "It doesn't say you have to do it during that period, only that it's harder if you don't."

"True."

"So, we can do it tonight. Then if it doesn't work, we can try again in two weeks."

"Good idea." Skye turned back to the sink. "Let's get these dishes done, then go kick some ghostly butt." She plunged her hands into the hot, soapy water. "If nothing else, maybe Mrs. Griggs will be scared into behaving herself when Wally's around."

"Oh." Trixie stopped dead as she walked toward Skye. "I almost forgot. Sam mentioned that if you do the ritual wrong, instead of warding off negative spirits, you might end up inviting them over for a playdate."

"It says we need to wrap the sage branches with string, making loops about a half inch apart." Trixie squinted as she read the directions to Skye. The two women were sitting at Skye's kitchen table and Skye was attempting to assemble the smudge sticks.

"Now close your eyes and visualize positive energy flowing into the sage," Trixie continued, then giggled. "What do you think positive energy looks like? Maybe a lightning bolt made of chocolate?"

"Shh." Skye shushed her friend and concentrated for several minutes.

"Hey." Trixie poked Skye. "Did you fall asleep? Come on, *CSI* is on at eight."

"Fine." Skye was beginning to regret allowing her friend to participate, but truth be told, she was a little scared of doing the ritual by herself. *Crap!* She probably should have checked with Father Burns before she started this. What if they conjured up a demon from hell? Refusing to think about it, Skye asked, "What's next?"

"Light that sucker on fire and smoke the meddling old ghost out of—" Trixie stopped short as her purse flew off the counter and hit her in the back of the head. "Ouch! What the heck? How did that happen?"

"See. You thought this was a game, but Mrs. Griggs is here and now she's clearly ticked off." Skye glanced fearfully around the room. "Maybe I should have asked Father Burns for some holy water."

"We could always make our own." Trixie's mouth twitched. "You know, just get a big pan of water, and boil the hell out of it."

"You are so not funny," Skye scolded, then shivered as she felt a chill go up her spine. "Come on. We'd better do this quickly before Mrs. Griggs decides to throw knives instead of your handbag."

"It was probably Bingo." Trixie looked doubtful, but clearly refused to believe in ghosts. "He must have jumped up on the counter, brushed against my purse, and it . . . ." She trailed off.

"Yeah." Skye sneered. "That was Wally's excuse, too. But the trajectory is all wrong. Let's get this show on the road before she starts breaking dishes or something blows up in our faces."

"Right." Trixie sobered at Skye's words and said, "You're supposed to start at the back of the house and walk the perimeter of each room until it fills with smoke." She stopped. "I hope we have enough sage branches. This old place has a lot of rooms."

"Maybe they burn slow." Skye got up and stood next to the back door, a box of wooden matches in one hand and the sage in the other.

"Wave the smudge stick around all the windows and doorways," Trixie continued, then read from the directions. "You're supposed to say 'I banish all negative energies, spirits, and ill will from this dwelling. Go now and do not come back.'"

"Got it." Skye moved through the house doing as Trixie had instructed.

Trixie followed Skye, and when a window rattled, she muttered, "This place sure is drafty." When a door slammed shut in front of them, she shrugged. "I didn't know it was so windy out tonight."

An hour later, when the two women came to the foyer, Trixie squinted at the sheet of paper she still held. "Do the front door three times and say, 'By the powers of three times, only positive energy

251

shall enter thee,' then immediately put the sage outside."

Skye complied. Next she and Trixie sprinkled sea salt across all the doorways and windows, and left a small pile in the corners of all the rooms. During this trip through the house, a picture fell off the wall in the bedroom, and in the parlor the glass in the front of the étagère cracked as if punched by a fist.

Both women were a little breathless and a lot freaked out when they finished. Skye said, "I sure hope that's all of it."

Trixie dug the instructions out of her jeans' pocket and said, "Not quite." She tilted her head toward the front porch, where they had put the used-up smudge sticks. "Now we have to cover the sage branches with salt and bury them. Then we shower and have a snack." Trixie giggled. "Eating. Finally something that doesn't require walking up and down the stairs a thousand times."

Trixie took the bathroom on the main floor and Skye lent her a robe. Skye put their smoky clothes in the utility room, then headed to the master bath. She would shower as soon as she heard the water from Trixie's go off, then start the washer as soon as she was finished. Even with new plumbing and a new water heater, she wouldn't risk doing all three at the same time.

Once they were settled in the sunroom with a

bowl of popcorn and two glasses of wine, Trixie said, "Well, I hope that worked."

The lights flickered, and Skye pointed at the TV as it wobbled. "Oh, oh!" Before either woman could get up, the set fell to the floor and smashed into several large pieces.

They sat in appalled silence until Trixie said, "I think you might need to call in a professional."

CHAPTER 20
All Cats Are Gray in the Dark

When Trixie left for home shortly before ten, Wally still hadn't called. Skye wasn't sure if that meant the police were still searching Wilderness Falls for Elijah or that he'd been caught, in which case Wally was busy interrogating the ex-doctor. And she wasn't sure which scenario she preferred.

While she wanted Alexis's murderer arrested and behind bars, in her heart of hearts Skye didn't believe Elijah was the guilty party. Not, as Wally alleged, because she felt sorry for the poor damaged man, though she did, but because she was convinced it was impossible for someone with Elijah's brain injury to pull off an elaborately plotted murder.

He didn't have the ability to organize his thoughts, think quickly, and concentrate long enough to carry out his plan. Whoever had left Alexis's car in front of Kyle O'Brien's house had executed an intricate scheme to throw suspicion off him- or herself and implicate the victim's ex-boyfriend. If Elijah killed someone, it would be in a fit of rage, and he wouldn't be capable of covering up the crime afterward.

She frowned, unhappy with the events she had set in motion and equally unhappy that she couldn't stop thinking about Elijah. If he was going to take up space in her mind, he should at least be paying rent.

Skye tried to distract herself from what was going on in Bolingbrook by taking the next step in planning her wedding. And that meant inviting her old friend, and new sister-in-law, Loretta, to be her bridesmaid.

If Skye waited much longer to ask her, Loretta might hear about the wedding plans from someone else, and she would be hurt that Skye hadn't been the one to tell her. Although May had promised to keep quiet until Skye had spoken to all her friends, Skye knew that her mother would burst if she had to keep the news to herself for long. So the window of opportunity to make the announcement herself was closing faster than a subway train door at rush hour.

It was late to call the typical Scumble Riverite, but Loretta was from the city, and Vince's years as a drummer in a rock band had made him a night owl. There was no way either of them would be in bed before midnight, at least not to sleep.

Loretta answered on the first ring, her smooth contralto sounding mellow and contented—quite a change from her usual stressed-out lawyer's voice.

"How's it going?" Skye asked.

"Wonderful." Loretta chuckled. "It's so nice to finally find that one special guy that you can aggravate for the rest of your life."

"You and Trixie should get together and do a comedy routine."

"Glad to hear you think I'm funny," Loretta countered. "Now that that's settled, what's kept you up past ten o'clock, sis?"

"We've set the date for the wedding," Skye blurted out. "It's December thirtieth." She paused. "And Mom is okay with me marrying Wally."

"Congratulations. On both setting the date and winning May over. How on God's green earth did you do that?"

Skye explained the process, then said, "And I'd like you to be my bridesmaid."

There was a silence, and Skye held her breath. Was Loretta angry that she hadn't been asked to be the matron of honor? *Shoot!* This better not be a repeat of what had happened with Trixie.

Finally, Loretta said, "Of course I'd love to, but . . ." She trailed off and Skye heard a muffled conversation, then Loretta said to Skye, "You've got to promise me you won't say a word to anyone."

"Except Wally." Skye had been burned by vowing confidentiality before.

Loretta let out a loud sigh, then carried on another muffled conversation before agreeing. "Wally, but no one else."

"I swear."

"We're trying to get pregnant, so I may be huge by your wedding day."

"Oh, my God!" *Heck!* Skye shook her head. She'd just taken the Lord's name in vain. There was another Lenten slip she'd have to confess. Pretty soon she'd need to start writing them down so she didn't forget any. "I hate to tell you this, but Mom already suspects. Wally saw her knitting a baby afghan at work, and her concrete goose is wearing a diaper and carrying a bottle."

This time Loretta obviously didn't bother to cover the receiver because Skye heard the handset go *thunk* and her friend yell, "Vince Denison, did you tell your mother we're trying to have a baby?"

"No." Vince's tone was defensive. "Why do you think that?"

"Because she's knitting baby blankets and her goose is dressed like an infant," Loretta shrieked. "If you didn't tell her, why is she doing that?"

"How should I know?" Vince's voice cracked. "I swear on my drum set, I didn't say a word to anyone." He tried to calm his hormonally crazed wife with humor. "Maybe Mom has ESP, or she's been rifling through our trash can and saw all the pregnancy-test kits."

After a few more minutes of bickering Skye interrupted. "It's probably just wishful goose dressing. Doubtlessly Mom has been planning the birth of her grandchild since the moment she found out you and Vince got married."

"Maybe." Loretta sounded skeptical. "But if she knows before my mom, someone's goose is going to be cooked, and it won't be mine."

"Anyway . . ." Skye didn't know what else to say. Having met Loretta's mother, she sympathized with her friend's panic. Mrs. Steiner was even scarier than May. "I still want you in my wedding even if you have to waddle down the aisle. It's not how you look, it's that you're the person I want with me on that day."

"Then of course I'll be your bridesmaid," Loretta assured her, then laughed. "Unless I'm already pregnant and just don't know it yet. In that case, the baby may be born the day of your wedding."

"No." Skye shuddered at the thought of May crazed with both a wedding and a birth. "I'm ordering you to hold it in until I get back from my honeymoon."

"Sure," Loretta mocked. "I'll get right to work on that."

Loretta and Skye talked for another half hour before saying good-bye. Skye hung up and yawned, then looked at the clock. *Holy mackerel!* It was going on eleven. Why hadn't Wally phoned? She had call-waiting, so she knew she hadn't missed him.

Skye shivered. Maybe he was hurt. What if

Elijah had attacked him? Wally wouldn't want to shoot an unarmed suspect, so he might have tried to take down the huge man on his own and been injured. As worse and worse scenarios piled up in Skye's mind, she heard the door opening.

She ran to the foyer, saw that it was Wally, and flung herself into his arms. "Are you okay?" she asked with a catch in her voice. "What happened? It's been so long that I was getting nervous."

"I'm fine, darlin'." He hugged her close with one arm and stroked her hair with his free hand. After kissing her eyes, cheeks, and lips he said, "Sorry to worry you. But you were right. Jacobsen was hiding in the miniature golf course, just like you thought."

"So you got him?" Skye asked. "And no one was hurt? Not any of the police officers or Elijah?" When Wally nodded, she stepped out of his embrace and took his hand, tugging him fully inside the house.

"It took us a long time to search Wilderness Falls," Wally explained as she led him into the kitchen. "What with the batting cages, the arcades, and the two golf courses there was a lot of ground to cover."

"But he was there?" Skye asked, wanting to hear again that she'd done the right thing in sending Wally to the amusement area.

"Yep." Wally took off his utility belt and tie, then sank wearily onto a chair. "And lucky for us, this time of year the place shuts down at dark so we didn't have to worry about civilians being in harm's way while we searched."

"Are you hungry?" Skye wanted to hear all the details, but Wally looked so worn-out, she made herself wait to question him. "I've got some leftover lasagna and garlic bread I could heat up."

"I'm starving." He rubbed the back of his neck. "And I'd kill for a beer."

Skye opened the fridge, grabbed a Sam Adams, and twisted off the top before handing the bottle to Wally. While he drank, she microwaved his dinner, then put the steaming plate of food in front of him.

She waited patiently until he had eaten, then got him another beer and said, "Start at the beginning and tell me everything."

"Four Bolingbrook police officers were at Wilderness Falls when we arrived and they had already explained the situation to the manager, so we were able to start searching immediately." Wally got up and opened the freezer. "The batting cages and arcades were easily eliminated, but the golf courses are full of places to hide."

"I bet." The picture on the coupon had shown a cave and a waterfall.

"The forty-foot mountain was the hardest." Wally came back to the table with a container of Ben and Jerry's Chocolate Therapy.

"So where was he hiding?" Skye demanded, dying to know where such a large guy could hide from six police officers for so long.

"Inside a bear." Wally handed Skye a spoon and dug in with his.

"What?" Skye stopped in midbite. "He gutted a bear and crawled inside?" Did Illinois even have bears? She was fairly sure it didn't.

"Not exactly." Wally licked his spoon. "Wilderness Falls hosts a lot of events, and someone had brought a bear costume for a party and left it there. Jacobsen borrowed the getup and has been wearing it around the mini golf course for the past several days."

"I'm surprised whoever owned the costume didn't come back to pick it up. Surely he or she missed it. And aren't those outfits expensive?"

"It looked pretty cheap to me. Probably under a hundred bucks." Wally polished off the remaining ice cream in the carton. "I'm guessing whoever left the thing only got it for the party and didn't care enough to go back for it. Or maybe they lived out of state."

"And no one noticed that there was a bear walking around that shouldn't be there?"

"The employees thought he was a new mascot, and the shift supervisor thought corporate had hired him. They already have a moose." Wally shrugged. "The kids loved him and he didn't cause any trouble, so . . ."

261

"Then how did you figure out Elijah was in the bear costume?"

"The manager was going over the list of employees, and I noticed that no one was scheduled to be a mascot," Wally explained.

"That was smart." Skye patted his arm. "Where did Elijah sleep and how did he eat for the past four days or so?" she asked slowly, still trying to picture the ex-doc dressed up like Smokey.

"He camped inside the arcade." Wally got up, stretched, and yawned. "There were plenty of pizzas, hot dogs, and sodas around."

"Hmm." Skye cleaned off the table. "How did he get to Bolingbrook if his car was found at the rec club?"

"Jacobsen claims God told him to park the car at the club and make his way into the wilderness on foot." Wally made a face. "Anyway, he said the only wilderness he could think of was the Wilderness Falls he'd seen advertised on a coupon, so that's where he headed."

"Just like I thought."

"Uh-huh."

"But that has to be at least a forty- or forty-five-mile hike." Skye visualized the route between Scumble River and Bolingbrook.

"He said it took him two days." Wally started to wash the dishes. "He slept in some barn along the way."

"Did he resist arrest when you nabbed him?" Skye dried a plate and put it away.

"Not at all." Wally shook his head. "Actually, he seemed relieved."

Once they were finished tidying up the kitchen, Skye and Wally climbed the stairs, both turning in to the master bath. When Wally stepped into the shower, Skye was tempted to join him, but his fatigue was evident. Not to mention that Mrs. Griggs's ghost was clearly still haunting the house.

Sighing, Skye brushed her teeth and applied moisturizer around her eyes, then put on her comfy nightshirt. This was clearly not the time for a sexy nightgown.

When Wally finished drying off, he put on a clean pair of boxer briefs, brushed his teeth, and they both headed into the bedroom.

As Skye set the alarm for six a.m., she asked, "Where is Elijah now?"

"The county jail." Wally pulled down the covers and stretched out on the mattress. When his head hit the pillow, he let out a blissful sigh, then said, "We took him straight there from Bolingbrook."

"So you're going to interrogate him tomorrow?" Skye asked as she crawled into bed and snuggled against his side, listening to his heartbeat.

"There's no need," Wally mumbled, already half-asleep. "He confessed."

CHAPTER 21

Catcall

Despite setting the alarm the night before, Skye and Wally overslept. They didn't wake up until a few minutes before seven, when Bingo meowed in their ears demanding his breakfast. Skye took one look at the clock and made a leap out of bed that might have earned her a spot as a prima ballerina in the Bolshoi Ballet.

If Skye didn't sign in at the high school by seven twenty, Homer would read her the riot act. Even though he rarely got there before eight a.m. himself, when he did arrive, the principal scoured the time sheet for any employee who had been late. Once he found a victim, he tracked the unfortunate person down and loudly harangued his prey.

A screaming principal would be an unpleasant way to start a Friday morning—or any morning, for that matter.

Wally sat up and asked Skye, "Do you want me to get you a cup of tea or coffee?" Since his shift didn't start until eight, he had plenty of time to make the short drive into town. Besides, he was the boss, so there was no one to hassle him even if he showed up late.

"No." Skye rushed past him into the bathroom, calling over her shoulder, "Besides, all the coffee beans in Kona and all the tea leaves in China won't make me a morning person."

"Okay," Wally said to her back. "I'll feed Bingo and give him fresh water."

"Great." She added, "Don't forget to clean his litter box. We don't want any unpleasant surprises in our shoes from Mr. Fastidious."

With no time for a shower, Skye twisted her hair into a loose bun on top of her head, threw on black slacks and a leopard print twinset, and applied a dusting of bronzer to her face. After a quick inspection, she also added a sweep of mascara, patted on some under-eye concealer, and applied bronze lipstick.

Ten minutes later, as she sprinted for the front door, Wally handed her a paper sack and yelled after her, "Meet me at the PD when you finish work today."

"Thanks, sweetie." Skye's words became more and more indistinct as she ran down the porch steps. "See you around four."

Hoping that the fact that she was sleeping with the police chief would save her from a speeding ticket, Skye pressed the Bel Air's accelerator to the floor and raced the Chevy down the road at twice the speed she usually drove. Four minutes later, tires squealing, she turned into the high school's faculty lot. It was already seven nineteen, and of course there were no spaces anywhere close to the building, so she was forced to park in the worst spot—the one by the Dumpster at the very back of the lot. Grabbing her shoulder bag, she bolted out of the car and dashed for the school's front door.

She tore across the threshold and glanced at the massive clock hanging on the wall to her left. She was a minute late. There was no one at the counter, and as she approached, Skye could hear the Xerox machine whirring in the adjoining office. Opal must be busy making copies, which meant she hadn't seen Skye's entrance.

Picking up the pen chained to the sign-in clipboard, Skye hesitated. Could she get away with writing seven twenty instead of seven twenty-one?

She looked around. There were no witnesses. She chewed her lip, trying to come up with a good rationalization for the deceit, but nothing came to her. Putting down the wrong time was cheating. If Homer yelled at her for being sixty seconds late, she would just remind him of all the occasions when she had stayed for meetings long after the official end of her day. Yeah. Right. That would work.

After signing in with the correct time, Skye retrieved the papers from her mailbox and headed toward her office. She greeted several teachers on her way down the hall, then settled in behind her desk and flipped open her appointment book. There was only one entry—a reminder about the Doozier homework transport. No PPS meetings, parent consultations, or multi-disciplinary committees. *Wow!* She might actually be able to work with some kids today. Easing back in her chair, Skye took the bag Wally had handed her out of her tote and opened it. Inside, he had packed her both a breakfast—Diet Coke and a package of brown-sugar cinnamon Pop-Tarts—and a lunch—a ham sandwich and a Raspberry Zinger. *Shoot!* Another day when she wouldn't make her healthy-eating goal. And when had he found her stash of Hostess snack cakes?

After opening her soda, she tore off the top of the pastry's foil pouch, and enjoyed her delayed breakfast. As she ate, she planned her schedule.

Late morning, after finishing the academic assessment of a student going through a re-eval, Skye phoned the junior high to see if Junior's assignments were ready for her to pick up and deliver.

Ursula Nelson, the school secretary, answered with a brusque, "Yes." She was a gruff woman who didn't seem to like anyone, and who, when spoken to, always appeared annoyed at the interruption.

After Skye made her inquiry, Ursula said with a snort, "Mr. Doozier called a few minutes ago. Apparently he is too busy to deal with his son's missing work and feels the teacher can catch him up on Monday."

Before Skye could inquire about Earl's hectic calendar, Ursula hung up. As per her usual habit, the secretary did not say good-bye.

Although Skye was happy not to have to interrupt her day with a trip to Doozierland, she was a bit concerned. The Dooziers were famous for being bone-lazy, so a busy Earl was almost certainly up to no good. He was probably knee-deep in another get-rich-quick scheme, like the petting zoo from which the lion he had rented escaped, or the paintball adventure that had resulted in Skye's resembling an Oompa-Loompa.

Still, not having to make the trip saved her at least a couple of hours, which meant she could complete another portion of the psychological evaluation, and then perhaps even get a start on scoring the tests.

When Skye took a breather at noon, she realized that Homer hadn't come looking for her regarding her late arrival and she had wasted all that angst for nothing. Either Homer had bigger faculty to fry, or he was taking the day off. She'd noticed that lately he was rarely at school on Fridays. Did she dare to hope he was using up his sick days and this was a sign that he might be retiring soon?

Deciding to have lunch with Trixie, Skye took her brown bag to the library workroom. Ever since Trixie had made up her mind to write a book, she almost always spent her breaks there. As they ate, Skye told her friend about Elijah's arrest and confession; then for the next twenty minutes the women discussed the case and Skye's wedding.

As Skye got up to go back to work, she mused, "I wonder why Mrs. Griggs will let Wally and me sleep together in the same bed, but not make love? She seems fine if we cuddle, but not much more."

Trixie ate the last bit of her Suzy Q, then said, "Maybe she doesn't believe in premarital sex, and once you're legally wed she'll be okay."

"Wouldn't that be nice?" Skye threw away their trash. "Hmm. If your theory is true, maybe it wasn't Mrs. Griggs who turned off my alarm this morning. I suppose Bingo could have stepped on the OFF button."

"I wouldn't put it past him. He's a smart cat." Trixie wiped the worktable down with a napkin, then said, "On a completely different subject, how do you feel about Elijah pleading guilty?"

"I just don't understand how he did it." Skye wrinkled her brow. "With his brain injury, I would have sworn he was incapable of pulling off that kind of crime." She paused. "Guess I was wrong."

After saying good-bye to Trixie, Skye headed back to her office, her mind on Elijah. Even though he had confessed, she still felt sorry for him. The poor man had been through so much in his life—losing both his profession and his fiancée. The only scenario Skye could come up with was that he had killed Alexis in an impulsive act of rage brought on by the woman's continual bullying. But then, how the victim's car had ended up in front of Kyle's house remained a mystery.

Certainly Alexis's harassing behavior didn't justify Elijah's murdering her. No one deserved that. Nevertheless, Skye hoped his sister would find him a good attorney.

When Skye arrived at the police station at a little after four, Wally greeted her at the door. Instead of his uniform, he was dressed in black jeans, a black long-sleeve T-shirt, and a leather jacket. While explaining where they were going, he hustled her out of the building, across the parking lot, and into his personal vehicle, a sky blue Thunderbird.

"Uncle Dante wants you to do what?" Skye asked. "And you agreed?"

Wally slid into the driver's seat. "I'll tell you all about it on the way."

As Skye buckled up, she demanded, "But why did you agree to be Uncle Dante's security guard at his self-storage facility auction?"

"Because the mayor requested a police presence." Wally put the T-Bird in reverse.

They had only found out five months ago that Dante owned a self-storage business, when he admitted that some of the police files—the ones that were over ten years old—were warehoused there. Without informing Wally, Dante had had the city hall custodians move everything from the

PD's basement to his place and was charging the city rent.

If Skye didn't know how small-town government worked, she might have wondered how the chief of police could be unaware of where all the records were kept, even documents that were stored long before he became the boss. But in a good-old-boy regime, unless you knew the right question to ask, no one would volunteer the information.

"So you're the police presence?" Skye twisted to look at Wally.

"Yes." Wally's gritted his teeth. "Since his facility is in Laurel, it's out of my jurisdiction, and more important, I refused to have my men do Dante's private work while on the public's dime."

"So, instead of compromising your officers, you're doing it on your own time for free. Right?" Skye asked with a sidelong glance.

"It seemed the lesser of two evils." Wally turned onto the road that would take them toward Laurel. "Dante's request was more like an order, and I thought it was best to pick my battles."

"But why am I coming along?" Skye asked. "Surely, my uncle didn't ask for the psych consultant." Her uncle had often voiced his opinion that the Scumble River PD didn't need any blankety-blank shrink on staff.

"Not exactly." Wally grinned. "But he did demand two security guards."

"Really?" She giggled. "I'm the other security guard? He won't be happy."

"I'm not sure why he thinks he needs guards anyway." Wally scowled.

"Probably because he's as much of a jerk to his customers as he is to everyone else. He's afraid someone will object to his selling their possessions when they're only a couple of days overdue with the rent—or whatever the legal limit is. You do realize I'm more likely to throw the first tomato at my uncle than save him."

"Good." Wally decelerated for a dump truck turning into the local landfill. "If there's trouble, which I doubt, I'll handle it. You head for the car and call the Laurel police."

Skye hid a smile. Wally had to know she would never leave him alone in that kind of situation, but instead of pointing that out she demanded, "Tell me about Elijah's confession. How could you drop a bomb like that, then fall asleep before giving me the details?"

"I knew you'd be upset." Wally's expression was sheepish. "Sorry."

"Fine." Skye crossed her arms. "Now, how did you make him confess?"

"Believe me, I wish I could take the credit, but it wasn't any great interrogation skill on my part." Wally's expression was rueful. "We handcuffed him, read him his rights, and he said he did it."

"Son of a gun!" Skye wiggled in her seat. "Did he say why?"

"Because God told him to." Wally tapped his fingers on the steering wheel. "Supposedly, sometime toward the end of the bowler disco party, Jacobsen received a heavenly message to go to the basement and kill the vic because she was an unrepentant sinner."

"So how did he get Alexis to go down there with him?" Skye asked.

"Jacobsen claims he doesn't recall that part." Wally concentrated on navigating the T-Bird around a curve. "He says his memory's bad."

"Did he bring the cat toy with him?" Skye asked. "And why did he use it instead of something more lethal?"

"He also claims he doesn't recollect committing the actual homicide." Wally blew out an irritated sigh, then muttered almost under his breath, "In fact, when we asked him to describe how he killed her, he said he stabbed her with his pocketknife."

"That's odd." Skye knew the details of the homicide hadn't been released, but the murderer should know how he had done it.

"I think he's just setting himself up for an insanity plea." Wally's lips formed a thin white line. "Despite his so-called brain damage, he seems to have some flashes of intelligence and cunning. Unfortunately, Zuchowski made a rookie mistake and blurted out that Alexis was strangled with a cat toy, and then Jacobsen quickly changed his tune."

"Oh. Anything else from Elijah's confession that struck you as strange?" Skye didn't bother to explain the nature of a head injury again. It was fairly clear that Wally didn't believe that the ex-doc's issues were real. "Did he remember leaving the bowling alley?"

"He says he woke up, saw the body, and just went home." Wally twitched his shoulders as if his neck was stiff. "It seems God didn't tell him to stick around or tell anyone that he killed her."

After a few minutes of contemplation, Skye asked, "When did God tell him to go into the wilderness?"

"The next morning." Wally passed a slow-moving Grand Am with its windows down. The weather had warmed up into the seventies and the Pontiac's driver was clearly enjoying the pleasant temperature.

Skye let her thoughts wander; then as Wally guided the T-Bird into the self-storage lot, she said, "So that's that. Case closed?"

"Yep." Wally parked the T-Bird beside an extended-cab pickup. "Jacobsen confessed and we don't have any other leads to follow, so unless something new turns up . . ." He trailed off, shrugging his shoulders.

"And you really, really think that Elijah is the guilty party?"

"Not entirely, but as I said, he confessed, so without new evidence, it's out of my hands." Wally's tone held a hint of impatience. "I went over everything with the county prosecutor today and he's satisfied. Unless something comes up in the pretrial motions, the police department's role is officially over."

Skye let the matter drop even though she was far from happy with Wally's explanation, and she was silent as he opened her door. Exiting from the low-slung sports car, she examined the storage facility. She'd been here once before while searching for a missing police file, and she still thought it looked like a fifties-style motel, although the fact that it was windowless and surrounded by a six-foot-high chain-link fence with razor wire strung across the top tended to spoil that illusion.

There were two types of lockers available. The smaller size had a regular pedestrian entrance, but the larger units had a heavy metal panel that rolled up into the ceiling like a garage door. The siding was a dirty tan, and the place reeked of bad luck and desperation.

While Skye was pursuing that thought, Dante waddled up to them and bellowed, "It's about time you got here." Short, squat, and with an enormous beer belly, the Scumble River mayor could have been a stand-in for the Penguin on the old *Batman* TV show. "The auction starts in ten minutes. Where's the second guard at?"

"Right here, Uncle Dante." Skye waved from beside Wally, then hid her grin behind her hand when the older man's face turned red.

"What the hell?" Dante sputtered, rounding on Wally. "I told you I wanted two of your people here to protect my property."

"And you have two." Wally's face was expressionless, but his fists were clenched. "Skye works for the police department and so do I."

While Dante ranted about insubordination, Skye observed the throng gathered near the office. The parking lot was almost full. Most of the spaces were occupied by pickups, but there were a few SUVs, a snazzy sports car, and an expensive sedan. But the vehicle that caught her attention was a beat-up Buick Regal.

The Buick's exhaust pipe was sticking out from under the passenger door and suspended by a seat belt. Shifting her gaze, Skye saw that the windshield had a spider-web crack and the side mirror was duct-taped to the body. She closed her eyes and shuddered.

It couldn't be. She quickly scanned the crowd, waiting for the auction to start. Was that a familiar badly dyed blond hairdo near the front? *Oh, oh!* She couldn't see with all the people milling around.

Skye glanced over her shoulder. Wally and Dante were still arguing, or rather Dante was throwing a fit like a little kid who didn't get what he wanted for his birthday. His pointy, beaklike nose was twitching and he was stamping his foot on the asphalt.

Skye edged closer to the horde of potential bidders, but before she could get a good look, she heard, "Whoo-ee! If it ain't Miz Skye."

In front of her, waving his arms as if he was directing a 757 to a gate at O'Hare, was Earl Doozier. The pint-size man was wearing red, green, and yellow print Zubaz pants, a white sleeveless T-shirt, and a purple gimme cap with a Copenhagen can embroidered on the front and his ponytail sticking out the back. He patted his little round belly and beamed a toothless smile.

Skye cringed. This was not going to end well. A Doozier's presence at an emotionally overcharged event like an auction guaranteed a disaster.

CHAPTER 22

Not Enough Room to Swing a Cat

After exchanging a few words with Earl, Skye told him that she didn't have time to say "howdy" to the rest of the clan that had gathered. While he was still nodding, she slipped away and quickly returned to where Wally and the mayor were standing. She pulled Wally to one side and whispered, "The Dooziers are here."

"All of them?" Wally's tone was a mixture of disbelief and horror.

"Just Earl, Glenda, MeMa, Junior, and Cletus," Skye reported.

"That's more than enough." Wally grimaced. "What are they doing here?"

"Hunting for treasure," Skye explained. "Glenda saw some TV show where people were buying old stuff at yard sales and making big bucks selling it online. So when Earl noticed Dante's ad in the paper about this auction, he figured it was easier to buy a bunch of junk in one place than to go from garage sale to garage sale."

"Shit!" Wally scowled. "I can't think of any valid reason to ask them to leave."

"Me, neither."

"But it would probably be best if we don't mention their presence to Dante." Wally glanced over at the mayor, who was screaming into his cell phone and shaking his fist in the air.

"Absolutely." Skye heartily agreed. "What my uncle doesn't know won't hurt us." Although she didn't know why, Dante had a profound hatred of the Dooziers. He wouldn't care about the niceties of the law; he would simply order the family's removal whether the action was legal or not. "Do you want me to distract the mayor?" Skye asked. "I speak fluent patriarchy even though it isn't my mother tongue."

It took Wally a second, but he finally chuckled and said, "I'll deal with Dante." He tipped his head at the crowd. "How about you hang around with Earl and his merry band while the sale is in progress?"

"That's probably a good idea." Skye smiled bravely. Best-case scenario, she could act as a buffer between the family and the rest of the attendees. Worst-case scenario—no, she didn't even want to think of the worst-case scenario, since it would probably involve her getting between an enraged gang of Dooziers and an even more infuriated mob.

While Wally headed back toward the mayor, Skye went looking for the Dooziers. Earl wasn't where she had left him, so by the time she found the family, her uncle and his police escort had made their way to the front of the crowd and the mayor was trying to get everyone's attention.

He wasn't having much luck until the woman standing beside him handed him a megaphone, which he used to shout, "Okay, folks, listen up."

Apart from the scuffle of feet and the heavy breathing, people quieted. Everyone, that is, except Glenda Doozier, a tall, meaty blonde wearing a camouflage miniskirt and a matching crop top that were riding up to reveal stretches of dead-white skin both above- and belowdecks. Hair dyed one shade beyond believability was swept into a towering beehive with a huge swirl riding low over her forehead. Her earrings, made from bullet casings, dangled nearly into her cleavage.

Peering out from behind the enormous curl, Glenda narrowed her rodentlike brown eyes and said to Skye in a high-pitched, pain-inducing voice, "Cain't you find nowheres else to stand than beside my man?"

Earl's wife was not a fan of Skye's, and she was vocally unhappy that her husband didn't feel the same way. Earl had learned through painful experience that disagreeing with his wife was futile, but he darted an apologetic glance at Skye and made a distressed sound.

MeMa cackled at the drama unfolding between Glenda and Skye. The elderly woman had a face like a sock puppet, and was the clan matriarch as well as Earl's grandmother—or maybe great-grandmother. It was hard to keep track of the Dooziers' twisted family tree since every time someone shook it a bunch of nuts fell out.

Wearing a neon orange muumuu and her signature red high-top sneakers, MeMa was clearly having a wonderful time. She leaned on a debonair-looking black cane, which she used to prod anyone who got in her way, while voicing loud opinions of the weight, attractiveness, and intellect of those around her.

Next to MeMa, Junior and Cletus, Earl's son and nephew, respectively, giggled and elbowed each other in the side. Skye noticed that they both had large backpacks strapped across their shoulders and she wondered what was in them. In times past, she had warned Earl about allowing the teens to carry guns and he'd promised they would leave the weapons at home. She hoped he had kept his word.

Dante squinted in the direction of the Dooziers and Skye held her breath. She crossed her fingers that because her uncle was too vain to wear his glasses, he wouldn't be able to detect their faces in the crowd.

Apparently Dante didn't spot the Dooziers among the other people, since after a few seconds, he continued with his speech. "Cash is king. I'm not taking credit cards, checks, IOUs, or sob stories."

A discontented murmur rose from the audience,

but Earl hooted, "I's got the money, Sonny. So let's stop wastin' my time."

Dante frowned, seemingly still unable to see who was heckling him, then raised his voice. "Here are my rules. Once the door of the locker is opened, you got five minutes to look around. You can't go inside, open any boxes, or touch anything. I don't want any rough stuff and if you bid, you better have the dough."

With that, Dante nodded to the woman next to him. "This here's Willie Jo. She manages this place for me and will be collecting the payments."

A statuesque platinum blonde waved a bunch of keys in one hand and a pair of bolt cutters in the other, then yelled, "Let's go!"

Dante stuck out his arm, Willie Jo rested her hand on it, and the mismatched couple led the way through a maze of lockers. As Skye struggled to keep up with Earl and his family, she examined the attendees. They ranged in age from teenagers to octogenarians, affluent to hard up, diminutive to gargantuan, and average-looking to downright odd. For once, the Dooziers fit right in.

Skye hadn't realized the facility was so large. Previously, she'd seen only the front strip of lockers. But finally, after trekking down row after row, Dante and Willie Jo stopped in front of one of the larger units.

Dante shouted, "This is a ten by twenty-five. Cut the lock, Willie Jo."

The blonde snipped off the padlock, rolled the metal door up, and quickly stepped aside as the pack descended. Skye stuck to Earl's side, peeking into the dark, somewhat spooky interior. It held old appliances, particleboard furniture, and a mountain of bulging black plastic trash bags.

Earl turned to his wife and whispered furiously, gesturing avidly at the locker.

"I don't care if you saw somebody's great-aunt's girdle go for a thousand dollars on eBay," Glenda hissed. "We may a' got married for better or worse—you couldn't do no better and I couldn't do no worse—but . . ." She pulled the V-neck of her camo crop top away from her body and pointed down to her boobs. "Iffen you go over two hunert, you'll never play with these babies again."

"But, honey pie," Earl whined. "Don't youse see that big ol' doll thingy in the back? I bets we could get a ton a money for that."

Glenda bent forward and Skye quickly moved behind her to block the view as the woman's camo micro mini crept up, revealing a dimpled derriere that should never have made the acquaintance of a thong. All they needed was Earl having to defend his ladylove's honor from some guy with a smart mouth or a fast hand.

"Two hunert," Glenda repeated. "Ain't no headless green plastic woman with a phone in her belly worth more than that. The furniture's nothin' but cheap crap, and we don't got no idea what's in those bags."

Earl's bid was quickly overtaken by a tall guy with slicked-back hair. His neck was the size of a Sunday ham, and he was dressed in tight black pants and a red silk shirt. He carried a small leather bag.

As he passed the Doozier clan to claim his locker, the man smirked and said to Earl, "Step aside for a real player, Shorty."

Skye recoiled, waiting for the first punch.

But Earl just narrowed his beady little eyes and said, "Dumbass, I ain't short. I is fun size."

Mr. Silk Shirt paused as if to turn back and say something more, but someone from the crowd said to him, "Word to the wise. Let it go."

Word to the wise? Skye shook her head. Really? Shouldn't that be word to the stupid?

Earl murmured something to Glenda, who nodded, and the pair moved on.

The next few units were filled with brown paper grocery sacks overflowing with used clothing and more black trash bags holding who knew what. A couple of them smelled so bad they made Skye's eyes water. She'd seen everything from dirty diapers to unwashed dishes, and couldn't believe the rubbish people paid good money to keep in storage.

The bidding had been lackluster, but the final locker of the sale perked everyone up. According to

Dante, it was ten by thirty feet and big enough to store the contents of an entire moving van. As the lock was cut, a wave of excited chatter rose from the attendees, and immediately the crowd surged forward to get a better view. The unit was packed with what appeared to be new merchandise.

Skye was shoved over the threshold and into a stack of cartons. Steadying herself on a pile of boxes that bore pictures of lawn mowers, weed whackers, and leaf blowers, she noticed the words stamped in red ink along the sides and top: PROPERTY OF THE CITY OF VIDERVILLE.

She frowned. Viderville was a municipality about twice the size of Scumble River, located fifteen miles south of her hometown. Why was its property being stored in Laurel? Almost before Skye could form the question, her uncle grabbed her arm and yanked her out of the locker.

Shouting above the multitude of excited voices, the mayor addressed the crowd. "Sorry, folks. Wrong unit. The ink was smudged. This is three-six-six and we wanted eight-six-six."

Grumbling, the mob followed Dante and Willie Jo to another large locker. This one contained an industrial oven, several rolling metal racks, and a mixer the size of a ten-year-old. There were also fifty-pound bags of flour, cornstarch, and sugar, as well as a huge white plastic tub of rainbow sprinkles and several gallon jugs of cooking oil. It looked like a bakery had gone out of business, and

Skye heard the folks around her murmuring appreciatively.

After a quick huddle with his wife, grandmother, son, and nephew, Earl started the bidding at two hundred dollars. It swiftly climbed upward, and the potential buyers dropped out one by one until Earl and Mr. Silk Shirt were the only two left.

Glenda tugged furiously at her husband's hand as he shouted, "A thousand!"

"Is that all you got in you?" Mr. Silk Shirt sneered. Then he yelled, "Eleven hundred."

"Twelve," Earl countered. "Youse got more than that in your itty bitty purse, Mr. Girly Man?"

Skye overheard Glenda hiss at her husband, "If youse fell into our fishpond, we'd be skimming stupid offen the top for a month."

"But, sweetums . . ."

"Don't sweetums me." Glenda dug her nails into Earl's arm. "We only got thirteen hundert on us. Do youse want to give Leofanti a reason to mess with us?"

Silk Shirt checked the black leather bag hanging from his wrist, then screamed, red in the face, "Twelve fifty." Hatred shooting from his eyes like flames, he taunted, "Beat that, you river rat."

"Twelve seventy-five." Earl shook off Glenda's restraining hand.

Skye winced. Earl would surely pay for that insubordination.

"Dante, let me write you a check," Silk Shirt pleaded. "You know I'm good for it."

"Cash on the barrelhead." Dante crossed his arms. "And if you bid more than you got, I'll have you arrested." He nodded in Wally's direction.

"Jerkwad," Mr. Silk Shirt snarled, but he didn't raise Earl's bid.

"Going once." Dante scanned the throng of people. "Going twice." He paused, and when no one raised the bid he said, "Sold for twelve hundred and seventy-five dollars to the man in the purple cap."

Skye pursed her lips. Apparently her uncle still hadn't recognized the Dooziers. Either that or he didn't care that they were attending the sale as long as they had the cash to pay him.

The crowd quickly dispersed. Those who had bought lockers settled up with Willie Jo and went to find out if they had hit it rich, and those who were departing empty-handed hurried toward the parking lot.

The mayor insisted that Wally accompany him and the money box to the office. Before leaving, Wally shot Skye a look, and she nodded that she was okay. She pointed behind her, indicating that she would stay with the Dooziers for a little while longer. The family had disappeared into their unit and she could hear excited exclamations as they discovered new treasures.

As Willie Jo, Dante, and Wally vanished around

a corner, Skye let out a sigh of relief that the auction hadn't resulted in a Doozier dustup. However, before she could fully relax, a smirking Mr. Silk Shirt sauntered into sight. With him were two muscle-bound men armed with baseball bats and badass expressions.

Shoot! Skye looked around. They were at the end of a corridor and there was no other way out. She dug in her purse for her cell and her can of pepper spray, wishing she had her Taser.

She was willing her phone to hurry and find a signal when Earl stepped into the locker's open doorway. He looked at the men coming toward him and fished a pair of spiked brass knuckles out of his pocket. Instantly, Glenda and MeMa materialized next to him. Glenda reached into her ankle-length high-heeled boot and pulled out a switchblade, and MeMa unscrewed the handle of her cane, revealing a fifteen-inch stainless-steel blade.

It always amazed Skye that the Dooziers seemed to be able to sense when one of their own was in trouble, and they appeared as if out of nowhere to fight side by side. Did they have some sort of psychic bond or did they emit a pheromone like a queen bee signaling her drones? And speaking of drones, where were Cletus and Junior?

While Earl, MeMa, and Glenda lined up, blocking the entrance of their unit, Skye moved as far away as she could get. If the boys appeared, she'd have to try to protect them, but the adults were on their own. She told herself that facing your fears might build strength of character, but running from them offered a terrific cardio workout.

The Silk Shirt gang backed up when they saw the Dooziers' weaponry, but the leader grunted something to the others, and they resumed their positions.

"No one has to get hurt," Mr. Silk Shirt said. "All you have to do is turn over this locker to me and we can walk away."

Earl chortled. "Oh, yes, somebody does got to get hurt." He bared the few teeth he possessed. "Ain't no one threatens a Doozier and lives to tell the tale." Looking behind him, he yelled, "You boys ready?"

"Inna second, Pa." Junior's gleeful voice rang out from the unit's interior.

Skye tensed. What were Junior and Cletus up to? She glanced at her phone; still no bars. Everybody loved their cells so much, but what good were they if they never worked when you needed them?

The Silk Shirt gang exchanged uneasy glances, but the leader said, "Don't be wusses. We can take one scrawny redneck, a woman, and an old broad." He flicked a scornful look at Skye. "And that fat chick won't be any trouble. Will you, babe?"

Until then Skye had been hoping to stay out of the fray, but she really hated being called a fat chick, and *babe* was almost as bad. Her fight-or-flight instinct had been triggered, and since she couldn't flee, there was only one option left. She slung her purse strap across her chest, checked that her pepper spray was aimed outward, and moved next to the Dooziers.

The thugs hesitated, clearly unsure of their next move. And as if picking up on their apprehension—sort of like a pair of guard dogs in a junkyard—Cletus and Junior burst out of the locker. They wore matching maniacal grins and held bright blue, oversize Supersoaker water machine guns.

Skye raised her eyebrows. So that's what the boys had had in their backpacks. Evidently Earl had kept his promise about not allowing the boys to go around with actual weapons, and had compromised by buying them squirt guns. Honking huge squirt guns that could probably shoot twenty-five feet with the power of a water cannon.

The teenagers were pumping the levers as they advanced, and before the Silk Shirt gang could react, Junior darted forward and slid back the handle of his Super Soaker. A stream of oil arced into the air and drenched the three stunned tough guys. Immediately, Cletus followed with his own spray, which appeared to be a mixture of flour and rainbow sprinkles.

The teenagers continued showering their foes with alternating cascades until their adversaries were coughing and sputtering. The two henchmen stumbled away, but Mr. Silk Shirt charged toward the boys, swinging his bat like an enraged baseball player coming after an umpire who had made an unfavorable call.

Without considering the consequences, Skye threw herself between the man and the teenagers, aimed her can of pepper spray, and pressed the button. Simultaneously, Cletus and Junior pumped their Super Soakers and fired.

While Mr. Silk Shirt turned and ran, clawing at his eyes, Skye was hit with the full force of the oil and flour sprays. Who knew that rainbow sprinkles propelled at a high speed could hurt so much?

CHAPTER 23

Has the Cat Got
Your Tongue?

No way. No how." Dante shook his head. "She is not getting in my car." He took a step backward, as if to avoid contamination. "She looks like a giant donut and smells like a rancid bagel."

"If you want me to escort this creep to the Laurel PD," Wally said, his tone brooking no argument, "you will give your niece a ride home."

Wally had explained to Skye that he'd spotted Mr. Silk Shirt as the guy fled past the storage facility office. Since the man looked suspicious—most of the bidders who were leaving the auction were not covered in goop—Wally had stopped him. Then when the man refused to answer any questions, he'd decided to detain him.

The slime path led Wally to Skye and the Dooziers, and after hearing that Mr. Silk Shirt had tried to force Earl into giving him his locker's contents by threatening him with a baseball bat, Wally had handcuffed the thug and called the local police.

Now, Wally stood with a firm grip on the guy's upper arm as he waited for a Laurel officer to arrive. He stared at the mayor, an unyielding expression on his face.

"Don't you forget that I'm your boss," the mayor blustered. "I can make sure that the city council votes not to renew your contract."

"Uncle Dante." The flour and oil mixture was starting to harden on Skye, and she was rapidly losing her patience. "I don't think you've considered the whole situation. Do you really want me to call your sister and tell her you're refusing to take her daughter home?"

"She'll understand." Dante stood firm. "May doesn't like a mess any more than I do."

"Maybe. But I'm positive she won't appreciate your threatening to fire my fiancé." Skye brought out the heavy artillery. "Especially since it means I would have to leave Scumble River when he took a new job elsewhere."

A nerve near Dante's right eye twitched, but he whined, "It's a brand-new Cadillac with leather seats. You'll ruin them."

"Think what Mom will do to your car when her grandchild is born in another state. A little damage to the seats will seem like nothing in comparison to the wrath of May." Skye stared down her uncle, then hastily added, "And no, I'm not currently pregnant."

"Fine." Dante pouted. "But I'm washing you off and wrapping you in garbage bags." As he left to find the hose, he said over his shoulder, "And you have to promise not to touch anything. Especially me."

"Fine." Skye turned to Wally, who was having some difficulty keeping a grip on his flour-and-oil-covered prisoner, and waved him away. "Go ahead. I'll be fine, and if Uncle Dante tries to strand me here, I'll get Mom on the phone to straighten him out."

"It shouldn't take more than a couple of hours to process this scumbag." Wally started toward the Laurel squad car that had just pulled into the lot. "The Dooziers are meeting me at the PD tonight to press charges, but I'll tell the chief that you'll come over Monday afternoon to give your statement." He wrinkled his brow. "How in the heck did you ever get Earl and his kin to cooperate?"

"I told them that either they pressed charges against this guy"—Skye pointed to Wally's prisoner—"or I pressed charges against them for assaulting me with a deadly water pistol."

"That explains it."

As she walked over to her uncle, who was motioning with one hand and flapping a hose in her direction, Skye asked over her shoulder, "Are you coming by my house after you finish at the Laurel PD?"

"Absolutely."

An unfamiliar vehicle was parked in front of Skye's house when Dante steered his Cadillac between the wrought-iron gates. She squinted at the late-model sedan, trying to figure out who her visitor might be, but couldn't think of anyone she knew who drove a dark blue Chrysler Sebring. Uninvited guests were rarely a nice surprise, and she braced herself for an unpleasant encounter.

While most of the males in her family would have asked if Skye knew her visitor, Dante seemed indifferent to his niece's safety. He had barely pulled his Cadillac into the driveway when he squealed to a stop and shoved her, and the plastic bags he had enveloped her wet body in, out the door. As soon as Skye's feet hit the gravel, he threw the car into reverse, zoomed backward onto the road, and sped toward town.

Skye yelled a sarcastic thank-you at the retreating vehicle. It took her a few seconds to fight loose of the plastic, but once free, she gathered the trash bags into a ball, hitched up her purse, and headed toward the front porch, her feet squishing with every step.

Most of her had dried off during the forty-five-minute trip from Laurel to Scumble River, but her shoes were still soaked from the hosing to which her uncle had subjected her. Although she had never quite understood how waterboarding torture worked, she was getting a glimmer of an idea now.

As soon as Skye neared the house, she saw Spike sitting on her porch swing. Relief washed over her—at least it was a friend and not another crisis coming to visit—and she called out, "Hey,

Spike. I wasn't expecting you. I hope you weren't waiting long."

"No." Spike got up, and after Skye climbed the stairs, she continued, "And since you didn't know I was coming, it would be my own fault if . . ." Spike stuttered to a stop when she got a good look at Skye. "What in the world happened to you?"

"It's a long story and I really need to take a shower before I become a papier-mâché statue." Dante's hosing had helped, but getting rid of flour mixed with oil really required soap, and lots of it.

"I can see that," Spike said.

Skye inserted her key and turned the lock. "Can you give me fifteen minutes to clean up or is there something you need in a hurry?"

"I'm just here to see you. I've tried a couple of times, but never caught you home. I guess I should learn to call first." Spike followed Skye inside. "I'll make us a hot drink while you unmold. Just point me to the kitchen."

After Skye had bathed, dressed in a pink and black velour tracksuit, and clipped her hair on top of her head, she joined Spike, who had entranced Bingo with a bag of treats she must have produced from her purse. The cat was lying across her lap purring like a diesel engine and literally eating out of her hand.

As they sipped tea and munched on Oreos that Skye had retrieved from her cupboard—she still hadn't replaced her cookie jar—Spike said, "I really miss my sweet kitty."

"Chopsticks, right?" Skye remembered Spike mentioning him in her e-mail.

"Right." Spike stroked Bingo's sleek black fur. "I found her in back of a Chinese restaurant with her head stuck in a carryout container."

"Is your grandfather bringing her when he moves to Illinois?" Skye asked.

"Yes." Spike nodded. "I haven't had a chance to look for an apartment or a car, so I have no idea when that will be. The station is providing me with a rental and putting me up at an extended-stay hotel until I find my own place. And since it's a studio, there's no room for Grandfather, and it doesn't allow pets."

"Are you still tracking down small-town government corruption?" Skye unscrewed the two chocolate wafers of an Oreo and scrutinized the cream center. After an experience with doctored cookies that had made her ill, she always checked to make sure that nothing had been added to the filling before she ate an Oreo. Some people might have avoided Oreos altogether after an experience like that, but Skye was made of sterner stuff.

"Yes." Spike watched Skye without comment. "But I'm getting discouraged. As I'm sure you know, it's hard to get people around here to trust a stranger, especially one who doesn't exactly look like their neighbors. I think I'd have an easier time

297

if I was blond with a Swedish last name like Anderson or an Italian one like Votta."

"Maybe. But I do think that the local residents are getting more tolerant. At least I hope so," Skye added, thinking about Loretta, Vince, and their future biracial offspring. "Is your suspect's identity still top secret?"

"I guess not." Spike wrinkled her nose. "Just don't call up a rival reporter."

"Cross my heart." Skye took a sip of her tea, then put her cup down.

Spike reached into her purse and pulled out a folder. She flipped it open and pointed to a group photo of two women and eight men. "It's the Viderville Village Board, which consists of six trustees plus the city attorney, the comptroller, the clerk, and the mayor."

Skye scrutinized the faces. "They look pretty typical of a small-town board."

"Don't they?" Spike scratched under Bingo's chin, sending the cat into a fit of ecstasy. "However, the tipster claims that any contractors who want to do business within the corporate limits of the village have to obtain a special license. Which means plumbers, builders, electricians, lawn crews, et cetera have to pay to play, as they say in Chicago politics."

"Isn't it usual for towns to charge some sort of fee to verify that workers are legitimate and not ripping off the citizens?"

"The tipster claimed the money wasn't going into the town coffers, but rather into the trustees' pockets," Spike explained. "In fact, apparently the mayor and his cronies are making a ton of money skimming from their constituents."

"Hmm." Skye half closed her eyes. Why did she think she knew something about that?

"Anyway," Spike continued, "I've got an appointment with Mayor Todd Urick tomorrow at eleven a.m. He's been putting me off, but he must have gotten tired of me calling every hour so he finally agreed to see me." She sighed. "Although since I have no clout, I can't figure out how I can make him tell me anything important."

"Oh, my gosh." Skye covered her mouth, having just remembered what she'd seen earlier that evening at the storage facility. "I think I might know how to get him to talk."

"How?"

Skye explained about the auction and the brand-new merchandise with PROPERTY OF THE CITY OF VIDERVILLE stamped on its unopened boxes. She finished with, "So I bet they order materials and equipment that on paper they claim are for various city departments. They use money from the city's budget to pay for the stuff, but when it arrives, they never add it to the departments' inventory. At my school, for instance, we have to stencil the items with a number that corresponds to the master list that the principals keep. But in

299

Viderville, the mayor and his cronies sell the unopened goods and pocket the cash themselves."

"That's it." Spike leaped from her chair, scattering her papers and dumping an outraged Bingo from her lap "Sorry, boy," she apologized.

"Hiss!" The feline's response was sharp as he ran from the room.

"Now I've got Mayor Urick right where I want him." Spike pulled Skye to her feet, hugged her, and danced her around the kitchen.

After Spike had calmed down and picked up her strewn documents, they discussed what Skye had seen in more detail. Once Spike had wrung every last scrap of information from Skye, she leaned back and smiled. "Now that I have leverage, this is going to be fun."

Skye agreed. Then, at the urging of her growling stomach, she got up and opened the refrigerator. Peering inside, she asked, "Are you hungry?"

"Starving."

"There's not much in here," Skye reported, "but I've got a pepperoni and mushroom pizza in the freezer. Is that okay with you?"

"My favorite."

While they ate, the two women discussed their mothers, their jobs, and their cats. Skye had considered asking Spike to be a bridesmaid, but since her friend was also Simon's half sister, it might be awkward, so she contented herself with inviting the younger woman to the wedding. She intended to ask Bunny, too, though she was undecided whether to invite Simon.

It was nearly ten when Spike left, and a few minutes later Wally walked in the door. While he finished up the leftover pizza and drank a bottle of Sam Adams, Skye jogged his memory about Spike's story. Once he was reminded of her investigation, Skye told him about the merchandise she had seen in the storage locker.

"If the Viderville board is guilty, I hope Spike nails them," Wally said, draining his beer. "There's nothing more despicable than a dishonest politician."

"Betrayal of the public trust should be a hanging offense," Skye agreed.

While they watched the late news, Wally said, "I was thinking that since we've arrested Jacobsen and the case is closed, you and I should go somewhere for a weekend getaway. How does Starved Rock State Park sound? There's the main lodge and a couple of other resorts in the area. We could do a little hiking and have some time alone."

"Perfect." Skye snuggled against his side and kissed his cheek. "I'll ask Trixie to come over and feed Bingo while we're gone."

"I'll call now and see if I can get a room." Wally took out his cell.

"Wonderful."

It took a couple of calls, but Wally eventually

reported, "Check-in is at four, so we should probably leave here about noon. We can swing by my place so I can grab a few things, then stop somewhere along I-80 for lunch. Morris or Ottawa would be good."

"That means we don't have to set the alarm." Skye stretched. "I'm exhausted."

"Me, too." Wally yawned.

Upstairs, Skye dawdled in the bathroom until she was sure Wally was asleep. She was afraid of what Mrs. Griggs might pull if they tried to make love. Crawling into bed beside him, she made a mental note to ask Father Burns about an exorcism. The ghost was ruining her love life, and it had to stop.

CHAPTER 24

Cat-o'-nine-tails

Skye and Wally slept until nine thirty the next morning. Then as they lingered over a late breakfast, she noticed something on the floor, wedged between a cupboard and the stove. Curious, she got up, walked across the kitchen, and fished it out of the crevice.

"What's that?" Wally looked up from the newspaper as she sat back down. Since he'd begun spending the night more frequently, he'd ordered Skye a subscription to the *Chicago Tribune*.

"A picture that Spike had in her small-town corruption file. It's a photograph of the Viderville city board." Skye laid the glossy page on the table and pointed to the group portrait. "Her folder fell to the floor yesterday when she jumped up to hug me, and she must not have seen the snapshot when she picked up the other documents."

"Oh." He turned back to the business section. "Do you think she needs it?"

"Probably not." Skye ran her finger over the shiny paper, smoothing the creases, then leaned closer. *Hmm.* Why did the mayor look familiar?

"If you're finished eating, you'd better start getting ready." Wally put aside the sports page and picked up the book section. "I know how long it takes you to decide what to wear, so I'm sure packing will be a lengthy process."

"What?" Skye stared at the photograph, not listening to Wally. Before he could repeat himself, she said, "I think that Viderville's mayor was the deejay at Bunny's bowler disco party. Isn't that odd?"

"Not really." Wally shrugged. "Lots of people moonlight."

"But he was wearing a wig and had a beard when he was at the bowling alley." Skye fetched a black marker from her junk drawer and added a beard and DJ Wonka's elaborate hairstyle to the picture of the bald mayor.

"He probably wears it to keep his personas separate," Wally countered.

"I suppose that could be it." Skye got up and cleared the table; then when another thought hit her, she froze with her hand on the faucet. "Bunny said DJ Wonka was from Chicago. I'm sure the mayor of Viderville has to live in town, so he fibbed to her about that."

"I'll bet he thinks people will be more likely to hire someone from the city, so he lies about where he lives." This time Wally's explanation didn't sound as confident as his previous two excuses.

"True, but don't you think if an area mayor was also a deejay, we'd have heard about it? I mean, surely the local paper would have done a story.

And the *Star* covers news from Viderville as well as Clay Center and Brooklyn."

"Why are you so interested in this guy?" Almost before he finished his sentence, Wally shook his head. "Let me guess—you're still not convinced that Jacobsen is the murderer."

"No, I'm not. Convinced, that is." Skye crossed her arms. "He didn't even know how she was killed. He claimed to have stabbed her."

"I admit that has been troubling me, too," Wally said. "But why did he confess? It certainly isn't for the fame, which is what fuels most false confessions. No one around here seems very interested since the vic wasn't a celebrity and wasn't from town."

"People with Elijah's type of brain injury are very suggestible." Skye pursed her lips, thinking. "Maybe somebody told him to."

"God?" Wally quirked an eyebrow. "Seriously? You're suggesting that God told Jacobsen to admit to a crime he didn't commit?"

"Of course not." Skye blew a raspberry. "But I do think we should call Bunny and see how she came to hire DJ Wonka in the first place."

"Maybe you're right. I haven't been happy with the resolution of this case, but between the county prosecutor being satisfied with Jacobsen's confession and no other leads to follow, there wasn't much more I could do." Wally pulled his cell phone from his pocket, and dialed. After identifying himself to Bunny, he asked, "How did you find the deejay for your bowler disco party?"

Skye strained to catch the other side of the conversation, but could hear only Wally's responses, which consisted of, "Oh. I see. That was convenient. Uh-huh."

When he disconnected, Wally turned to Skye with a thoughtful expression. "It seems DJ Wonka contacted Bunny and applied for the job. She says he did it for free."

"Which together with everything else seems strange," Skye commented. Suddenly, snippets of conversations in which she'd taken part were sliding into place like the last Legos of a complicated structure. "You know, a group of girls at the high school said that they'd heard the music sucked. That it was as if the guy had never deejayed before."

"Well, that's certainly interesting." Wally stroked his chin.

"Did Bunny ask for references or question him as to why he wanted to work without pay?"

"He told her that he'd heard some of the judges were bartering their services in exchange for the chance to participate in the cat show and speed dating and he'd like the same deal." Wally pursed his lips. "But he didn't take part in the activities. He hung around, but he didn't enter a cat in the show or sign up for the speed dating or attend the awards brunch."

"Did he go to the after party at the Brown Bag?"

"No." Wally got up. "In fact, Bunny said he didn't socialize at all."

"Did he have any other alibi for the time of the murder?"

"No. All the servers had alibis, but the bartender, bouncer, and deejay didn't." Wally paced the length of the kitchen. "Since they had no contact with the vic, I didn't think they were viable suspects, so I put them at the bottom of the list."

"Which was reasonable at the time," Skye assured him. "You have limited resources and you needed to use the manpower you had to investigate the most likely suspects."

"Maybe." Wally walked back and forth. "However, now I'm beginning to think I should have scrutinized this deejay/mayor guy more closely."

"That's easy to see now, but you didn't have all the information when you reached your original decision." Skye hated to see Wally beating himself up over a choice most people in his position would have made.

He shrugged, clearly not convinced.

A few seconds ticked by. Then Skye narrowed her eyes as another piece of the puzzle slipped into its slot. "Frannie mentioned that Alexis's last temp job was for a city official. What if she worked for Mayor Urick and somehow discovered his embezzlement scheme?"

"That would give him motive, and we've established he had means and opportunity."

"Holy crap! We need to stop Spike before she confronts him." Skye checked the clock above the sink. "It's ten fifty-five. She's probably already in Viderville."

Skye searched frantically for Spike's cell number—why hadn't she programmed it into her phone? She finally located the scrap of paper she'd written it on, stuck in her address book, and dialed it while Wally put on his loafers and fetched Skye's Keds.

She was slipping the tennis shoes on when the call went directly into Spike's voice mail. She shot Wally a worried look.

He nodded and said, "We'd better get over to Viderville and see if she's okay."

They rushed outside and jumped into Wally's Thunderbird. Once they were buckled up, he threw the sports car into gear and they tore out of the driveway. Skye held on to the dashboard and watched the speedometer climb.

After a few seconds, Skye caught her breath and asked, "Should we call the Viderville police chief? Maybe he could check things out."

"No." Wally concentrated on the road. "We can't be sure Chief Eden isn't mixed up with the embezzlement. I can't imagine how the mayor would pull it off without someone on the PD being in on the scheme."

"Maybe I should call city hall and ask to speak to Spike." Skye hated sitting and doing nothing while her friend might be in danger. "I could tell her to get out, or at least to wait for us before she talks to the mayor."

"Go ahead and give it a try, but unless Urick is keeping her cooling her heels, she's already with him. Because if what we suspect about him is true, I doubt he wants her sitting around the waiting room talking to city employees. Or anyone else."

A couple of minutes later Skye reported, "No one's answering. I tried three times and the machine always picks up. The message says that due to a gas leak, city hall is closed for the weekend."

"Son of a buck!" Wally tightened his grip on the wheel and pressed down harder on the accelerator. "That doesn't sound good at all."

"Do you think the mayor cleared everyone out so he can get rid of Spike if it turns out she knows too much?" Skye felt her stomach clench. If only she'd put the pieces together earlier.

"It crossed my mind."

Wally made the fifteen-mile drive in less than ten minutes.

When he parked the T-Bird, Skye asked, "Why didn't you pull into one of the spaces in front of the city hall? They were all open."

"Exactly." Wally reached into the glove box and withdrew a black calfskin case and a small flashlight. His gun was already in a holster under his leather jacket. He tucked the case and the light into the pocket of his jeans. "If our car is the only one sitting there, the police might run its plates. And when they come back to me, they might mention it to their chief, who might—"

"Contact the mayor," Skye said, finishing his sentence. "Gotcha."

Wally took her hand as she got out of the Ford. "We're going to casually stroll by the front entrance and scope out the situation."

There were only a couple of people around. The city hall was on a side street, and the businesses nearby were mostly law offices, real estate firms, and insurance agencies. Skye hesitated when she saw a CLOSED sign on the door, but Wally didn't break his stride, tugging her along and then walking her around the corner.

"What do we do now?" she asked when they were safely out of sight.

"This way." Wally led her toward the back of the building to an unmarked door. "Stand in front of me and pretend we're having a fight."

"Why?" Skye asked, as he drew the leather case he'd taken from the car out of his pocket. Then: "Those are lock picks, aren't they?"

"Yep."

"Where did you get them?" She moved into place, blocking Wally's actions from the view of anyone who might happen to glance down the alley.

"I took them off a burglar when I was a rookie." Wally's voice was distracted. "My sergeant told me to keep them because they'd come in handy someday."

"Have you used them before?" Skye was fascinated with this side of her fiancé. He was usually so persnickety about breaking the law.

He ignored her question. "Got it. Now we slip inside as fast as we can."

With one last glance behind them to make sure they weren't being observed, Wally eased the metal door open a few inches, waited for Skye to go through, then followed her, quickly shutting them inside. The room they had entered was windowless and pitch-black.

Wally produced his flashlight and illuminated the area in front of them. This was obviously a catchall space, full of boxes, old office equipment, and cleaning supplies. Skye felt her nose twitch at the odor of ammonia, and prayed she wouldn't sneeze.

"See that door to our left?" Wally whispered. "I'm betting it leads into the rest of the city hall, so we have to be extremely quiet."

Skye nodded, glad she had on her tennis shoes. She put her purse strap across her chest—a location she was beginning to think of as her fighting position—and carefully squeezed past the haphazardly piled paraphernalia blocking her path to the exit.

As they stepped through the door into a dimly lit passage, Wally extinguished his flashlight. Now they had a choice: Take the hallway in front of them or the one that veered to the right.

"Let's each go a different way," Skye suggested, worried that they were already too late. "What if we go the wrong way and by the time it takes us to backtrack something happens to Spike?"

Wally hesitated, then reluctantly nodded, prodding Skye toward the side corridor. She stood firm, knowing he thought the one he'd chosen for himself led to the lobby and thus the mayor's office.

He nudged her again and she shook her head, digging in her heels.

This time he pushed her a little harder and whispered, "I'm the one with the gun."

"Point taken," she murmured and reluctantly allowed him to follow the more likely route.

She made her way down the hall in her assigned direction, passing offices on both sides. When the corridor took a sharp turn, she emerged into a reception area. Looking around, she spotted the words MAYOR TODD URICK stenciled in gold leaf on a large interior window. The blinds were drawn, but light seeped between the slats.

Skye wondered where Wally had ended up. She heard his voice inside her head telling her to wait for him, but she ignored it. What if her hesitation resulted in Spike's death? She would never forgive herself, or be able to look Bunny or Simon in the eye again.

The whole building had an eerily deserted feeling. Skye shivered, then forced her feet to move forward. She crept toward that office, and as she neared it, she could hear a loud whirring noise and raised voices.

Skye was relieved to see that the door was slightly ajar, which meant it wasn't locked. Either something had made Spike nervous or luck was on their side. Skye tiptoed to the gap between the hinge and the door and peered into the office.

Once her eyes adjusted from the dim lobby to the brightly lit room, her gaze swept the area. Spike was handcuffed to the arm of the chrome chair in which she was seated. Duct tape covered her mouth and bound her ankles. A man Skye recognized from the board's photo as one of the trustees was shoving papers into a shredder and Todd Urick stood a few feet from Spike, pointing a gun in her direction.

The man who was shredding yelled at Urick above the noise, "How did this bitch find out about the money? Did you tell that big-mouth wife of yours?"

The mayor snorted. "She didn't know anything, Garth. Until you burst in here waving a gun, she was just guessing. She had no proof. I told you on the phone that I had everything under control. All you had to do was to sit tight and keep your cool. I would have taken care of it."

"Like you took care of that nosy temp worker?" Garth ran his fingers through his thinning blond hair and sneered. "We told you to shut her up, not kill her."

"If you all hadn't insisted I give her the hundred thousand from my share, none of this would have happened," Urick snapped. "I already bought her a new car to keep her quiet. If we'd split the cost of the blackmail, it would only have been twenty grand apiece."

"No way. We didn't cause the problem. Why should we pay for it?"

"Then since you caused this problem, you get rid of this chick." Urick handed the pistol to Garth and pushed him toward Spike.

Skye felt as if she couldn't breathe. She had to save Spike. Praying that the door wouldn't squeak, she had just started to ease it open when a hand snaked out and grabbed her arm. Swallowing a scream, she whirled around. Wally had his finger to his lips. He jerked his head, motioning for her to get behind him.

While Skye was trading places with Wally, Garth said in a wheedling tone, "Look, Todd, you already killed one bitch. What's one more?"

Wally had his gun out and was poised to rush into the office, but as the men argued, he paused. He was clearly waiting for the best time to intervene.

"And who am I going to convince to confess for this murder?" Urick retorted.

"How did you get that loony guy to say he did the other one?" Garth asked. "You never said."

"It wasn't part of my original plan." Urick leaned his butt on the desktop. Apparently he was a man who loved telling a good story. "I was only going to tell Alexis that blackmailing me was a dangerous way to earn a living, and that if she didn't stop she might end up dead."

"Which she did."

"The bitch laughed in my face when I threatened her." Urick shrugged. "I wasn't sure what my next step was going to be, but then she pissed off that cuckoo bird, Jacobsen. So when he attacked her, it came to me." The mayor snapped his fingers. "Here was my chance to get her out of my hair permanently, and throw the blame on him."

"But how did you know he wouldn't have an alibi?" Garth had managed to hand Urick the gun and was surreptitiously backing away from Spike.

"I drugged his soda. I always carry a few roofies in my pocket in case I want to get lucky, and I knew if the crazy guy acted strange, no one would notice." Urick shook his head. "He barely made it into the basement before passing out."

"But how did you get him to go to the basement?" Garth asked.

"I didn't." Urick's mirthless laugh was like a

seal bark. "God did. I heard Jacobsen talking to the Man Upstairs whenever he got stressed out, so I figured it was time for the Big Kahuna to answer him. Then all I had to do was have one of the waitresses pass Alexis a message from me that said I'd reconsidered, and the money she had demanded was in the basement utility closet."

"But, how—"

"Enough," Urick interrupted his coconspirator. "I'm not conducting a Murder one-oh-one class."

"So-o-o-rry." Garth elongated the word like a teenage girl. "Anyway. I'm almost done with the documents. Then I'll go to the storage facility and move the merchandise while you get rid of Ms. Nosy Reporter."

"No way." Urick's demeanor turned belligerent. "It's time for you to man up."

Garth fed the last paper through the shredder. "I don't know what you mean." He sidled toward the door, his pear-shaped torso giving him a pregnant silhouette.

"I'm not killing her." Urick waved the gun toward Spike. "You are."

"Uh-uh."

Urick advanced until he was face-to-face with the other man.

Wally put his mouth to Skye's ear. "I'm going in. Stay here."

Skye felt Wally tense; then, when Urick tried to shove the gun into Garth's hand, Wally burst through the door with his weapon leveled and ordered, "Drop the gun and put your hands up."

Urick hesitated.

"Can you run faster than twelve hundred feet per second?" Wally's voice was conversational. "Because that's the average speed of a nine-millimeter bullet."

Skye held her breath. Was Urick going to refuse? She dug frantically for the fresh can of pepper spray she'd tucked into her purse earlier. Her fingers had just curled over the cool metal when the mayor grabbed his partner and held his pistol to the other man's temple.

"I'm leaving here and if you try to stop me, I'll shoot him," Urick threatened.

"Fine." Wally shrugged. "One less criminal the county has to provide an expensive trial for."

Urick's shocked expression was almost funny, but Skye wasn't laughing. She knew Wally would never let the mayor shoot the other man, but what was his plan?

There was no other entrance, so she couldn't sneak up on the guy. She could phone for help, but as Wally had said, they didn't know which Viderville authorities they could trust. Should she call the county cops or maybe one of the Scumble River police? Who knew how long it would take either of them to get here? Maybe she was supposed to stop Urick when he came through the door.

Skye caught a glimmer of a movement out of the corner of her eye, and saw that Spike had somehow slipped out of the handcuffs and was tearing at the duct tape binding her ankles. The two criminals had their backs to Spike, and Wally was focused on Urick's gun. It seemed that no one except Skye had noticed that the young woman was freeing herself.

As Spike ripped the last piece of tape from around her legs, the metal cuffs, which were still attached to the chair's arm, rattled and Urick's head whipped toward the noise. At that moment Wally lunged toward the man, grabbed his arm, and wrested the weapon from his hand.

While Wally shoved Urick flat on the floor, Garth made a run for freedom. As he rushed through the door, Skye stepped back, took aim, and, for the second time in two days, emptied a can of pepper spray into the astonished face of a bad guy.

EPILOGUE

The Cat Who Swallowed the Canary

It had been a long, hectic week. Skye had had to give two police statements—one concerning the storage auction bullies and the other regarding what she had witnessed in Todd Urick's office. She had barely seen Wally, who had been inundated with interrogations and paperwork.

Not only did he have to deal with the Scumble River homicide, but he was also a key player in two additional cases—Spike's abduction, which had become part of Alexis's murder, and the Viderville corruption mess. As Wally had feared, Chief Eden had been involved in the embezzlement scheme. The Viderville sergeant had been appointed acting chief, and he was leaning heavily on Wally for support and assistance.

In addition to Mayor Urick, Chief Eden, and Garth Anders, the city clerk and the comptroller were also in on the scheme to pilfer the town's coffers. They all denied that they had any knowledge that Urick had killed Alexis, but the county prosecutor wasn't buying their claims.

With Wally occupied and her television set broken, Skye spent her evenings making wedding plans. She'd had a stroke of good luck and been able to book an appointment at Á L'Amour Bridal Boutique in Barrington for Saturday morning at eleven. It was a long trip from Scumble River, but according to Trixie, who had been scouring the Internet, it was *the* place in Illinois to buy a bridal gown.

Because Skye's superrich cousin Riley was footing the bill for the wedding dress as part of the payment for Skye's help the previous summer as a wedding planner, Skye was determined to get the dress of her dreams no matter what the cost. After all, her future in-laws were Texas multi-millionaires and she didn't want to embarrass Wally.

Skye had invited Trixie, Loretta, Frannie— whom Skye had asked to be her third brides-maid—and her mother to accompany her. May's invitation had come with a caveat—she was not to make any remarks regarding her daughter's weight, dress size, or other figure flaws.

Thanks to Loretta's speedy driving, they arrived at the upscale shop nearly a quarter of an hour early. After being shown into a private room and provided with coffee and tea, they were promised that their personal consultant would be with them in a few minutes.

As they sipped their drinks, Trixie and Frannie exchanged meaningful glances until Trixie finally asked Skye, "Do you mind if we ask you a few questions about the murder while we wait?" She wrinkled her nose. "Or would you rather not talk about it today?"

"Go ahead." Skye blew out a breath. She'd been surprised no one had brought up the subject during the hour-long ride to the store.

Most of the story had been on TV, since Spike had been recording everything that happened in the mayor's office with a lipstick camera that she had rigged so its lens peeked through a flower pin she had on her jacket. But there was a lot that Wally hadn't shared with the reporter. And only the night before had he given Skye permission to reveal certain details.

"How did Todd Urick convince Elijah that God was telling him what to do?" Trixie asked, leaning forward and resting her elbows on her knees. "I sure wouldn't believe something like that without a miracle or two."

"The messages came by way of Elijah's cell phone," Skye explained. "He tended to pray out loud, and Urick overheard him. The mayor then used that information to persuade Elijah that the texts he sent were from God." She combed her fingers through her hair. "You also have to realize that due to his brain injury, Elijah was much more open to suggestion than the average person."

"What I don't understand is the sequence of events," Loretta said, setting her cup of herbal tea down. "How did Todd Urick even know Alexis would be at the cat show, let alone figure out how to set up his DJ Wonka identity?"

Skye started at the beginning, mostly because the circumstances were confusing even to her. "Alexis was on the phone with Bunny about the show during the month she was working for the mayor. During that time, Alexis answered Urick's private phone and discovered his embezzlement scheme. Once she started to blackmail him, he remembered that she was going to attend the Cat's Meow event, and decided that was the perfect place to confront her."

"So he got himself hired as the deejay by Bunny so he could attend without anyone seeing the real him there," Frannie interjected. "How did he pull that off? Most people don't have deejay paraphernalia just sitting around their garage."

"He borrowed the equipment from his coconspirator Garth Anders, who had deejayed in college. Urick thought that he could intimidate Alexis into backing down."

"But why didn't Urick just call Alexis or text her or e-mail her or even go talk to her at her apartment?" Trixie demanded.

"He didn't want any record that he'd had any contact with her." Skye crossed her legs. "He was really very clever." She shook her head. "But Alexis didn't give an inch, so Urick came up with the plan to kill her and blame Elijah, because there was no way he was going to pay her a hundred thousand dollars."

"Why do men constantly underestimate women?" May asked. "Do they really think that there would ever be a second-born child if we were afraid of a little pain?"

"The problem is if they ever admitted to themselves how strong we are, they'd have to treat us like equals," Skye said with a half smile.

After they all agreed with Skye's statement, Loretta asked, "How did Urick manage to kill Alexis and set Elijah up for the murder?"

"Just before the disco bowler party ended, Urick sent Alexis a note via one of the cocktail waitresses saying that the blackmail money she had demanded from him was in the utility closet." Skye glanced at the door, not wanting the salon consultant to hear them talking about murder. She might be too frightened to be any help finding the perfect dress. "Once Urick gave the server the note for Alexis, he put on the last song, hurried to the basement, and waited in the dark for his victim to arrive."

"And he garroted her with the wire part of the cat toy when she walked into the room," Frannie guessed.

"Right." Skye nodded. "He used the cat toy because he hadn't come prepared to kill her." She paused, gathering her thoughts. "Then, having already drugged Elijah's drink, Urick, claiming to be God, texted the ex-doctor to come to the basement."

"How did Urick have the drugs handy?" Loretta asked.

"He told Wally that he always carried those roofie pill things in his pocket," May answered, then quoted Urick, "He said, 'You never know when a girl in a bar will need a little chemical persuasion to put out and spread her legs.'" May's mouth puckered in distaste. "He really is a crude and vulgar man."

"Ew." Frannie made a gagging sound. "That's just totally gross."

"Yes, it is. And something you should remember when you go down to U of I in the fall," Skye told Frannie, who had announced on the drive that she'd been accepted into the University of Illinois journalism school.

"Yes, Mother," Frannie shot back, then added, "as if I'd ever be that stupid."

Skye raised a brow, then went on. "Urick watched Elijah come to the closet and pass out; then he wiped his prints from everything and hid until the cleaners were finished and Bunny went to bed. Once the coast was clear, he simply unlocked the front door—the dead bolt has a thumbturn on the inside—and left. He lucked out that Bunny hadn't set the alarm, but even if she had, he'd have been long gone by the time the police arrived, and Elijah would still have been the prime suspect."

"As you said, he's a clever one all right," Loretta commented. "The criminals I end up defending are usually dumb as dirt."

Skye gave her sister-in-law a thoughtful glance. Was Loretta getting tired of being a defense lawyer? Mentally shrugging, Skye resumed her account of the crime. "After Urick killed Alexis, he took her car key from her purse, drove her MINI Cooper to Kyle O'Brien's, and parked it in front of the house. Next he wiped his prints off the car, jogged back to Scumble River, picked up his own vehicle, and drove home as if nothing had happened."

"Urick's wife told Wally that he'd suggested she visit her mother that weekend," May added. "So Urick didn't have anyone wondering where he'd been or why he was so late getting home."

"Right," Skye nodded. "Urick knew from when Alexis worked for him that she had dated Kyle, and he wanted a second suspect in case Elijah somehow wiggled off the hook."

"So let me see if I have this straight." Trixie jumped in, her eyes gleaming. "Sometime later, Elijah wakes up, sees the body, thinks he killed Alexis per God's instructions, and goes home?"

"Yes." Skye looked at her watch. It was almost eleven. She needed to wrap this up so she could concentrate on selecting a dress. "Then the next day, Urick texted Elijah for the last time and told him to park his car at the rec club, turn his cell phone off and throw it into one of the lakes, and then walk into the wilderness."

"Why did he do that?" Frannie asked.

"So Elijah would look even guiltier." Skye shook her head. "What a creep."

"True, but he was really ingenious." Loretta's voice held a hint of admiration. "How did you and Wally get into city hall to save Spike?"

"The back door was open," Skye lied. Wally had sworn her to secrecy regarding his lock-picking skills. "Now *I* have a couple of questions."

"Oh?" Loretta looked nervous, which made Skye wonder what her sister-in-law had been up to, but she decided that was a subject for another day. Instead, she turned to Frannie and asked, "What's the deal with Bunny's mysterious boyfriend?"

"Why do you think I know?" Fannie's expression was innocence personified. "Miss Bunny says she doesn't have a boyfriend."

"If you ever want another scoop from me you'll spill," Skye threatened.

"Fine. Be like that." Frannie exhaled noisily. "He's some old-timey movie or television star with oodles of money. He was one of the few who realized that CupidsCatsMeow.com was a dating service, and it turned out he had seen Miss Bunny dance in Las Vegas."

"Why all the cloak-and-dagger?" Skye demanded. "The guy sounds like a good catch."

"We-e-ell . . ." Frannie drew out the word. "The

thing is, he's not quite divorced and so he's afraid his wife will try to get a bigger settlement if she finds out he's dating." She grinned. "Believe me, it's killing Miss Bunny not to be able to show him off."

"Okay." Skye could understand that. "One more thing. Have you and Justin made up?"

"Yeah." Frannie's grin widened. "He called me the other night and admitted he was wrong."

"Good." Skye beamed back, glad the two young people had patched up their differences.

There was a knock on the door and while everyone was distracted by the consultant's introductions, Trixie whispered to Skye, "Did you ever talk to Father Burns about an exorcism for your house?"

"Nope." Skye shook her head. "I decided to wait and see if your theory about Mrs. Griggs's aversion to premarital sex is correct. I really hate to kick the old lady out of her own home."

"Do you think that's a good idea? After all, the wedding is *nine* months away."

"All I know is that you have to lead with your heart and everything else in life will follow." Skye shrugged, then winked. "And there's always Wally's place."

As Trixie giggled, Skye turned and saw the beautiful wedding dress the consultant had brought into the room. Her throat closed and tears of happiness welled up in her eyes. This was it. She was really getting married.

Center Point Large Print
600 Brooks Road / PO Box 1
Thorndike ME 04986-0001 USA

(207) 568-3717

US & Canada:
1 800 929-9108
www.centerpointlargeprint.com